FOR THE RECORD

Books by Regina Jennings

FOR THE RECORD

REGINA JENNINGS

BETHANYHOUSE

a division of Baker Publishing Group
Minneapolis, Minnesota

© 2016 by Regina Jennings

Published by Bethany House Publishers
11400 Hampshire Avenue South
Bloomington, Minnesota 55438
www.bethanyhouse.com

Bethany House Publishers is a division of
Baker Publishing Group, Grand Rapids, Michigan

Printed in the United States of America

Library of Congress Control Number: 2016942750

ISBN 978-0-7642-1142-3

Scripture quotations are from the King James Version of the Bible.

This is a work of historical reconstruction; the appearances of certain historical figures
are therefore inevitable. All other characters, however, are products of the author's
imagination, and any resemblance to actual persons, living or dead, is coincidental.

Cover design by John Hamilton Design

Author is represented by Books & Such Literary Agency

16 17 18 19 20 21 22   7 6 5 4 3 2 1

To Bob and Glenda Jennings
in honor of
their crowning achievement

CHAPTER 1

October 1885
Pine Gap, Missouri

Only a limited patch of Earth could claim the privilege of belonging to Texas. Not that he despised the rest of the world for its misfortune, but there was a difference.

Deputy Joel Puckett dropped his saddlebags on the platform of the depot and surveyed the wall of mountains that surrounded the valley. He hadn't seen all of Texas. It'd take more years than his twenty-four to visit every town from the badlands of El Paso to the swamps of Beaumont, but he knew now that a native Texan could sense when he'd been separated from his homeland, and he felt the loss keenly.

The train's chugging had ceased to thunder through the hills, and yet no one came out of the depot to greet him. Rustling started at the top of the hill as a gust worked its way down the mountain, tumbling autumn leaves across the rocky expanse in front of the train station. The stars had already appeared above the mountain, and the air was cooling. Joel lifted his Stetson and ruffled his hair. According to Governor Marmaduke, the people here were desperate for help, begging for relief from the outlaws who razed their homesteads. So if they were anxiously awaiting his arrival, where were they?

His boots echoed on the platform as he strode to the depot building and rattled the door. Locked. The brim of his hat bumped against the glass as he peered through the lone window but found no one. No help coming from that quarter.

Joel scanned the dense woods that surrounded him, but couldn't make out anything in the darkness. He picked up his saddlebags and studied the rocky road that passed along the railroad tracks. When they'd arranged for him to ride the train, he hadn't counted on being afoot once he arrived. He should have insisted on bringing his horse. Who knew what kind of mount they'd be able to provide? For now he'd have to make use of his own two feet. Uphill or downhill? Which would take him to civilization sooner?

The sounds shifted. Joel froze as his hearing instinctively separated the routine noises from the new element. Years of tracking had honed his senses so that any change alerted him. An unknown entity had entered the area and was even now racing toward him.

Hooves on rocks. Many hooves. Voices raised, calling to each other not in anger but in a boisterous excitement that usually preceded acts of derring-do. They were coming down the hill fast. Most men would've stepped out of sight until they knew what they were facing, but the thought never occurred to Joel. His hand flexed at his side, and he didn't have to check that his six-shooter was in place. His feet were spread wide in classic gunslinger pose. What if he was in over his head? What if he'd made a mistake? With the horses barreling out of the trees, it was too late to second-guess himself.

His blood chilled at the sight of the first rider—a torch-toting apparition straight from hell, complete with a disfigured, blackened face and horns. As more of them raced from the trees,

Joel realized the masks were burlap sacks, holes cut out for eyes and marked with white paint to make terrifying faces. Cones had been attached at the corners like horns, tassels streaming in the wind from their tips.

Hooting and hollering, the riders raced into the clearing, straight at him. Who were they? If they meant him harm, he was hopelessly outnumbered. With coats turned inside out and socks over their boots, the only identifying markings would've been those of their horses, but even they looked to be rubbed with soot. Dozens of them appeared, some waving a bundle of switches in one hand instead of a torch, but they paid him no mind. Streaming past the depot, they continued their ghastly calling as if he were of no more consequence than the squirrels darting about for acorns beneath the oaks.

Instead of being relieved, Joel fumed. He was not used to being ignored. As the men were disappearing into the trees, he cupped his hands around his mouth and hollered a challenge.

"Hey! Don't you see me standing here, or are y'all afraid to stop?"

He was downright affronted that no one thought enough of him to break stride.

Save one.

Just before his horse dipped out of sight, one man reined hard to the left. Gravel flew as his horse cut and circled around the depot clearing. The man was massive, and the loose sack over his head only added to his bulky profile. One of his horns had twisted and pointed down like a crazed bull's. His horse plunged its head, wanting to rejoin the herd, but the masked man held it steady and steered it directly toward Joel.

With the disguise, Joel couldn't make out much about the man besides his size and his attitude. A leader—definitely. Fearless and arrogant. Someone he'd lock horns with sooner or later.

Might as well be sooner.

Joel stepped to the edge of the platform and looked down on the rider. Every nerve was taut. Every sense sharpened.

The man's expression was not visible through the mask. He shifted in his saddle, and before Joel knew it, he felt the cold wooden handle of his own gun in his palm. But the man hadn't drawn a gun on him. Instead of bullets flying his way, a bundle of switches skidded across the platform and landed at Joel's feet.

One glance to see they posed no threat, and then Joel had the rider back in his sights.

The man's horse pranced as the noise of the other riders faded into the woods.

"A bundle of sticks?" Joel said. "What's that supposed to mean? Who are you?"

The white painted circle over the masked man's mouth distorted and stretched with his answer. "I'm the law."

Turning his horse, the rider spurred it, and they shot off like a cannonball to catch their companions, thundering across the clearing and ducking where the road entered the woods.

Joel's scalp crawled. Releasing a long breath, he holstered his gun and only then allowed himself to consider what could've happened. They'd warned him that the mountains were dangerous. He'd thought the risk better than the fate that faced him at home, but now he wasn't sure. Whatever he'd expected on his arrival, this wasn't it.

Nope. This definitely wasn't Texas.

CHAPTER 2

While we think your writing shows promise, our readers have no interest in the ineffectual attempts of a mountain sheriff to apprehend criminals in the Ozarks. If you find a topic that would be of more interest to those unfamiliar with your area, please submit again—

Betsy Huckabee folded the letter along its well-established creases. Good news, bad news. She could tell a story, but there wasn't any story worth telling in Pine Gap, according to the Kansas City paper's way of thinking. How could they not find the clash between the various gangs and outlaws fascinating? But they claimed their readers couldn't relate to the incidents. While they might live in the same state, the mountaineers didn't catch the attention of the city folk. If she wanted to start her career, she'd have to come at it from a different angle.

Stuffing the letter into her skirt pocket for the hundredth time, Betsy took up the wooden spoon and scraped it against the bottom of the iron pot, loosening what had stuck while she was distracted. There was more onion than squirrel in the pot. While the onions filled the cabin with a pleasing aroma, they wouldn't keep her stomach from rumbling all night. The hams, shoulders, and middlin' meat of the recently butchered pig were curing in the smokehouse, but they would have to stretch through spring, and evidently Sissy was already worried about running short. Betsy took a stick of walnut, tossed it in the cookstove, and then set to stirring again.

Maybe she could write a sentimental story for the ladies' page—some fictional piece that would put her name in the paper and some money under her mattress. It wouldn't hurt to try. She needed to think of something to help her earn a place of her own. The current situation wasn't conducive to her well-being.

A whistle shrilled from outside. Was that the train? Betsy glanced at the clock on the fireplace mantel. Eight o'clock, and there the whistle went again, probably to alert the town that some poor soul had been abandoned at the depot. She set the kettle on the table and wiped her hands on the checkered dishtowel. She might be hungry, but she couldn't stir onions when there was a mystery afoot.

"Uncle Fred? Did you hear the train?" Pushing open the door between the newspaper printing office and their living quarters, she found him leaning over the press, arranging a troublesome line of type.

He brushed at his forehead. His stained sleeve protector branded a smudge of ink right above his glasses. "The train? It's certainly late."

The outside door flew open, and Betsy's fifteen-year-old cousin Scott burst in. "That was the train, Pa." Even thin as he was, the way he wiggled, you'd think there was a whole litter of puppies beneath his shirt. He rushed to his pa, nearly bumping the typesetting tray onto the floor. "Do you reckon the new deputy was on that train?"

Uncle Fred caught the tray by the corner and tugged it to

the center of the desk. "Go tell Sissy that we're coming in for supper. You aren't going after a train."

Betsy waited until her cousin, arms dangling and lip protruding, sulked into the cabin. As soon as the door fell closed behind him, she turned to her uncle. "What about me? Am I going after a train?"

Uncle Fred placed the quoin lock into the chase to lock down the print before stepping away from the press. "I am awfully curious about that new deputy from Texas." He flashed his ready grin, then waved an inky palm back toward the kitchen.

The family was already seated at the table. Sissy—or Aunt Sissy, as she was to be called now—had finished feeding Baby Eloise and commenced to dish out the squirrel and onions. Scott held his other half sister, Amelia, on his knee, bouncing her and eliciting squeals of delight. Now that he was nearly grown and had a stepmother to look after him, Scott didn't need his older cousin Betsy anymore. No matter how she helped in the newspaper office, her presence was a strain on the growing family—a strain that none of them would mention, but it troubled her sorely.

Betsy took her plate from Sissy and dove in.

"Sit down and eat with us for once, Betsy." Sissy wasn't that much older than Betsy, but she tried to make the gap feel wider with sternness. "Between the chores and the press, you've been on your feet all day."

Ignoring the sitting down part, Betsy shoveled in a few more bites. It was full-on dark, and that was when things started happening among the steep cliffs and deep hollows. She wouldn't find a fantastic story sitting at the table with Uncle Fred and Aunt Sissy. Her destiny was bigger than that.

Tossing her plate into the sink, Betsy planted a kiss on Amelia's little cheek as she hurried past. She didn't quite hear what

Sissy was calling, so she waved a hand over her head as she entered the office and shouted back, "I'll be careful."

She grabbed her cousin's coat off its hook and pulled it over her calico dress. No clouds out tonight, so she'd be able to see well enough. Her desk rattled as she opened the drawer. She removed the letter from her pocket, gently placed it alongside the other rejections she'd collected, closed the drawer, and then extinguished the lantern and snatched a hat of her uncle's before heading outside.

Pausing next to the house, she heard Sissy's words through the window. "I know she's always scuttled around unaccompanied, but it really isn't fitting. She's a young lady—"

Betsy growled. Not true. She was no longer a young lady. She'd already weathered the painful season where everyone from the postmaster's wife to the auctioneer tried to get her hitched to some yokel. That was behind her. They'd finally given up, leaving Betsy to live the life she enjoyed, free from having to justify her decision to any chaw jaw who wanted to opine on the matter. She'd rejected every available man who was interested, and since there was no one new to strike up speculation, she was safe.

At the sound of thundering hooves, her heart sped. They were riding tonight. Where were they going? Had they found Miles Bullard? How she wished she could join them and see the action firsthand.

Betsy jogged to the corner of the town square so she could better see them as they passed. She began her mental tally of those she suspected and those she'd cleared. Down the street, Postmaster Finley was pulling his shutters closed on his family rooms above the post office. She hadn't expected that the shady postmaster was one of them, especially since his family usually fell on the wrong side of the law. What about Doctor Hopkins?

He'd been to town earlier. Had he had time to get decked out in his ruckus-raising clothes?

Here they came, shouting excitedly and some waving their bundles of sticks over their heads. They looked a fright, but Betsy wasn't scared of them. They were all local men, most of them quite decent and law-abiding until the law failed them. As much as she liked Sheriff Taney, he had let them down. If he couldn't handle everything on his own, then they were lucky someone was willing to step in.

She watched as the riders streamed by and tried to memorize the various masks and disguises. Clive Fowler was easy to recognize. Couldn't hide size under a burlap sack. But besides him, she couldn't positively identify anyone. They raced by, whooping it up, but one of them seemed less gleeful. He rode a fine horse that she suspected was from the Calhouns' farm. He wasn't Jeremiah . . .

"Hey, Mr. Pritchard," she called.

It was a shot in the dark, but it struck the bull's-eye. The mask turned to her. She couldn't see his expression, but she did note the long hair emerging from the bottom of his hood. Yep, another Bald Knobber identified.

He raised his branches and shook them at her. A warning, but Betsy smiled. She didn't mean any harm, and Mr. Pritchard knew it. She just couldn't stand to leave a mystery be. Not if there was a chance on her figuring it out.

Leaves scattered as the riders turned on the square and headed down toward the river. Whatever campaign they were on would be finished by the time she reached them. Following them was out of the question, but maybe she'd spot a few of them sneaking home after she checked on the train.

Shoving her hands into her pockets, Betsy started up over the hill toward the depot. Even she didn't like to walk outside of town after dark, not on the road anyway. Come around the wrong bend, and you might see a fight commencing. You might see someone sneaking home after a night of carousing. But what was worse, someone bad might see you. Although Betsy had no enemies herself, outlaws of all persuasions found the heavily wooded Ozarks a good place to lie low, hide their loot, and live off the land . . . or at least live off whatever sundry goods they could appropriate from the locals. You didn't want to stumble across those folks on a lonely trail. Even the sheriff found it safer to stay at the jailhouse or out at his cabin of a night.

But not Betsy. Once she got out of the safety of town, she'd take to the brush and cut through thick patches. Besides, the Bald Knobbers were riding tonight. They'd done a lot to quell the orneriness. If you didn't mind their methods, you'd have to say Pine Gap was much improved by them.

Betsy reached the crossroads at the ridge. Straight ahead led to the depot. Take a left, and she'd end up at the sale barn. Instead of either of those options, she'd step off the road onto a rabbit trail and proceed from there. Aunt Sissy thought she was in danger, but once Betsy was in the shadows, no one would see her.

But she wasn't in the shadows yet, and here came a stranger.

The man wore a rumpled suit, cheap shoes not made for walking, and a floppy hat so big you could bathe a pig in it. His nose was bulbous while his chin was meager. He came down the hill roughly, like his knees were popping out of control with every footstep.

He took her measure as he approached. Betsy waited calmly. If this was the new deputy from Texas, she wasn't going to disgrace her fellow woodsmen by gawking over him.

Mustering all the poise she'd ever learned from her friend Abigail Calhoun, she lifted her chin and wiped every last sparkle of orneriness from her gaze. "Good evening, sir." Her accent was Abigail's, although slightly altered by her Ozark cadence.

He didn't even give her a second glance. "I suppose I'm on the right road to get to Mrs. Sanders's house."

How she wished she had her slingshot, but he was the new deputy. Getting into his good graces could help her career immensely.

"The widow Sanders lives right here at the corner. Is that where you're staying?"

The man ignored her and plowed past to the small cabin she'd indicated. Widow Sanders had the most ambitious garden in town. You couldn't find a corner of the yard that wasn't bedecked with the product of some bulb, flower, or vine. And the deputy strode through it like it was a field of nettles.

Betsy hesitated. Surely Widow Sanders knew he was coming. She'd self-designated her home as the town's boardinghouse, so Betsy had to assume she was prepared. And yet it seemed unthoughtful to leave a single woman to meet a strange man alone. Betsy would think of some excuse to insert herself into the conversation.

The deputy had reached the front porch, but instead of knocking on the door, he burst right through. Betsy gasped. What was he thinking? It was straight-out evening, and he just busted plumb into a woman's house? Was that how deputies in Texas operated? The hair on the back of her neck pricked up. Walking backwards, she found a spot beneath a cedar where no light reached. Maybe she'd just sit a spell and watch. If everything looked all right—

A scream sounded from inside. Betsy's blood ran cold, then hot. She had to get help. She had to go—

Betsy sprinted from the trees, but before she could breach the widow's property line, she plowed right into another man and ricocheted off his solid mass. She was falling, on her way to a sharp landing on the rocks, when he caught her by her arm.

"I don't know what kind of place this is where men wear their clothes inside out and women fall out of trees," he said.

The first thing she noticed was the low drawl of his voice. The second, since she was dangling just above the ground, the pointy toes of his boots. A cowboy?

Before she could form an opinion, he jerked her upright and removed her oversized hat. "At least I think you're a woman. You could be another rabble-rouser in disguise."

She finally caught a look at his face, and for the first time in her life, Betsy couldn't speak. He was perfect. Not cute, not adorable, but strikingly handsome with enough power in his gaze to send a twinge of concern up her spine.

He was talking. Pointing to Widow Sanders's house. She watched his lips move. A trim beard covered his cheeks and jaw, and those eyes—what color were they?

Still holding her arm, he shook her a little. "Of all the cotton-picking—" He dropped her arm, smashed her hat back on her head, and ran to the house.

Now she looked at the rest of him. Taller than she was by a good half a foot and well built. Dressed for traveling with a red cavalry-style shirt beneath his leather vest and coat. Where had he come from? To just show up at night in the middle of nowhere—

Another scream rang out. Betsy blinked. Good thing the new man hadn't forgotten Widow Sanders, because Betsy was slap out of smarts. Quickly she followed.

"Widow Sanders," Betsy called to the open door. "Widow Sanders!"

The cowboy stopped at the door and turned back to her. "Do you know the man who just walked in there?"

"He's the new deputy," Betsy answered.

He frowned—which was very attractive as far as frowns went. "Something ain't right."

"Betsy? Is that you?" Widow Sanders came to the door carrying a candle with shaking hands. Her face looked like it'd been whitewashed. The deputy appeared behind her. He'd ignored Betsy before, but now he was grinning like she was his best friend.

"Betsy? It's not Betsy Huckabee, is it? You were still a baby when I left."

"Who are you?" she asked.

"I'm Mr. Sanders, finally home."

Betsy looked to Widow Sanders, usually a well of competency, but she'd shrunk as if drained. "Mr. Sanders? I thought you were dead."

Widow Sanders's eyes widened. "I never said that. I never told anyone he died. He was just gone . . . for a very long time."

Betsy wanted to pry, but the fear in the woman's eyes stopped her.

"You weren't on the train," the cowboy said. "How'd you get here?"

Still reeling from the notion that Mr. Sanders was alive, Betsy could only now stop to wonder about the handsome one. Who was he?

"I walked clear from Indian Territory," Mr. Sanders said. "But if you'uns don't mind, it's getting late, and my wife and I have a lot of catching up to do." He stepped forward, directing them away from the house.

The cowboy's jaw hardened. His gaze caught Widow Sanders dead to rights. Betsy shivered at the pent-up strength. "As long as you're all right, Mrs. Sanders. I can stay if you'd rather."

Betsy's jaw dropped open. This man had just stepped out of

the bushes, and here he was acting like it was his job to protect Widow—Mrs.—Sanders. The nerve.

The former-widow Mrs. Sanders watched her husband—Betsy couldn't quite wrap her mind around that word—with wary eyes, then nodded. "I'll be fine."

The words *thank you* hadn't left her mouth before the door shut, throwing Betsy and the stranger into the shadows.

They stood side by side, looking at the closed door. Already Betsy was running through her mind the conversation she'd have with Uncle Fred. Imagine, Widow Sanders had a husband! But maybe Uncle Fred knew already. Was this one of those things adults didn't discuss in front of the children and then forgot to tell them once they grew up?

"What made you think he was the deputy?" the cowboy asked, obviously unconcerned with the very important internal discussion going on in Betsy's head.

She looked him over again. On occasion, Betsy was known to overindulge on candy and sweets, then later have a bellyache and wish she hadn't gorged so. That was what she feared now, studying him. Tomorrow she'd need some coffee and jerky to chase away all the fluff.

Only then did she notice the pistols gleaming from his gun belt. Another look at his cowboy hat and fancy boots, and a piece of information surfaced . . . a deputy from Texas. A handsome, young deputy from Texas.

The inspiration for her story had just arrived.

CHAPTER 3

If the train had arrived on time, Joel would have met with the town fathers and would already be in his room, turning in for the night. Instead he'd stumbled into a bewildering maze of crooked trails, dense forests, and strange characters marauding through the night. He'd been told that another deputy had already arrived and then found that man involved in terrorizing a widow. Even worse, it looked like his best hope for an introduction to town was this starry-eyed miss. And Joel had sworn off starry-eyed misses.

She threw him a sidelong glance, watching him through a stray lock of blond hair that danced in the breeze. A coy smile played about her lips. Uh-oh. She was fixin' to be cute.

"I just figured he was the deputy because he was slightly overweight, dull-witted, and smelled like he'd been sleeping in a vat of pickles."

Joel was tired, it was late, and he really didn't have time for this. "You must be very observant," he said. "So I reckon you could direct me to the nearest boardinghouse?"

"Without introductions? I don't know how it's done in Texas—"

"Who said anything about Texas?"

He'd caught her off guard. She waved her hand before her face. "Did I say Texas? I meant—"

"And if you know I'm from Texas, then you've already figured out I'm the new deputy. You can call me Deputy Puckett. And you are?"

She paused just long enough to give weight to her words. "Going home." She flashed a devastating smile and spun on her heel. "Good night," she called over her shoulder, "and good luck."

He hadn't seen that coming. But she was going, disappearing down the hill, her sure steps never faltering on the uneven terrain, and if he had any hope of finding a roof for his head, he couldn't let her get away.

"Wait a minute." He jogged to catch up with her. She walked with the easy stride of a young boy but with the prickly attitude of a railroad baron's daughter. "The boardinghouse, if you don't mind."

"Behind us. Widow Sanders is the only one who takes in boarders, but I doubt she's looking to take anyone in tonight."

They'd reached a small hamlet. A few houses dotted the lane while lights shone between the trees, giving evidence of more buildings ahead. The lady had slowed and seemed to be listening for something, and then he heard it. An echo, a cry—surely the ruffians he'd seen at the train station. Why hadn't he insisted on bringing his horse?

Holding on to her hat, the young woman tilted her head back, almost like a wolf sniffing the air. The moonlight fell on her face. Quick eyes, intelligent brow, and a mouth designed for mischief. Did she have connections with the gang? She could've been sent to keep an eye on him while they conducted their devilment.

"Where can I find Sheriff Taney? Surely he'll help me make arrangements," he said.

"Sheriff Taney lives out past Dewey Bald. You won't want to walk out there tonight."

"Why not?"

"That's where the gang is right now."

"Where the sheriff is? Then he'll need my help."

"To do what?" she asked. "Sit by the fire and pretend he doesn't hear them? I'd say he's doing that well enough alone."

"Then I'll go by myself."

"It's not safe."

"Says the woman who's traipsing around after dark."

She dismissed that comment with a wrinkle of her nose. "I used to have a pet skunk. It behaved itself right smart as long as you acted real calm, but the last thing you wanted to do was surprise it. Once Jeremiah ran up on it—"

"I'm not in the mood for a story, Miss Huckabee."

There. He'd surprised her again.

"How did you know my name?" Her eyes narrowed before widening in realization. "Mr. Sanders. He said it, didn't he? See, you're not all that clever. A clever man would've made arrangements before nightfall."

No use in reminding her that the train was late. He'd find no sympathy, nor did he desire it. Dark cabins lined the street on both sides of them, and a cleared green of some kind waited ahead—the town square, from the looks of it. He raised his head to follow the silhouette of the mountains before him. More cheers rang out, thinned over the distance. A dog barked incessantly, and a volley of gunshots made his teeth grind.

She sighed. "Sounds like the fun is over and I missed it again." Whatever surprise had rendered her speechless earlier had lost its effect. She lifted a hand and flopped it in his direction. "Jailhouse is straight ahead. Probably locked up, but you can catch some shut-eye under the hanging oak if the raccoons don't bother you. Just stay out of sight from the road. Loitering after dark isn't admired around here." She shivered and tucked her hands into her coat pockets as she turned to walk away. "Sleep tight and welcome to Pine Gap."

Betsy swung the cabin door closed and peeled off her coat as fast as she could. The heat from the fireplace made her skin prickle, and the coat itched like the dickens once she was out of the cold air. Sissy was singing to one of the babies, probably suckling Eloise in the rocker in her bedroom. Quietly Betsy eased into the printing office and tossed the hat on her cot.

Until Uncle Fred had married Sissy, Betsy had been the woman of the house. Fourteen years ago, her aunt had died, and Betsy left her parents' farm to come to town and take care of her younger cousins—cooking and cleaning like Mama had taught her. 'Course she still had plenty of time to wander town while they were in school and sort of educated herself by asking questions and watching people as they practiced their trade. Uncle Fred said she had a journalist's heart, the way she could sniff out a story and was never satisfied until she knew everything. Poking her nose where it didn't belong had given her more practical knowledge than most people twice her age. As far as book learning, well, she read anything she could get her hands on, including her cousins' school books and newspapers from around the nation, making her one of the more well-informed people in town.

Betsy was smart, but Sissy now occupied the head position in the cabin. Once Sissy and Uncle Fred started adding to their family, Betsy's cot was moved to the office, and no matter how much they tried to ease the situation, she couldn't help but feel in the way.

Sitting at the desk, Betsy found her pencil and notepad. She supposed that most every child had a maiden aunt to dote on them and fill the gaps when Mother wouldn't suffice, but she hadn't reckoned on filling that position once her little cousins had grown. One by one, the boys left home to get married and live on their own homesteads, leaving only Scott and Betsy behind.

What did she want? She wanted to be out of Uncle Fred and Sissy's way, but she didn't know how. God had put her amid good friends and family, but she hadn't found her place here. Like getting a stiff new pair of winter boots, her toes were getting pinched every time she barged into the kitchen, which used to be her domain, and found Sissy at the stove. But after living in town, going home to live at her parents' farm seemed a banishment.

Uncle Fred's little newspaper didn't make enough to allow him to pay her much. Not enough for her to buy a cabin on her own. She'd have to write for a bigger paper for that, which was exactly what she'd been attempting.

Week after week, Betsy reported on the vigilante groups that protected the hills, but similar reports were coming in from all over southwestern Missouri. Whether they called themselves the Bald Knobbers, the Anti-Horse-Thief Association, the Regulators, or the Honest Men's League, they all operated in much the same way, and Kansas City wasn't buying any reports from a novice like her.

Now with the governor appointing a new deputy to end the Bald Knobbers' reign, there'd be even less to write about.

Unless . . .

She chewed on the end of her pencil. Her submissions before had reported the facts. She'd described the various crimes, expounded on the fears of the citizens, and detailed the activity of the bad guys, but the stories weren't that unusual. She had to do something different. Instead of reporting only the dry, indisputable facts, Betsy would write a serial fiction piece just like Dickens did, but not as wordy. She would craft articles for the ladies' section of the paper and fill it with characters that they found fascinating.

And the inspiration for her most important character had just dropped into town like a gift from heaven.

Clive Fowler did an able job as leader of the Bald Knobbers, but he wasn't hero material. What *would* keep the ladies waiting for the next installment of the newspaper would be reading about one man against the gang, one lone lawman from Texas who spoke with a slow drawl and wore a double-breasted cavalry shirt, tall boots, and a shiny star. She'd be careful what she said about him in the stories—she'd even give him an alias—and if her story ever saw the light of day, it'd be in faraway Kansas City. No one from Pine Gap would ever know.

Naturally, the deputy must never find out. The memory of his stern brow caused her a moment's unease. He wouldn't appreciate the interference, but he wasn't the only one with a job to do. There was no reason that they couldn't both accomplish their objectives without troubling his handsome face. Betsy smiled. She wouldn't have to exaggerate his looks, that was for certain. As long as he was brave and capable, she'd have plenty to work with. He needed to love the Lord, keep his neck clean, be good with children—that always wrung the hearts of the female readers—and be respectful of his elders, polite, charming. Let one smile of his send the ladies into vapors—

Snap! Betsy's pencil broke in her mouth. She'd gotten carried away. She spat the pieces into her hand, picked a splinter of wood out from between her teeth, then with a frown flicked it away. The sharp end still functioned.

Time to get to work.

CHAPTER 4

By dawn's light, Betsy was scrambling through the printing office, searching for another blank tablet. After working half the night, she'd gone to bed thinking about the deputy—or the idea of him, anyway—and now she was itching to get the rest of her nocturnal musing on paper.

This man, in which all the attributes of manliness since Adam were assembled, surveyed the sleepy village in the valley. It would be his domain, under his protection. He would guard her as a jealous lover, and woe to the man who dared trifle with her. But although he'd determined that her care was his life's work, he had yet to win her heart. First he had to pry her away from the destructive hold the evil one had on her and woo her to himself.

As he sat on his snow-white steed, he heard the sound of unholy merriment ricocheting off the hills. His blue eyes held the secrets of the prairie sky, changeable and danger-ous, striking fear into the most reckless outlaw's breast.

Were his eyes blue? Betsy started to chew the end of her pencil but met the jagged edge from last night's break. She really didn't remember his eyes, or maybe she hadn't seen them clearly in the dark. Well, she'd see them today. Hopefully he'd play along and do something heroic. After seeing his response to Widow Sanders's dilemma last night, she had full confidence that he'd dive right into the fire. But even if he didn't, she'd take what she got and embellish it to fulfill every female hope and dream.

She needed to come up with a first name for him, though. It should be something good. Tex? Ulysses? Maybe something foreign sounding, like a Spanish landowner. Alejandro? Eduardo?

Through the door to the cabin, she could hear Sissy stirring in the kitchen. Betsy set aside her draft, then, after double-checking the curtains on the front of the building, she shed her cotton nightdress and pulled on her shirt. The air in the office was cold, but the morning promised a sunny day. Good thing, because there was no telling where the deputy would lead her. She stepped into her skirt, worked it over her drawers, and tucked in her shirttails. She didn't dare miss his first meeting with the townspeople. The whole situation was ripe for conflict, and she wanted to be there for every moment of it.

She rolled her nightclothes up beneath her pillow and tidied the bed. The door creaked as she pushed out of the office and into the cabin. The babies must still be asleep, because Sissy put a finger to her lips as Scott came in carrying the firewood.

The scent of Uncle Fred's shaving soap warred against the aroma of eggs and bacon. His razor paused at his neck, and he shot Betsy a glance in the mirror. "What'd you find out about the train?"

Sissy tsked. "She should be home in bed, not gallivanting about."

Betsy stole a piece of bacon straight from the skillet and sat on the table. "I forgot about the train. Can you believe that? So much happened."

"It's not fair." Scott dropped the armload of kindling in the wood box. From the bedroom, they heard a baby begin to fuss.

Uncle Fred shook his head at his noisy, unrepentant son, then turned to Betsy, his face still foamed with soap. "Well?"

"First off," Betsy said around a crunchy bite of bacon, "the Bald Knobbers were riding. I saw them pass through town, and then it sounded like they went up on Dewey Bald."

"Do you think they were after Miles Bullard?" Scott asked.

"They had the bundles of sticks with them to give a warning. Bullard is wanted for murder. That's a piece past a warning. If they find him—"

"You stay away from them," Sissy said. "Those men are dangerous."

"Pshaw." Betsy waved away her concern. "They wouldn't hurt me. I figured out another one, Uncle Fred. Mr. Pritchard—"

"Betsy!" Sissy stomped her foot. "You will not name a single member of that gang in this house."

"Can we go in the office?" Betsy asked.

"I figured Pritchard was involved," Uncle Fred said.

"Fred . . ." Sissy warned.

Uncle Fred twisted his mouth to the side, and Betsy nearly laughed at his predicament. He knew he shouldn't encourage her to spy on them, but he was as curious as she was. And one never knew when such information might lead to a story—although like as not, it was information that couldn't be published.

"Listen to your aunt," he said. "Your parents wouldn't appreciate me letting you tangle with them."

Betsy was a full-out adult, but there was no use in fussing over it with Sissy. Uncle Fred didn't mean it anyway.

"But the Bald Knobbers aren't the best of it, by half. Did you know Widow Sanders was married . . . *is* married? I supposed, being a widow, that there'd been a husband at some time, but he showed up last night. Nearly scared her to death, and I surely didn't know what to do."

"Mr. Sanders is alive?" Uncle Fred exchanged a worried glance with Aunt Sissy. "What did she say?"

"She screamed like she'd been doused with ice water. After a bit she calmed down, but she still looked none too pleased. I don't have a good feeling about him, Uncle Fred."

He turned to the mirror and thoughtfully scraped the last of the shaving soap off his face. "I'm trying to remember what I heard of him, but to tell the truth, everyone just assumed he'd died in the war. Widow Sanders never wore mourning, now that I think of it. And she never asked for any sympathy, either. I'm ashamed to admit it, but I guess we just forgot about him."

"He doesn't seem to be the type that likes to be forgotten. He ran us off before we could ask too many questions."

"Us?" Uncle Fred dried his neck.

Betsy crunched the bacon. "Yep. Me and the new deputy."

"I knew it!" Scott hopped out of his seat and Sissy waved him back down.

Uncle Fred smiled wide. "You *were* busy."

"Mm-hmm. His name is Puckett, and he sure enough is from Texas—big hat, shiny guns, and cowboy boots."

She didn't mention that he was as handsome as Adam on the first day of creation, but Sissy cleared her throat and raised an eyebrow. Betsy swallowed a smile. Obviously her young aunt already had her suspicions. Betsy would have to work on convincing everyone that she thought him as plain as rye bread. If he knew how she described him on paper, she'd never have the upper hand.

Uncle Fred nudged Betsy. Obediently, she repositioned herself to the bench as they took their seats and bowed their heads.

As her uncle said grace over their breakfast, Betsy added her own prayers. Automatically she prayed for Ma, Pa, and her younger siblings, for her brother Josiah, his wife, Katie Ellen, their children and soon-to-be-born baby, but then she said a prayer for blessings over her new venture and thanked the Lord for the dual gift He'd given her in the form of a deputy and the idea to make the most use of him. She prayed she'd be a good steward of the inspiration and not let a single movement of his go to waste.

The amens were said, and Baby Eloise called out from her crib. Sissy got up to get her, and Uncle Fred watched her leave. As soon as the coast was clear, he leaned forward. "What's the deputy like? Any chance he'll make a difference around here?"

Betsy thought of his determination, his fearlessness as he charged toward the Sanders house when he heard a woman's cries. "He's going to stir things up, no doubt about it. Whether he fixes something or only gets himself killed remains to be seen."

"Why would he come here? You gotta know that when the governor of a state invites outsiders to come rule over the people, it ain't going to sit well. No one in their right mind would want the job . . . unless they're running from something," said Uncle Fred.

Betsy mulled that over. Sheriff Taney had been elected by the people. Overturning the election results and sending in a replacement hadn't been popular. So why had the deputy come? Maybe he'd made a mistake in Texas? Killed the wrong person? Failed to protect his partner? Let a bandit get away? There had to be some sort of hot water boiling beneath his feet, or he would have stayed put. Absently she twisted a button on her cuff. What if her deputy was less than heroic? That took some of the fun out of her project.

"Seems like since the Bald Knobbers organized, things have settled down," Uncle Fred said. "But you know the government. They can't have people taking care of anything on their own. Only a genuine representative of the state is qualified. That's how it's been ever since . . ."

Betsy didn't have to listen to know exactly where her uncle's speech would wander next. States' rights, individual liberty, government corruption—she'd heard it all repeatedly. Uncle Fred thought of himself as a statesman, but his best material never made it into his newspaper. Instead he published stories about whose kin was in town for a visit, the rising or falling price of timber, and notices of the winners of the school board elections. Nothing controversial enough to lose readers or bring any threats to his door.

Not taking time to fix a drink of her own, Betsy drained Sissy's cup just as her aunt returned with a tousle-headed tot in her arms.

"I declare, I wish you'd stop filching off my plate."

"It's a cup, not a plate." But Betsy reached for a new mug and sloshed the last of the milk from the can into it for Sissy. Messing the blond hair of her little cousin, she said, "I'm going on out. Don't want to miss the introduction of the deputy to the people. It could be the most entertainment we've had around here since Miranda got attacked by the headless chicken."

"Umm, Betsy," Sissy said, "before you go, I've been meaning to ask if you could give me a hand with the rabbits. I'm hankering after some rabbit stew, and we need to thin out the cages." Judging from Sissy's no-nonsense scowl, her timing was no coincidence.

Betsy flashed a desperate look at Uncle Fred, who suddenly took an avid interest in the bottom of his mug. Why this morning of all mornings? Because this morning was precisely the morning Sissy wanted Betsy home and out of trouble. Just when things started to get interesting, Sissy had to remind Betsy that no matter how many years passed, she was still a junior member of the family with no rights. Which was why she couldn't wait to have a place of her own.

"How many rabbits do you want?" Betsy rolled up her sleeves in preparation for her task.

CHAPTER 5

It'd been a long night. Joel leaned against the thick oak and watched as the sky turned a rosy pink. It'd be nearly nine o'clock before the sun made it over that mountain. Used to the open plains of northern Texas, Joel felt like he was in the bottom of a rust-colored sack, surrounded by these mountains. At any moment someone might pull the drawstring and the sky would be swallowed up from view. He ran his finger beneath the bandanna that hugged his neck. Such thoughts were fitting when one slept beneath the hanging tree. The limbs rustled above his head. How long since they'd had need for the tree? Hopefully he wouldn't be called on to utilize it.

A rooster crowed up the hill, but no one stirred. Back home in Garber, the restaurateurs and delivery men were up before dawn. Then again, they weren't out terrorizing the county in masquerade costumes at midnight, either. Those men had to sleep off their activities, which might be a start in identifying them. The early birds wouldn't be as suspect, while everyone dragging around after sunrise . . .

What had she been up to, that Betsy lady who'd run out of the woods like a bear was chasing her? At the time he'd thought she'd hit him blindly, but now he wasn't so sure. He couldn't trust anyone, if the reports were true. Even before the war, the feuding ran so deep that the law couldn't be trusted to be impartial. That was why he was there—so that both sides had someone without a history, without any partiality, who could judge fairly. So he had to be accurate with his first impressions. In a town as divided as this, everyone would be trying to paint the other side in the worst light possible. He couldn't pay much mind to their reports. Better to start with a clean slate and judge each by his actions as they went.

Joel opened the flap on his saddlebag and dragged out his Bible. Before he could contemplate judging this town, he had to make sure his own heart was right. He didn't take his responsibility lightly. In Texas, he'd operated under the auspices of Sheriff Green, but here he had no direct supervisor. In essence he was the acting sheriff in a town where he knew no one and no one knew him, but that was for the best.

He flipped to the book of Psalms and took up where he'd been reading on the train, at number forty-three.

Judge me, O God, and plead my cause against an ungodly nation: O deliver me from the deceitful and unjust man. For thou art the God of my strength: why dost thou cast me off? why go I mourning because of the oppression of the enemy? O send out thy light and thy truth: let them lead me; let them bring me unto thy holy hill, and to thy tabernacles.

After last night, Joel was of the opinion that nothing in these hills was holy. Had God's light and truth led him here, or was he just running from the deceit of the unjust? Either way, Joel hadn't had a choice, but that didn't excuse him from doing his job. No matter what people back home said about him, he'd do the best he could to bring law and order to this far-off nation.

As good as those intentions sounded, they didn't solve the immediate questions of where he was supposed to eat, sleep, or wash up in this town. He brushed the dead grass off his coat. Speaking of first impressions, he couldn't help but notice which house Betsy Huckabee had gone to last night. It was the cabin just up the street. Smoke puffed out the chimney, but no one had opened the door yet. As much as he wanted to take a look around, something told him that poking between buildings wasn't a safe occupation for a stranger.

Instead he'd best get a spit and polish before meeting the sheriff. Standing, he dusted off his trousers and buckled on his gun belt. On the way down the hill last night, he'd crossed a creek. Retracing his steps, he found it easily. As the sky lightened, more activity was apparent—doors creaked and banged shut, children shouted, the unoiled wheel of a well's pulley squeaked. Soon he'd be discovered.

He knelt at the creek and found it spring-fed and cold as ice. No matter how sorry he'd slept the night before, Joel was braced up now.

Drying his face with his bandanna, he started back to town, pleased to see some people out. The jailhouse was still locked up, but he took a seat on the bench against the wall. A barefoot boy crossed before him, driving a flock of white geese with a crooked stick. The boy nearly twisted his neck off staring as he passed and even walked backwards a piece before hurrying away. A woman across the road walked out of her cabin with a basket of laundry. She'd lifted a towel to her clothesline when she spotted him. Fumbling for the towel, she picked up the basket, hurried inside, and closed the door with a thud. Joel wasn't here to make friends, but it might help if everyone wasn't scared to death of him.

A man rode around the corner on a mule, took one look at Joel, and reined his mount in the opposite direction. He had to spur it three times for the ornery thing to take off, making Joel wish for the hundredth time that he'd insisted on bringing his own horse. Well, it shouldn't be long. The townsfolk wouldn't want to spend the rest of the day hiding behind locked doors. Soon someone would have the courage to come out and talk to him.

And here came a man from the same cabin that Miss Huckabee had gone to last night. The man's clothes were worn, but evenly. No one who wrestled animals or traipsed through the forest would keep cotton clothes unripped long enough for them to wear that thin. He spotted Joel through smudged glasses and turned his steps accordingly. There was no fear or threat evident in his presentation. At first glance his hair looked entirely gray, but after a second look it was clear that there was still a healthy amount of blond hair involved, hanging on against time.

His approach was the tipping point on the scales of bravery. Doors began opening, and men who'd only peeked out the windows before waited until he passed before joining him. Funny how the news had spread without a single word being spoken. Were there connecting tunnels beneath their cabins that allowed them to communicate unseen? Joel wouldn't be surprised.

"Morning, Fred." A rough mountaineer nodded as the man passed. "Pritchard has already headed up the hill to get Clive."

Fred didn't acknowledge the statement but continued until he reached Joel. By this time Joel was on his feet, back to the wall, and facing nine men, none of whom looked happy to see him.

"I presume you're the deputy?"

Joel took that back. Fred seemed to be enjoying this very much.

"Yes, sir. Deputy Puckett. And who might you be?"

"I'm Fred Murphy. Thought I'd welcome you to Pine Gap since Sheriff Taney hasn't made it to town yet."

Brown tobacco juice was slung into a puddle at Joel's feet by a scruffy old-timer. "Whatcha going to do about Sheriff Taney, anyway? We never asked for you to replace him."

Fred waited for his response. Everyone did.

Joel forced his chin to stay level. He knew what his orders were, and so did Sheriff Taney. Too bad Governor Marmaduke wasn't there to explain. "Sheriff Taney and I will work it out. All you need to know is that I'm here to apply the law. I don't know you and I don't know your neighbor. Frankly, it's none of my business what happened last year or last week. There'll be no vengeance, no vigilante justice. It's over. Everyone starts out today with a clean slate. Don't run afoul of the law, and you'll have nothing to fear from me."

The crowd parted as a bear of a man pushed through. In his late forties, the hammer-fisted mountaineer with the neck of an ox overshadowed two of the men standing in front of him. His appearance brought mixed reactions from the group, and Joel was quick to note who shied away from him and who cozied up.

"Clive Fowler." He spoke his name like he'd earned it in the trenches of a hard-fought war. "What pretty little plaything did good Governor Marmaduke send us?"

The bare twitch of a mouth was all the humor the men showed. Joel's heartbeat slowed. Something told him he'd already met this man.

"You got your coat on right side out today, Mr. Fowler." Joel looked him square in the eye, not hiding his meaning. "I didn't rightly know what to do with those sticks you tossed me, so I started a little fire to keep warm by last night."

Judging by the response of their audience, they thought Joel was poking a mad bull with a dull stick, but Clive wasn't shaken. He presented like a worthy opponent, one Joel would do his best to change into an ally.

"Those sticks represent a warning—a promise of a thrashing to come if one doesn't mend his ways. For the most part, those warnings have been heeded, so I'm not convinced that we need any outsiders interfering with our business. We've got it handled."

"I'm not here to interfere with legitimate business. Everyone behaves themselves, and we'll get along just fine."

"And if they don't?" His words didn't sound like a threat, more like a challenge—a challenge to do better, but a challenge just the same. Perhaps this Fowler character wasn't looking to cause problems as much as he wanted to fix them.

"If they don't, I'm going to do my dead-level best to put them before a judge."

"Not everyone is partial to that idea."

Joel didn't blink. "I didn't ask for permission, did I?" Feathers were getting ruffled. He shrugged. "Now, y'all know better than I what's been going on here, and you know the challenges we're going to face to get it cleaned up. But in the end what we all want is a place where your cattle aren't disappearing, where a disagreement doesn't end with someone dying, where you don't have mysterious riders harassing people after sunset."

From the back of the group a man blurted, "Why do you think they're riding? To do just what you said, and the Bald Knobbers have done a fine job of it, too."

Bald Knobbers? Was that what they called themselves? Joel nodded. "And maybe some are grateful for their help, but I don't expect anyone to do my job for me. It ends now. That doesn't mean your information isn't important. You're welcome in my office anytime."

"As soon as someone unlocks it for you." Low chuckles rumbled over the group.

Now that they mentioned it, Joel was in a helpless position. No key. No horse. No breakfast. He rested his hand against his gun belt, an unconscious move that seemed to happen whenever he felt at a disadvantage. "I look forward to meeting Sheriff Taney. In the meantime, where do I go about getting something to eat?"

Cold stares met his request, and instead of answering, men broke off in twos and threes, heads bent in lazy discussion. Only Clive Fowler and Fred Murphy remained.

Clive stood as rock solid as the mountain behind him. "I don't want you to get the wrong idea, son. I'm a God-fearing man. I don't take from no one and I don't suffer any nonsense. You come to town saying you're the law—well, we've heard that before. There are those here who don't care two bits what the law says. The sheriff turned a blind eye to the goings-on. Under his watch a killer escaped not once but twice. But the men of this town have brought order. That was us—volunteers, not some appointee by a politician up in Jefferson City. So sorry if I don't act relieved to see you here. I'll wait to shake your hand once you've actually done something worthwhile."

With that he turned and strode away. Every eye on the square followed his path, and then they grouped again, probably trying to guess what Fowler said to Joel and probably guessing correctly.

Joel eased the tension out of his knuckles, but there was no time to relax. He'd be under suspicion from dawn to dusk.

"About breakfast . . ." Fred Murphy's round spectacles

looked like they'd dive off his nose if it weren't for the gold wire anchoring them on his ears. "My wife wouldn't mind cooking you up something to eat. She's a fair cook and it's probably the best offer you'll get."

"I'm beholden to you." Joel gathered his saddlebags and followed his host.

"You haven't met Sheriff Taney yet?" Fred kept his head down and hidden by his floppy hat brim.

"The train was late. By the time I got here, no one was about."

Fred glanced sideways at him. "No one?"

Joel's teeth ground together. He wouldn't be discussing the encounter with the gang, and he certainly wasn't going to mention any late-night meeting with a lady. He'd learned that lesson from a harsh teacher. "No one who would help me."

Something about that comment amused Fred. He clasped his hands behind his back and leaned into the hill as it grew steeper. Joel's slick-bottomed boots didn't grip so well on the rocky incline, but Fred didn't seem to notice the pitch at all. It was a wonder all these little cabins didn't just slide off into a pile at the foot of the mountain.

They stopped before a cabin that was held level by a rock foundation. A room of sawn planks with its own door was attached to the cabin. Newspaper columns and notices fluttered from two boards hung on either side of the door.

It was this newer part of the building that Fred entered. He paid particular attention to the cot in the corner before allowing Joel inside. Curious as to what he was looking for, Joel could see nothing unusual. Clothes tucked beneath a pillow and a trunk at the foot of the bed. An apprentice, obviously.

And for what trade? The scent of ink made him want to sneeze. A stack of blank paper was held down by rocks on three corners and an iron on the fourth. Newspapers from around the country were spread on a rack to the left of the door. A newspaper printer? If Joel's expression wasn't already dour, it doubled up on the spot. No wonder Mr. Murphy offered to feed him. Knowing the news was his bread and butter.

"Have a seat." Fred paused with his hand on the door that divided the room from the cabin. "I'll see what Mrs. Murphy can round up for you."

Joel would sit, but not just yet. He scanned the newspapers folded on the rack, either for resale or perhaps for reprinting the news. What news did they have out here? Any from home? He picked up a copy of the *Hart County Herald* dated from the last week. Nothing newer on the stand, but what did he expect? A daily in this area? The front page boasted illustrations of the various pieces of the Statue of Liberty being uncrated in New York as well as a drawing of what it should look like assembled, along with the news that the Calhouns had recently returned from visiting Mrs. Calhoun's family in Ohio. That was front-page news? He flipped the paper open to read an editorial by Mr. Murphy in support of free home delivery of the mail and what it would mean to Postmaster Finley to be compensated for bringing their mail around, and an unusually long article about a wealthy Boston family and their social calendar.

Maybe it'd been a quiet week, because in this paper Joel found no evidence of the supposed discord he'd been sent to quell. No reports of violence or mischief, no arrests, no ongoing trials—nothing. Perhaps Fowler was right. Perhaps he wasn't needed here. A few more pages only revealed trivial items like Widow Sanders's new recipe for rhubarb muffins and a book review of *The Adventures of Huckleberry Finn*.

He folded the paper and eased the creases back where they belonged. Interesting to see what Fred considered newsworthy, but he was relieved to find nothing about his anticipated arrival. The last thing he needed was mention of his whereabouts in a newspaper, and that was a fact. Not finding a chair at first glance, Joel took a seat on the cot. Too bad he hadn't met Fred last night. He would've slept a sight better in this quiet office than he did under the hanging oak.

He leaned back against the wall and let his shoulders relax. The room was warm. The smell of eggs wafted through the door with the sound of children's voices—

"What are you doing here?"

His hands flew off his lap as he jolted upright, knocking a pillow to the ground. He forced himself to stop and think before he moved again. No frantic fumbling from him. Not in front of this woman.

He gave her scowl long enough to set before answering. "Mr. Murphy invited me."

Betsy Huckabee had a bucket propped against her hip and looked more milkmaid by the morning light, but still bristling with restless energy. The roundness of her blue eyes gave her an innocent look, but the set of her mouth warned it was only an illusion.

"For what?" she asked.

"For breakfast." Then with a pat on the cot beneath him, he added, "And hopefully for a place to sleep."

How did she do that? Smile just so he knew there was something funny that he was missing? He wished he was free to plumb her secrets, but Joel couldn't mess up like that. Not again.

He'd picked up the pillow to set it over the nightshirt that'd been folded beneath it when he noticed a simple band of lace on the clothing. It only took one piece of lace to change a nightshirt into a nightdress, and that meant—

Joel crammed the pillow down and sprang to his feet. Just

imagine the rumors that could be started. He'd been alone with a lady and actually sitting on her bed. And he'd sworn that he'd be more careful this time.

Flinging the door open, Joel stomped outside, unwilling to consider what the startled lady thought.

CHAPTER 6

Betsy straightened the pillow so it adequately covered her night-dress. Jumpy fellow. He was observant, though. She'd credit him that. Most people either couldn't tell when she was laughing at them or didn't feel the need to demonstrate their displeasure so dramatically. Maybe he was easily embarrassed, but sitting on her bed wasn't a hanging offense. Then again, things could be different in Texas. She adjusted the bucket on her hip and went to close the door that he'd left open in his haste.

Uncle Fred popped his head into the room. "Where'd he go?" His eyes narrowed. "Betsy, what'd you say to him?"

"Nothing." She blinked a few times, and when that failed to convince him, she added, "Honest."

"No use in making him mad." Fred headed to the door. "You know how I enjoy hearing firsthand what's going on."

Hearing, but not printing it. "I have no reason to send him packing." And she had every reason to want him around. Her first Dashing Deputy story needed more material. As it was, she'd only introduced the hero—a valiant crusader with an eye for the ladies. She was raring to give him an adventure. She carefully swept the papers on her desk into a tidy pile. Had the deputy found her morning scratchings about his steely jaw and broad shoulders? Surely not, but she couldn't take any chances, even with her early drafts. "He was looking forward to breakfast," she said to Uncle Fred. "Maybe you can bring him back."

Uncle Fred called to Deputy Puckett from the step as Betsy entered the house to deliver the rabbit meat to Aunt Sissy. She plopped the bucket on the counter top. "Another breakfast?" she asked. "Today's my lucky day."

Sissy shot a worried glance at the fussing baby on the floor as she flipped the eggs. "Only enough for Fred's guest. Don't you go eating it all. You must have a tapeworm, girl."

Betsy picked up Eloise and bounced her on her hip. If she'd gone and done what everyone expected of her, she'd have her own progeny by now. She kissed Eloise on the forehead. Sweet baby, but she'd just finished raising the baby's half brothers when Uncle Fred and Sissy got hitched. Betsy was due a break before starting on another family.

The men entered along with Scott, who had been sent for a second pail of milk. Uncle Fred delightedly made introductions, but the deputy wouldn't even acknowledge Betsy. So he was tetchy? She'd better be on her best behavior if she wanted to shadow him. No more poking fun. If only it were that easy. Betsy handed Eloise a wire whisk to play with as she stepped away from the table to give them some room.

"You came all the way from Texas?" Sissy passed the deputy a plate. "Which part?"

"North central. A town called Garber."

"I bet it's real fine there." Sissy clasped her hands in front of her as he began eating. "Probably makes Pine Gap look pretty sorry by comparison."

Deputy Puckett swallowed down the first bite. "Yes, ma'am, it sure does," he said without lifting his head.

For crying aloud. If he were a real hero, he'd say something like, *No, ma'am. Pine Gap has a charm that the big towns in Texas could never hope to duplicate.* Or, *From what I've seen, Pine Gap excels in one area, in the beauty of its womenfolk.* Then he'd tip his hat and add an extra "ma'am" just for effect.

"But I might tolerate Pine Gap better on a full belly," he added.

Betsy rolled her eyes. This cowboy had a long way to go before he'd be quotable. "If Pine Gap isn't to your liking, then why did you leave Texas?" she asked.

He fixed her with a searing gaze. "It got too hot there," he said. And took another sip of milk, all the while watching her over the rim of the cup.

"Hot? The temperature, or—"

"Those are some right substantial pistols," Scott interrupted. "Can I shoot them?"

Sissy's gasp quickly smoldered into some heavy fuming. She took up the skillet with a trembling hand and excused herself to the sink. Uncle Fred suddenly looked a sight older than he had just minutes ago. Before Deputy Eduardo could answer, Betsy's uncle spoke up.

"My son has a fascination with the activity around here that we'd rather him know nothing about."

Only his son? Uncle Fred would've liked to shoot the guns himself if Sissy and Scott weren't watching.

Scott dropped his fist on the table. "All I've got is my .22 and that's only good for squirrels. How am I going to be able to protect my family if I don't get serious about this?"

This would be the perfect place for a hero to assure the family that he'd protect them—that there'd be no need for their boy to worry about the safety of his kin. Instead, Eduardo said around a mouthful of eggs, "I don't let anyone touch my pistols."

Scott slumped in his chair.

"Your hunting rifle is enough for now," Uncle Fred said. "As good as you hit squirrels, you don't have to worry about practicing with a pistol. And now that Deputy Puckett is here, what happens out in the mountains isn't our responsibility."

If only it were that simple. Again Betsy studied the deputy's smooth brow. How old was he? People didn't cotton to bossy youngsters. Still, he did a tolerable job putting on like he knew what he was about. Maybe he was older than he looked.

He glanced up. Betsy felt a jolt of lightning run through her when their eyes met again. He hadn't really answered her question about why he'd left Texas, but from the way he watched her, she dared not ask again. She turned away and crooned over the baby as if she weren't the least interested in the goings-on.

Scott spoke up again. "You ever wear chaps? Leather ones?"

Eduardo cleared his throat before answering. "And spurs, but I don't wear them unless my horse needs reminding who's boss."

Scott fidgeted and grinned. "I never thought I'd meet an honest-to-goodness Texas cowboy. Do you rope?"

"My roping ain't what it should be, but it's required learning in Texas. We got to be able to lasso the teacher or we don't get out of primary school." Betsy stole a peek just as the deputy winked at Scott, his normally stern expression showing just a touch of lightness. Then he cleared his throat and his voice dropped as he addressed Uncle Fred. "Since it looks like I've landed with the local journalist, I'd assume you know what's going on here. Anything you can tell me that a faraway politician might not know?"

Uncle Fred fiddled with the kerosene lamp on the tabletop. "It's not so bad now. If you were to go to Greene County or Christian County, they might need you."

"My orders are clear—Pine Gap, Hart County, to relieve Sheriff Taney."

Betsy's ears perked up. So did the man's who'd trained her. "When you say relieve him, do you mean you're going to help him or replace him?" Uncle Fred asked.

Deputy Puckett lowered his fork. "That's not my call. It's never been my call to make." He waited until Uncle Fred had the grace to look away before asking, "You say things are better. Why would that be? What's changed?"

"The Bald Knobbers." Scott plunked his elbows on the table. "They've been keeping the riffraff down. All except for that Miles Bullard, but he won't dare show his face as long as the Bald Knobbers are riding."

Sissy dropped a dish in the basin and walked out of the room—her usual response to the topic. Betsy cuddled the baby close, planted a kiss on her wispy hair, and made her way to the table.

"What does Bald Knobber mean?" Deputy Puckett asked. "Who are they?"

No discussion of the Bald Knobbers began without first glancing over your shoulder to see who could hear. Even though he was in his own house, Uncle Fred looked both ways.

"A bald knob is a mountaintop without trees—not very common in this part of the country. They meet on bald knobs so no one can sneak up and overhear their plans."

"What are their plans?" Deputy Puckett tapped his finger against his tin cup.

"They do the job that the law failed to do. Ever since the war, there's been all sorts of trouble out here. Bushwhackers, outlaws, moonshiners, everyone at each other's throats, and Sheriff Taney turned a blind eye. Finally, some of the men had

had enough. They banded together and took out after the troublemakers."

"Illegally."

Uncle Fred's face hardened. "It was a hard choice for many of them. Do something without the government's approval, or sit by and let your neighbors be killed. One's illegal, but the other is immoral. Which would you choose?"

Deputy Puckett didn't answer that question. A prickle of fear crawled up Betsy's back. Uncle Fred was right—things had simmered down. What kind of trouble would this man stir up? Would he actually punish those who'd helped them survive? Betsy had been nurtured by this town. She'd taken meals in nearly every kitchen in the hills. She didn't approve of an outsider coming in to straighten things up.

"Give me an example," the deputy said, "of some of this righteous, illegal activity."

Uncle Fred settled into his chair, and Betsy prepared for the story she knew was coming.

"Miles Bullard was a ne'er-do-well around these parts. Would get liquored up and play the fool in town, insult the ladies, and assault anyone he felt slighted by. Fowler's boys had finally had enough. They'd tossed him a bundle on his porch to warn him, but he hadn't heeded it. Next time he hit town all lit up, they hogtied him, threw him over a mule, and rode him out of town. Got him up the hill, and they lashed him with the same willow branches they'd thrown on his porch."

Deputy Puckett's face hardened. "Was he hurt?"

"Mostly his pride," Uncle Fred said. "But he didn't learn his lesson. That night Stony Watson, a good family man and the father-in-law of my nephew Josiah, got killed when he went to check on his open barn. Best anyone could tell, Bullard was poking around there, up to no good. Didn't take no time at all before the gang caught him and hauled him in to Sheriff Taney."

Betsy remembered that night. She'd pretended to go to bed early so she could sneak out and watch once they caught him. She'd never seen a man look so ill as Sheriff Taney did when Fowler presented him with a real-life murderer all trussed up and ready for trial.

"Was he convicted?" the deputy asked.

"Convicted?" Uncle Fred uttered a gruff laugh. "He wasn't even tried. Somehow he escaped Taney's grasp before the moon came up the next night. Taney's only response was to carry on about Bullard defending himself against the gang and being fearful for his life—as if the gang were responsible for Miles going to Stony's and shooting him in cold blood. But the gang stayed vigilant, and it wasn't too long before someone managed to wing Bullard on the run. He showed up at Doctor Hopkins's, but Fowler tracked him there and brought him in again. This time it only took Sheriff Taney a few hours to lose his prisoner. That's when we pretty much gave up on the sheriff and started looking to Fowler for help."

The deputy shook his head as if something were beyond his comprehension. "Why wouldn't Sheriff Taney hold him for trial? That's his job. That's the law."

Uncle Fred removed his glasses and polished them on his shirt sleeve. "I've spent many an hour cognating on that. I reckon he thought that it wasn't right of the Bald Knobbers to thrash Bullard in the first place. The sheriff didn't appreciate them getting in the way, so he probably figured that they brought it on themselves. Fact is, I couldn't tell you for sure that Stony was even a member of the gang. Likely his only offense was that he had something Bullard wanted to steal."

Poor Katie Ellen. She and her pa had been close. Katie Ellen would probably be hunting Bullard herself if she weren't expecting another little one. Betsy couldn't help but feel gloomy about it all.

"So when do you get started?" she asked the deputy in an effort to clear the air.

The deputy directed his answer to her uncle. "As soon as Sheriff Taney and I iron some things out. And I get a horse."

"You need a horse?" Betsy handed Scott the baby and took up a kitchen towel. "Are you sure? Mules do just fine in the mountains."

His mouth fell open, astonishment voiding his decision to ignore her. Pinning her with eyes that she happily realized were gray, he announced, "I'll not be riding a mule."

Betsy couldn't keep her mouth from twitching at the seriousness of his tone. She remembered her brother Josiah putting his foot down when Katie Ellen wanted him to build her her own carpentry shop on their farm. He'd caved like a sinkhole during flood season when she'd pouted sufficiently. You had to wonder what it'd take to get Deputy Puckett astraddle a mule.

Uncle Fred nodded to Betsy, her signal to take the dirty dishes. "I reckon you'll want to see Taney as soon as he hits town."

"I'm locked out of the jailhouse until then."

"Then what will we do with you?" Uncle Fred meant it in jest, but the deputy stood. His shoulders blocked the light from the lone window in the room.

"I've trespassed on your hospitality long enough. I've got to learn my way around."

Uncle Fred frowned. "I didn't mean to rush you off—"

"I'm not rushing." The deputy dropped his hat on his head and hesitated at the door, then with almost a guilty shrug, he turned and tipped his hat to Betsy.

Uncle Fred whistled as the door closed. "How long do you suppose he'll last?"

She only needed him long enough to inspire a few stories, but something told her that he might cause more trouble than he was worth.

CHAPTER 7

Joel treaded the rocky road to town. The whole situation was ridiculous. He felt like a fish without fins, a bird without wings, a porcupine without quills. What was he supposed to do? Wait until something illegal happened, then run over the mountains and try to chase down the bad guys on foot? From his instructions, he'd understood that the town was supposed to provide him with a mount, but no one in town seemed of a mind to. If the sheriff didn't show soon, he'd have to send a telegram. Surely someone here answered to the governor.

As the road left the newspaper office, it straightened out and headed . . . north? Northwest? Joel didn't even know which direction he was facing. The roads curved and wound like a worm left on the hook. He needed a map—needed to get the landmarks fixed in his head. Rivers, hills, bluffs. What could he use to orient himself in this bewildering landscape?

Coming down the hill, Joel spotted two horses tethered to the hitching post in front of the stone jailhouse. Well, a horse and a child's pony, to be exact, but finally, someone who would give him some direction. Sure enough, the front door was open, too. Looking better and better. Joel's pace quickened now that he knew his next step. He'd come here to help and didn't want to waste another minute.

The wind whirled around the building, tugging at his hat, until he stepped under the shelter of the porch. Even though the door was open, he rapped on the doorframe. Didn't want to make the wrong impression.

"Come on in."

The first things he saw upon entering were the soles of a small pair of boots. They belonged to a corpulent man with skin pulled as tight as a sausage casing. His thinning gray hair had sprinkles of red in it, which perfectly matched his freckled complexion. With a grunt the man swung his feet off the desk and fell forward, barely getting his elbows up in time to stop his momentum from throwing him face first on the desk.

"What have we got here?" He took his time taking in Joel's clothing, his gaze sticking at the gun belt and boots. "A real live cowboy, complete with all his tackle and trim."

Joel removed his hat and set it on the desk next to the man's rounded bowler. Even Joel's hat was four inches taller. "I'm Deputy Puckett. Who are you?"

The man leaned back in the chair, his feet dangling a half inch off the floor, and wiped his hands on his dingy white suit. "I'm Mayor Walters, your new boss." His face scrunched up in an awful imitation of a smile.

"I'm here on the governor's orders. Not yours," Joel said.

"He can order what he will, but I've not seen him around these parts. Not since the Battle of Hartville, but we don't talk about those days, do we? He's a loyal American now."

The boards beneath Joel's feet creaked. He'd been called here because the local politicians were too crooked to be trusted. No longer did the state have any faith that they would be impartial. In fact, according to his briefing, it was assumed in most cases that the local magistrates were involved in the illegal activity. Looking over the self-important man before him, he could easily believe it. Still, he had to proceed cautiously.

Joel stepped away. He turned and inspected the room—two cells, each with a lone cot. Dust had settled over the padlocks. Joel took one in his hand and rubbed until true black iron shone beneath his thumb.

"This cell hasn't seen much use lately." The padlock clanged against the iron bars as he released it. "Guess y'all don't have a crime problem after all."

"Not one that'd warrant a stranger coming in, that's for certain. We can take care of our own."

Joel nodded. "Then Governor Marmaduke was mistaken. I won't take any more of your time. If you'll direct me to the telegraph office, I'll let him know that you refused my service, and then I'll get out of here." *And back to Texas, where people are sane*, he wanted to add. If only going back to Texas were an option.

Mayor Walters wrinkled his nose. "You don't fool me, Deputy Puckett. That's a nice attempt at forcing my hand, but I didn't survive the last twenty years here without recognizing an ambush when I see one. No, you won't give the governor the chance to send in troops. One lawman is bad enough, but I think we'll be able to handle you." He pulled on a desk drawer. It stuck halfway open, then with a jerk he forced it the rest of the way. A brass ring caught the sunlight as he tossed a set of keys to Joel.

Joel caught the keys and dropped them into his vest pocket without breaking eye contact with the smug man. "That's my office. Now how about my transportation?"

The mayor smiled, ginger whiskers spreading like a curtain. "Your horse is outside."

Joel nodded again. If God had wanted him to walk

everywhere, He wouldn't have invented horses. Joel dropped his hat on his head and strode outside, the mayor hot on his heels. The black horse caught the sunlight and glistened. Obviously well groomed and well fed, it tossed its head as if it appreciated Joel as much as he appreciated it.

The diminutive Walters reached above his head and caught the saddle horn. He kicked his short leg off the hitching post to get one foot in the stirrup—the wrong foot. The black horse shook its head. Joel had to agree with the horse. This man needed to let it be.

"What are you doing?" Joel tried to steady the pacing horse before it threw the mayor off.

The mayor's face was slicked with sweat. Joel doubted he'd ever been on this horse before, or quite possibly any horse, but he managed to hold on until he got the correct foot in the stirrup. Then with a mighty effort he pulled himself into the saddle.

Joel had already untied the reins and reluctantly placed them in the mayor's outstretched hand. "Where are you going with my horse?"

The mayor couldn't answer immediately, not huffing as he was to catch his breath. He smiled between each wheeze. "This isn't your horse. That one is."

Joel looked around, but he didn't see another animal in sight—besides the pony.

"You've got to be kidding me," he said. "That ain't right."

"My regrets." The mayor yanked on the reins. The black horse didn't budge.

"Look here." Joel went to the pony and, standing flat-footed, threw his leg over its side. "This horse isn't big enough for me." He crammed his feet into the stirrups. "My knees are in the way."

Jabbing his horse with his heels, the mayor finally got it to move. "What a pity. Gonna be hard keeping up with those Bald Knobbers, ain't it?"

Joel let his legs drop to the sides, and his toes brushed the ground as he watched Mayor Walters ride away. On this horse, he'd be a laughingstock.

Back in Texas, the outlaws feared Joel and the townspeople respected him. The only thing he ever caught grief over was his refusal to court the fine daughters of Garber, and that was his undoing.

Joel had wanted to be a sheriff someday, and he was willing to work the extra hours and cover the extra miles to do it. That allowed no time for dancing attendance on a girl. Growing up in a house with three older sisters had made him gun-shy of matrimony. Frills and curls meant fussing and bickering, and he wanted nothing to do with that, much to the distress of the conniving mothers throughout Blackstone County. There wasn't a force on Earth more powerful than a Texas mama hunting a qualified son-in-law for her precious princess. Their combined efforts to shackle him had failed, until a lady resorted to dishonest measures.

The pony's ears twitched, then lay flat. Not only was it little, but it was also mean-tempered. Joel dismounted, or stepped off, and went to untether the reins as he mulled over the decisions that had led to this disaster.

That night a month ago, when Joel had ridden out to check on a wrecked buggy, he had no idea he was riding into a trap. By the next morning, Mr. Blount was in the sheriff's office insisting that Deputy Puckett marry his daughter, Mary. Joel's protests went unheeded. Sheriff Green was up for re-election and he didn't need the distraction. *"Marry the girl,"* he ordered Joel, *"and then get back to work."*

Joel refused, killing his career and his good reputation. The sheriff was generous enough to tell Joel about this position in the distant Ozark Mountains, but only if Joel kept the sheriff's recommendation secret. Sure, his parents knew where he was, but if word got back to the Blount family that he hadn't turned in his badge, they'd be incensed—still furious that instead of netting a son-in-law, their plans had only blackened their daughter's name.

They were responsible, but Joel had paid the price. And why had God allowed it? Wasn't God supposed to fight his battles for him? Wasn't God the vindicator of those falsely accused? Then why was he stuck in this backwoods town with only a disgraceful animal to help him?

By the force of his will, Joel stilled his heart. He scanned the rocky streets of Pine Gap. He had a fresh start here. No one knew about Texas, and Texas didn't know about Pine Gap. He was wiser now and better acquainted with the dangers of female connivances. True, no one wanted him here, but soon he'd earn their trust and these shenanigans would end. That was what he had to aim for. Until then, he'd keep his patience. Keep his eyes fixed on God and stay above reproach, above question.

He had to succeed here, because he was out of options.

CHAPTER 8

The pony twisted its head to nip at Joel's knee, which was way too close to those teeth as it was. No wonder it was in a foul mood. The little thing wasn't made to carry this much man. He felt foolish riding it, but the only other option had been to sit at the jail and gaze at the beautiful stallion tied up in front of Mayor Walters's dry goods store.

Seeing how coveting was breaking a commandment, Joel had decided to poke around town and introduce himself to the townsfolk instead. The morning had come and gone, and still the erstwhile sheriff had yet to appear. Time to find him and make his acquaintance.

The houses were close to the road but still hard to spot through the trees. Even where lawns had been cleared, saplings sprang up, attesting to the resistance of the forest. Must be a constant struggle to keep any space clear here. Back home people planted trees for shade. He guessed no one was ever satisfied with what they'd got.

He'd gotten as far as the edge of town when he recognized the house from the night before. Mrs. Sanders, was it? But last night he'd thought the sheriff's house had been in the direction that the bandits had ridden. He was all turned around and not even sure he'd set out in the right direction from the first. If only he knew who was trustworthy.

Joel hadn't counted on how hard it'd be to just jump in and start swimming. In Garber, he'd known from childhood who was a troublemaker, what parts of town were poison, and who could be trusted to tell the truth. Here, it'd take some time to figure it out. He suspected that those burlap sacks weren't the only masks being worn by the citizenry.

The pony was of a mind to turn to the left at the crossroads. Joel pulled on the reins to stop him. The ornery thing backed up a few steps. He loosened the reins just as its ears went back. It was getting agitated, and so was he. The horse danced sideways, balked, and then did what Joel had known was inevitable—tried to buck him off.

"No you don't." He tightened his knees around the horse's small barrel. If this little mountain pony thought it could throw him . . . It bucked again, curving its back with the effort. Joel's teeth jarred. The short legs connected with the ground before he was prepared. His timing was off, but he would prevail.

A giggle. Out of the corner of his eye, Joel caught the outline of a woman standing in the trees. The reins slipped. The pony reared, then plunged. Joel came out of the saddle, but he didn't fall off. Instead he landed smack-dab on the saddle horn.

The pain was intense. His legs went weak and his stomach cramped as he slid to the side and fell to the ground, which fortunately wasn't too far away. He held onto the reins as he lay on his side and tried to breathe again. A calico skirt danced into his limited view, accompanied by worn brown boots.

"Give me the reins," she said.

He coughed. Almost gagged. Forced his voice to steady. "No."

The boots shifted. The skirt swayed. "You're in no condition."

He rolled to his feet and forced his spine straight. The horse danced away from him, eyes wild and speculative. Joel jerked it closer. "We're not done yet."

Betsy shrugged. "Suit yourself." She stepped back and, with a sweeping arm motion, presented him the road on which to seriously injure himself.

He couldn't let the pony win. Had to get back into the saddle. He winced at the thought but had no choice. No mountain pony would get the best of a Texan. It wasn't in the natural order of things.

The horse tossed its head as he approached. Another tug on the reins to bring it around, and he got a foot in the stirrup. Quick as lightning he was astride it, but he took his time easing into the saddle. Completely focused now, Joel welded himself to the animal's back and let it spend itself. It was mean. It was stubborn. But it didn't have the strength of a full-sized equine, and he'd messed with a few of those.

Sides heaving, the pony began to break. Its head dropped forward. Its ears calmed. Resignation settled over it like a heavy dew.

Job done. Joel reached forward and patted its neck, murmuring soothing noises. He'd forgiven those who'd trespassed against him. He'd even turned the other cheek . . . in a manner of speaking. Not that he had any intention of keeping this pony, but they had to reach an understanding.

As for that woman . . .

"Where'd you get the horse?" she asked.

Watching that the beast didn't pull any more foolishness, he dismounted. "By our contract, the city had to provide me with one."

"Looks like they got it for half price. So much better than a mule." With hands deep in her pockets, she pulled her coat tight around her back and tucked her chin into her scarf. The blue of the coat brought out the blue of her sparkling eyes. "Where are you going?" Flecks of dried leaves floated down and landed on her blond braids, but she didn't seem to notice or care.

"I'm headed out to see Sheriff Taney."

"And who gave you directions?"

"Some fellow named . . ." He looked right, then left. "They steered me wrong?" The town looked so innocent from here on the top of the hill.

"And those are the townsfolk. Once you get out in the woods, you'll get shot before you get close enough to ask."

The horse's tail swished. Whatever truce they'd brokered was being rethunk even as he tarried. He might have to fight the beast again to prove himself, but he wouldn't give in. And the woman seemed more stubborn than the pony.

"I came here to do a job. If I can't ride outside of town by myself, how am I going to protect the womenfolk like you?"

He'd expected her to argue, but instead she beamed. Her eyes crinkled up, and he saw for the first time a dusting of freckles on her nose. "That was perfect," she said. "Inspired and inspiring."

Not the response he was expecting, but before Joel could comment, a scream pierced the air.

Joel turned toward the cry, surprised it came from beyond Mrs. Sanders's house. Here the road turned rocky and wide, but before he could get on the pony, Betsy Huckabee took off without him.

"Come on!" she said. "That's Katie Ellen. I'll show you the way."

She darted up the winding road, anticipating the dips and

turns as they went. Another shout for help, and a child's voice joined in.

"Katie Ellen, I'm coming," Betsy belted in twice the voice Joel had ever heard a young lady of his acquaintance use.

He held himself out of the saddle by standing in the stirrups, which the pony didn't appreciate, but it did seem content to follow Betsy. The road widened to expose a massive barn, probably an auction house, but no one was about. He slowed to evaluate the scene, but Betsy ignored the large doors in front and raced around the pens to the back. He didn't like rushing in until he'd had time to make a plan. What if this was some sort of ambush? What if that gang of rowdies was waiting for him around the corner? No one outside of this town even knew he'd arrived safely. He should've sent a letter home as soon as he got off the train, just to let his parents know that if he failed to write at Christmas, they should put the responsibility for his death on the tab of the good folks of Pine Gap.

Too late now.

He hurried around the pens, but instead of being greeted by hooded marauders, he saw a pretty woman, heavy with child, dancing around a well with a baby on her hip. At her side, a young boy bent over the well, stretching his arms over the rim.

"Poor, poor baby. Hold on for a little longer."

Betsy had the rope in her hand and was fishing it from side to side, lowering it and pulling it up tight. With dread in the pit of his stomach, Joel ran to the well, leaned over the rocky wall, and saw what was causing all the hubbub—a soaked, exhausted kitten.

"I was going to put the cover back on the well, but then you told me to go help Pa." Tears trembled on the brim of the boy's eyes. Another year and he'd be too old to cry about a kitten, but that didn't mean anything today.

Betsy held her tongue between her teeth as she concentrated. "Every time the bucket comes near the kitten, it bounces it under. It can't take too many more hits."

Joel reached down to catch his foot and yanked a boot loose.

Betsy turned and raised an eyebrow that was a tad darker than her blond hair. "You're gonna?"

"If you want the job . . ."

"Be my guest."

He tossed the second boot, unfastened his gun belt, and after a long hard look at Betsy, laid it on the ground behind him. He didn't like giving up his security, but hopefully taking a dunking of a cold morning would impress someone.

Standing barefoot he took another look down the well and shivered, but it wasn't getting any warmer. Betsy had already motioned the mother and son to come to her. The mother set the youngster down, and then they lined up with both hands on the rope and braced themselves like they were getting ready to take on a locomotive at tug-of-war.

"How much do you think I weigh?" he asked as he hung his feet over the edge.

"It's the cat that has me worried," Betsy said.

"There's only one pulley," the other woman said, "so the amount of force required is directly proportionate on a one-to-one ratio."

What was she? Some kind of engineer? Joel leaned forward to grasp the rope. The trio stumbled forward a few feet, then held steady. He didn't want to stay overlong. They couldn't hold him all day.

The well was deeper than he'd expected, but then again, they were on top of a mountain. Hand over hand he eased down, only then realizing he should've tested the spindle on the well before beginning this journey. The earthy smell of damp rocks grew even stronger as the circle of blue sky above his head shrank.

When his toes brushed the water, it made his toenails curl. Mountain-spring fed. Like ice. The water slipped over his ankles, then his knees. He gritted his teeth and tried not to whimper. He wished he could let go and plunge in, just to get it over with, but that would drown the blamed cat for sure.

Holding the rope with one hand, he unbuttoned the collar on his shirt, then reached down and grabbed the kitten by the scruff of the neck. The pathetic little thing shivered uncontrollably. Well, he knew how it felt. Still holding his body out of the water, he shoved the kitten into his shirt. Needlelike claws scratched him all the way down, but soon the kitten had settled atop his belt, its body quivering.

"Coming up," he hollered.

The rope wobbled, bouncing him with its movement as the ladies tried to pull him up.

"Just wait," he hollered. "I'll climb out."

He didn't need a boy and some womenfolk to hoist him out of a well, but by the time he reached the top, the idea had more merit. He grasped the spindle that held the pulley and swung his legs up and over the side. Walking his hands along the brace, he regained his balance and finally got his cold bare feet on the ground.

The boy's mouth trembled despite his fierce efforts for control. His eyes traveled from Joel's empty hands to the well behind him, but he didn't have the courage to ask.

Joel slid his hand into his shirt, which was now bereft of a button, and pulled out the raggedy animal. The tension in the boy's face melted, and his eyes rolled up as if in a prayer of thanksgiving.

"There you go. Safe and sound."

Joel didn't flinch, even as the kid threw himself toward him and wrapped his arms around his waist. Joel stood with arms upraised, unsure what to do. The mother was beaming at him, too.

Well, he'd needed to make allies. If a dunk in a freezing well was the best way to do it, then so be it.

CHAPTER 9

He'd saved a kitten from a well. A child in the well would've been better. Betsy looked at her nephew. No, she absolutely could not toss him in. Katie Ellen would skin her alive. But since she was writing fiction, it didn't matter who Deputy Puckett saved. She could make Eduardo Pickett's story read however she wanted. What if he rescued a little girl who was complected like a china doll and could sing like a mockingbird? Wouldn't the women swoon over that? Betsy smiled. All in all, the deputy had done pretty well for his first day, and she'd see to it that her fictional hero did even better.

And then there was his appearance. Deputy Puckett held his leg out to the side and shook it about. Betsy dearly wished that he'd slipped off the rope and gotten drenched. That'd make a better story, but she'd work with what she had.

Katie Ellen returned from the sale barn and handed Douglas a rag to wrap the kitten in. "My gracious, I didn't know how I was going to get that thing out of there," she said. "I'm Mrs. Huckabee, by the way. My husband, Josiah, works here at the auction house. I'm sure happy you came along when you did."

"Just doing my job," Deputy Puckett said with no little pride.

"What kind of job?" she asked.

"He's the new deputy we've heard tell of," Betsy answered. "Come to help Sheriff Taney."

Katie Ellen's face fell. Betsy hoped Katie Ellen would behave. If the Bald Knobbers had a parade on Main Street, Katie Ellen would deck herself in bunting and cheer them on. They were the only chance she had for getting justice for her father's murderer, and she wouldn't be partial to anyone getting in the gang's way.

"Name's Deputy Puckett," he said. "I guess you're kin of Miss Huckabee's?"

Betsy nodded when Katie Ellen failed to answer. "Uncle Fred told you about Mr. Watson. That was Katie Ellen's pa."

The deputy's jaw tensed. "My condolences."

Katie Ellen bristled. "Thank you for saving Douglas's kitten. We're mighty appreciative."

Yet from the way she herded her kids toward the barn, her thanks had come to an end. She called farewell to Betsy, then waddled inside with a second glance over her shoulder before disappearing into the giant entryway. Betsy didn't even have to hear the squawking of the hinges to know the doors were being pulled closed.

Eduardo tugged his gun belt through the buckle, then settled it on his hips. Putting his hands in front of him, he stood absolutely still, then quick as a hummingbird's wings, he had his guns in his hands. Betsy's eyebrows shot up. How'd he do that? It was like the guns leapt into his hands of their own accord. Pretty handy if someone was standing in front of you. 'Course, in the mountains he'd never see the bad guys coming.

His test seemed to satisfy him, because he returned the guns to their holsters and then with a sidelong glance noticed her watching him. He twisted at his ear and cleared his throat. Had he disremembered her so easily?

"Didn't peg you for an animal lover," she said. "That was right nice of you, going down that well to save a cat."

"I didn't do it to save a cat; I did it to save the well. Do you know how long it'd be before they could get water out of it if it had a carcass at the bottom? Dead cat hair floating in every bucket of water?"

Yeah, that statement definitely wouldn't make it into her story. And Betsy wouldn't bother telling him that they had a pump. The well hadn't been relied on for years.

They started down the hill toward town with the pony trailing behind.

"Still, it could go a long ways toward growing some friendly feelings for you," Betsy said. "On sale day, if you'd like, I could throw various animals in there for you to rescue. Then everyone would be beholden."

He stopped at a wide place on the road, the water running off his boots and making two dark spots on the ground. "Are you going to keep following me?" His eyes dropped as he rubbed his jaw with the back of his hand. "Traveling with a single young lady isn't proper. Surely you understand."

No, she didn't. "I'm not a young lady, and nobody around here worries about what I'm up to. As far as my reputation, there's not a man anywhere around here who's ever turned my head. I'm impervious, as my uncle says."

"I'm not worried about protecting your reputation, ma'am. It's my own I'm trying to protect."

Betsy frowned. When would this ornery man behave like a proper hero? He was forever saying the wrong things.

"I don't know what you have to gain from my company," he continued. "I'm not enticed by your beauty. I'm not charmed by your manners, and personally I'd rather fall off a cliff and land on a cactus than have to listen to a woman talk. You stand to gain nothing by being in my company, and I surely don't expect to profit from yours."

She realized her mouth was hanging open in surprise. No one had ever talked to her like that before. And for good reason. Everyone around these parts knew she could give back in equal measure.

"I'm so glad you explained yourself, Deputy. So considerate of you to protect me from wasting my time pining over you, but allow me to explain something. I am twenty-four years old. I see you grimace"—she waited for him to protest, which he didn't—"because you know that I'm well past marrying age. I had to work hard to get to this age without being shackled with a husband. I had to be rude at times, unfriendly, and withdrawn to keep the potential suitors at bay. None of those qualities come naturally for me. Since I've sailed those waters and have now arrived safely at port, I will revert to being the cheerful, friendly, gregarious woman I was born to be and will not pretend to be otherwise for you."

"All I'm saying is I don't—"

"Furthermore . . ." She paused to make sure he understood she was interrupting and he'd better listen. "Furthermore, I've been wandering these hills freely since I set feet in the dirt. At five years of age, I escaped from bushwhackers and ran for help when they took my parents hostage. At nine, I'd stay out all night with my brother Josiah, coon hunting. At ten, I left home to raise my nephews and help Uncle Fred when my aunt died. I come and go at will, where I will and when I will. These mountains are my territory, and I'll not be sitting by the hearth twiddling my thumbs just because a fancy Texas lawman stepped off the train. Is that clear?"

There. She'd said all she wanted, but if she'd hoped to make him mad, she was disappointed. He stood and studied her, his face devoid of any emotion, neutral of frustration or pleasure or the general reconciliatory ruse men usually affected toward women when they threw a fit. Had she not made an impression at all?

Finally he rolled his shoulders like he'd just been released from an overlong Sunday service. "Thank you for the sermon. Did I mention I'd rather land in cactus than listen to a woman talk?"

And he turned and walked away.

The pony rode about as smooth as a wagon with square wheels, but memories of a feisty blond woman kept Joel distracted for mile after bumpy mile.

Miss Huckabee hadn't asked for the dressing down he'd given her, but if he hadn't said those words, she could jeopardize everything. In fact, he felt rather foolish for even suggesting that she had designs on him, but the way she popped up everywhere had to be addressed.

Her uncle, the newspaper man, could he be putting her up to it? But if they were going to employ a spy, they should've used someone less intriguing. Betsy Huckabee and her quick smile were flypaper to Joel. He found himself stuck looking at her, no matter how he tried to get away.

Joel broke into a river bottom clearing dotted with hay stubble left from harvest. He felt like a goldfish in a bowl, the way the area was rimmed about by trees. Any number of people could be watching him and he'd never know it. When he rode outside of Garber, he might have to watch for someone hiding behind a tree, but never this, where there could be whole regiments standing shoulder to shoulder and he wouldn't be able to see them. Since when did an open field feel so threatening?

It didn't help that his horse couldn't outrun a glob of molasses rolling down a canning jar on a cold day. The dislike and mistrust between them was mutual. Surely Sheriff Taney would be understanding over the horse issue. Lawmen understood how important respect was to their profession, and no one could respect a deputy whose knees hit his elbows while riding.

Miss Huckabee had pointed out the hill ahead for him to be aiming toward. Even after their spat, she still looked fresh and sweet. The afternoon light had bounced off her cheek, scrubbed until it was as shiny as an apple. Maybe the blush was barely constrained fury, but either way, the sight raised his spirits.

So she thought she was impervious to any man's charms? Joel growled at the temptation to prove her wrong. She might not mean any harm, but his life had no room for a meddling woman.

He'd reached the hill, but he couldn't see any obvious paths from the clearing into the woods. A quick scan of the horizon revealed no smoke plumes to guide him. Well, if there wasn't a road, he could follow tracks. Just no telling where they'd lead.

After a few minutes of riding across uncharted wilderness, he found a wagon trail that looked recently used. Fallen leaves bore the creases of shod horse hooves, so hopefully the travelers were on their way home and not traveling cross-country. Luck was with him, because he found a cabin situated in the bottom of a hidden valley. Raccoon pelts were stretched across the cabin's walls to tan. A tree stump held an ax driven deeply into its heart, and a billy goat glared at him from atop the woodpile.

"Hello?" Joel called. It didn't take the hair on the back of his neck to tell him he was being watched. Even the goat looked nervously at the cabin. "Hello? Is anybody home?"

So intently was he watching the front door that he nearly

jumped out of his skin when a lanky fellow stepped out of the trees at his left. Realizing that he was nearly eye to eye with the man, even mounted, Joel quickly got off the horse. But it didn't seem to help his case.

"Howdy. I'm Deputy Puckett, and I was wondering if you could help me find Sheriff Taney's place."

"Well, I'm Bo Franklin, and I have trouble believing you're who you say you are." The young man's face was roughly shaved, although *why*, Joel couldn't understand. With cheeks as flat as his, a razor shouldn't have any trouble reaching every whisker. "If you're a deputy, then it seems to me you should've noticed that a crime has been committed right under your nose."

Joel bristled at the man's arrogant tone. His smirk needed readjusting.

"Right under my nose, you say? And what would that be?"

The young man spat a brown stream of tobacco. "Someone done stole half your horse."

Joel looked to the clouds. *Lord, even you had a decent animal to ride when you needed it.* Then he remembered that Jesus rode a donkey and left off his petitioning.

"And where does Sheriff Taney live?"

"If'n Taney wanted you to find him, seems like he would've told you how."

"Does Taney spend a lot of time hiding?"

Franklin lifted his chin. His body swayed, as if weighing his answer on the scales. "I'll tell you how to find him. The road splits just after the washout. Take the north branch and you'll come across Taney's place before dinnertime."

Joel sighed. Why'd it have to be this way? Why couldn't they understand that he really did want to help them? That he had no interest in interfering unless it was warranted?

Without a word he hopped into the pony's saddle. This

Bo Franklin didn't seem to be a dangerous fellow, but he bore watching.

"What's wrong with you?" Bo asked. "You don't seem none too happy over our conversation."

Thank goodness the pony had decided to behave. Last thing Joel wanted was to be curled up on the ground with another groin injury in front of this man. "I might not know these hills, but I know when someone's pulling my leg. What do you bet I take the south fork and I'll find Taney?"

Bo's mouth twisted into a smile. His eyes pulled tight into narrow slits, and a cut on his cheek glistened with new blood. "Do what you want, Mr. Deputy. You won't find people who care less than here."

CHAPTER 10

If people were cagey about something as simple as directions to the sheriff's house, then how would they act when an honest-to-goodness criminal was hiding? Joel brushed through the branches that stretched across the path. A wind chime of tin cans and wire jangled above his head. He'd just entered someone's domain, as the bawling coon hound was warning. He only hoped this was the one he was seeking.

The trees thinned to reveal a log cabin. Barbed wire stretched from trunk to trunk, making his path the only unchallenged approach—unchallenged besides the gray-haired man rocking on the porch with a banjo across his lap.

"Sheriff Taney?" Joel called.

"I've been waiting for you." His rocking chair halted as he sneered. "What in tarnation are you riding?"

Never more happy to get off a horse, Joel dismounted and tied the pony to a tree before continuing on foot. He nodded. "Isn't this what lawmen in the Ozarks ride? A miniature pony?"

"What would I be knowing about that? I don't reckon I am a lawman anymore."

Joel looked at the gnarled hands on the banjo and proceeded

with respect. "I'm Joel Puckett, sir. Pleased to finally make your acquaintance."

Beneath Taney's sagging brow, his sharp eyes traveled from Joel's big hat to his cowboy boots. "Well, don't you look purty? No wonder they gave you a toy horse. You're just a pretty little doll-baby."

Never before had Joel felt his youth so acutely. "I have a lot to learn, and that's a fact, but I aim to do my best."

"Unlike me? Is that what you're saying?"

"Not at all—"

"Listen, boy. You think everything is cut and dried. You think you can stop the bad guys and protect the good guys, but it ain't like that here. These fights have been going on for decades. They have long histories, and you won't make it right by swooping in and squashing the first person to step out of line. It's everyone for themselves, and the good guys catch all the blame."

What did Joel expect the man he was replacing to say? *Thank you for coming to do the job I failed at? Thank goodness they brought in someone with half my years to show me how to work?* Governor Marmaduke's office had warned him that more often than not, the sheriffs were part of the problem, which was exactly why someone from outside of the community had to be called in. Was Taney corrupt or merely inept?

"Any help or advice you can lend is mighty appreciated, but I still hold that right is right and wrong is wrong. Why someone breaks the law is none of my business. My job is to halt any criminal activity and to see that the ones perpetrating it are brought before a judge."

Taney's head wobbled from side to side. "What those people in Jeff City were thinking sending a lad out to do a man's job—"

"I take issue with that statement." Joel had always looked younger than he was, and even a beard didn't help. "I earned my rank as a deputy in a good-sized city. I've dealt with murderers, train robbers, cattle rustlers, and a host of ne'er-do-wells in Texas."

"This ain't Texas."

So he'd noticed. "It's not for me to boast, because ultimately my success lies in God's hands, but I wouldn't have come here if I didn't think I could do the job, and I'd much rather have your support than have you oppose me."

Sheriff Taney plucked a string on the banjo. The twanging sound seemed to climb right up Joel's backbone and rattle beneath his molars. Ignoring him, the sheriff stood and bent over a beat-up banjo case. He tugged a piece of lining loose, then ran the moth-eaten red velvet through his fingers.

"Reckon I have time to fix this case now that I've been put out to pasture."

"Sheriff, there are a lot of people in these parts who respect you. I've no mind to disabuse them of that sentiment. I'll leave it up to you how you want to explain my coming. You could even say you took a well-deserved retirement so you could—"

"I'm telling everyone that you cost me my job. That the dirty politicians in the capital thought a green cowboy from Texas could do better by them than their own elected official. That's what I'm saying. And mark my words, you coming won't bring nothing but trouble."

The branches rustled with the few leaves that were still hanging on until the first snow stripped them down. Joel understood Sheriff Taney's anger, but still he'd pray that the sheriff would reconsider his attitude. Joel wasn't his enemy, and Joel badly needed a friend.

"If you can feel good about that, then say what you will. For my part, I'm going to speak what I think will bring peace here instead of stirring up more trouble."

Joel said his good-bye, but Taney only responded with a snarl on his weathered face. Joel wished Taney was willing to help him get established, but then again, had he expected the sheriff to appreciate his arrival?

Back on the path toward town, Joel marveled at how much he missed his parents. He'd never been away from home this long. Never this far, either. It was funny because he'd spent the best part of his growing-up years trying to distance himself from his suffocating, although well-meaning, mother. Earning respect as a deputy wasn't easy when your ma still licked her hankie and cleaned your face on the boardwalk. He steered shy of her in public when he could, although he frequently stopped by his dad's watch-making shop to visit. Just knowing they were around, that he could pass down their street, that Ma would always have a piece of pie to accompany her lamentations over his failure to settle down, was a comfort.

No such comfort here, but he knew they were remembering him in their prayers. Just to picture them sitting at the table, his father's spectacles pushed up on his forehead, his mother wearing her apron, with their heads bowed over their dinner . . . he knew they were praying for him, and he held the thought dear. Why God hadn't answered his prayers was another question, but he'd do what he could not to let his parents down. He'd do nothing to break the trust they—and the state of Missouri—had in him.

A shotgun blast startled his horse. Not only was the pony small, but gun-shy, too? Joel tilted his head to listen for the sound ricocheting off the mountains. After sorting through the echoes, he thought his first reaction was correct. It came from the valley by Bo Franklin's house. After deciding that it wasn't faster to pick up the horse and carry it, he jabbed it with his heels and tore toward the homestead, grateful as he ducked beneath a gnarly limb that the horse wasn't taller, or he'd be sitting on the ground with a goose egg popping out of his forehead.

The sun was dipping behind the mountain, making for an early dusk, but there was plenty of light to see two men standing in the high patch of weeds in front of Franklin's cabin. A trace of gunpowder scented the air as Joel got off his horse. By the failing light he could make out his new friend Bo holding his shotgun on a horned caller with hands outstretched.

"If you shoot me, you'll rue the day." The visitor's words were muffled by the black sack over his head.

Joel's fingertips caressed the handle of his own six-shooter as he approached. "What's going on here, Bo?" One gun already drawn, and he'd bet all the cattle in Texas that the Bald Knobber was carrying.

"Found this jackanapes trespassing. With a bundle of sticks on my porch, there's no doubt what he's up to."

Having had a bundle of sticks thrown at his own feet, Joel was more than curious. Sure enough, the offending article was resting where Bo claimed.

Keeping one eye on Bo, whose sweat was catching the last rays of weak sunlight, Joel gave the Bald Knobber his attention. "Do those sticks mean what I think they mean?"

The man's shoulders went back and he stood a little taller. "Your friend Mr. Franklin has been stealing from Caesar Parrow's traps. Those coonskins on his wall don't belong to him."

The barrel of Bo's gun shook.

"That may be so," Joel said, "but the remedy is to tell me about it. Not to throw sticks on his porch. What good does that do?"

"It means that they aim to come back and flog me if I don't bless the ground they walk on," Bo said. "That's what that means."

The masked man crossed his arms over his chest.

"You don't deny that you mean to threaten him?" Joel asked.

"No, sir. I'm doing my part to see that justice is done, and I won't be apologizing for it."

Joel turned to his horse. He dearly wished that he'd had more time before any undertaking of this nature presented itself, but he'd been prepared to be disappointed. Lord, he hoped Ma and Pa were praying for him now.

Taking a length of rope from his saddlebag, he returned, and before either man knew what he was about, he'd tossed the Bald Knobber on the ground and had his knee in his back. "Mister, you are under arrest for trespassing and for threatening a citizen with bodily harm."

"Get off of me. You can't do this."

"You can't do this," Bo echoed. Now his gun was pointing at Joel. "Do you know how much trouble I'm going to be in if you arrest him?"

"Who is he, anyway?" Having secured both of the man's wrists, Joel tugged on the sack before realizing it was tied around the man's neck. The man managed to kick Joel's thigh while swearing but didn't land it hard enough to do any real damage.

"Don't pull his mask off!" Real fear tinged Bo's plea. "I'll give the skins back. I didn't know someone was looking for them."

"Nothing to fear," Joel said. "If you sure enough stole them, I'll deal with you on my next pass, but for now he's my greatest concern." The drawstring loosened and Joel yanked on the sack until it fell away.

"Uncle Pritchard?" Bo ran his hand through his hair. "Oh no. Ma's going to kill me."

"I wouldn't be worried about your ma, you idiot," Pritchard said. "If I end up going to jail because my half-wit nephew's been stealing Caesar's pelts, your name is going to be on the short list of every Bald Knobber—"

"Hey!" Joel jerked him to his feet. "Threatening him is exactly what you're in trouble for. Don't keep perpetrating the same offense right in front of me."

"I'm not pressing charges," Bo cried. "Let him go. Let's say I invited him here."

"Too late for that." Joel eyed his horse. Hauling in a miscreant should look better than bringing in a middle-aged man behind a pony.

"Don't I get a say? I'm the victim," Bo said.

"He's threatening you, which is exactly why you're afraid of him."

"It's not him so much. You haven't met my ma."

For crying aloud. Joel looped the end of the rope around the saddle horn. "It's not a far walk to town, and I seriously doubt the judge will go too hard on him, but this is exactly the sort of goings-on I'm here to prevent. Let's not make it more than it is."

Bo picked up the mask and hugged it to his chest. "I'll keep your mask clean for you, Uncle Pritchard. Nothing will happen to it while you're gone."

Joel marched back and pulled the mask out of Bo's unwilling fingers. "I'll take that," he said. "For evidence."

It hadn't taken long to get his hands on one of the disguises, and he had the feeling he was bound to see more of them ere long.

CHAPTER 11

"Betsy, Pa's looking for you."

Betsy stopped to gawk as her cousin Scott approached. His normal walk was afflicted by a very distinctive cowboy swagger.

"He wants to know if you've seen that deputy. What's the story?"

The story was that she'd been banned from ever speaking to the deputy again, which was downright inconvenient seeing as how getting him on paper was her ticket to independence.

"He's headed out to Sheriff Taney's. I'm watching for him to come back, though. It's nearly dark. . . ." Her words trailed off as she heard someone approaching. A horse, footsteps. Whoever it was was coming along slowly, dragging their feet like they had lead in their socks.

"Go on," she said to Scott. "I'll talk to him."

"Wouldn't it make more sense for me to talk to him? Man-to-man, you know."

Yes, it would. Then why was she so all-fired eager to send Scott away?

"Go," she said, falling into the bossy voice she'd used back when she was twelve and needed a restless three-year-old Scott to obey.

"Are you sweet on him, Betsy? Because if you are, you don't stand a chance. Every gal from here to—"

Betsy whirled around, hands on her hips. Scott stopped, but he refused to stop smiling.

"He is coming, and I don't want to be hanging around jawing with you. See, that's him now. . . ." And sure enough the deputy broke through the trees on his little pony, leading an irate Mr. Pritchard tied up behind him.

Scott whistled low and scratched the back of his neck. "I'm gone. Good luck." He jogged away.

There had to be some mistake. What was he doing with Mr. Pritchard? Betsy rushed forward to intercept him.

Deputy Puckett's face tightened. "I swear, woman. Stop jumping out at me like that."

But she was headed straight for Mr. Pritchard. "What are you doing? Why are you tied up?" She turned to the deputy. "Do you know who he is? He used to own the auction house before Isaac Ballentine. He's the seed salesman now. You aren't supposed to tie him up."

"He broke the law. That's all I'm interested in." The deputy kept plodding that tired pony toward the jailhouse, his face as set as granite.

Break the law? Mr. Pritchard? Betsy brushed off the dead grass clinging to the bound man's sleeve. "What's he talking about?"

"This young man doesn't understand. I was on official business, authorized by the leader."

Authorized? He had to be talking about official Bald Knobber business. "No, no, no." Betsy jogged a couple of steps to come even to the deputy's side. "You arrested him? Well, you don't understand." Then over her shoulder she said, "Forgive him, Mr. Pritchard. He'll let you go just as soon—"

"I'm not letting him go. He was threatening one of our citizens."

"Only Bo," Pritchard said.

Betsy waved her hand. "Oh, Bo? Was he raiding Caesar's traps again? Yeah, Bo don't care. He didn't tell you to arrest Mr. Pritchard, did he?"

"I don't expect a man who's being threatened to press charges. I'm the one responsible for his arrest."

Of all the pigheaded . . . "No, really, you don't understand." Betsy danced to stand in front of him, but now that the road had widened at town, Deputy Puckett maneuvered the horse around her. "This isn't right," Betsy sang. "The thing that you should do . . . this isn't it."

They'd reached the jail. Deputy Puckett dismounted and untied Mr. Pritchard from the saddle. Mr. Pritchard bristled as the deputy opened the door and dragged him inside like a dog on a leash.

"You're going to regret this," he said as he passed.

Betsy clapped her hand to her forehead. "What in the world made you think this was a good idea?"

The jail cell clanged closed after Mr. Pritchard passed through. With a huff, he settled on the cot and began untying his own bonds. Deputy Puckett took a seat at the desk and lit a lamp.

Betsy bent at the waist and rested her elbows on his desk as he opened a ledger. Trying her dead-level best to be persuasive, she scooted her face as close to his as she dared. "What I was trying to tell you," she whispered, "is that the Bald Knobbers have taken an oath. You can't take one of them without messing with all of them. This idea of arresting Mr. Pritchard, you might want to rethink it."

He looked up, and his gray eyes caught and held her in a

gaze that made her heart feel bigger. Her mouth went dry at the proximity of him. The ends of her fingers tingled. He really was as handsome as she remembered. The way his eyes shone so bright through dark lashes, making you certain that he was thinking of nothing else in the world but you. If she could get the way he made her feel into words, every paper in the country would run her stories.

But then his perfect lips moved and said, "You are the most bothersome woman I've ever come across," which pretty much ruined the moment. Closing the ledger, he rose and took two steps toward the jail cell before spinning to her again. "I take that back. You are the second most bothersome woman I've ever come across. Please, for the love of Pete, don't make being number one your aim."

Betsy didn't like being second place at anything. Mr. Pritchard's mouth twitched, appearing a sight more amused than a man facing incarceration had a right to be.

"I'm trying to save you from making a big mistake." Now she was speaking to Eduardo's back. "You're new, so they might cut you some slack, but arresting Mr. Pritchard for bringing his nephew into line won't be your finest moment."

But he'd stopped listening to her and said, "Mr. Pritchard, I hold stock with the wisdom of the natives, so I reckon you might be able to help me with my problem here. I have to in-terview you before I decide whether or not to release you to your own cognizance, but I cannot conduct an interview with a hostile third party present. Do you have any idea how I might go about ridding the premises of this nuisance without further alienating the populace?"

Betsy's mouth dropped open. He was talking about her. And making it harder and harder for her to keep the Dashing Deputy image untarnished in her mind.

Mr. Pritchard rubbed his formerly bound wrists. "The populace knows Betsy. Anything short of physical harm, and they'd be mostly forgiving."

"Mr. Pritchard!" she gasped.

"That's what I figured." Deputy Puckett marched to the door and held it open. "Thank you for your concern, Miss Huckabee, but right now the biggest obstacle to my success happens to be your own charming self. If you'd allow me to finish my job, then I'd be happy to review with you why citizens are not allowed to threaten other citizens, even if they do happen to be kin."

"It's not the kin part that worries me. It's that mask you have on your desk. That means more than blood ties to the men—"

"Go, Betsy," Mr. Pritchard said. "You aren't helping my case any."

She looked from one man to the other. To be honest, she really wasn't concerned about Mr. Pritchard. You'd be hard-pressed to find twelve men in Hart County who wouldn't laugh their heads off at the charges, so he was in no danger. No, it was the man who obviously didn't want her help who needed it the most. But he stood, feet planted wide, door held open with one hand and his other hand resting against his gun belt.

"Don't say I didn't warn you," she said and passed beneath his arm. If she wasn't wanted here, fine. She'd rather spend her time crafting a perfect hero—one who could only exist in fiction.

Betsy Huckabee marched past Joel with her back as stiff as a rifle barrel. Curly wisps of her hair trailed behind her like the tail of a runaway horse. Maybe she was trying to help him, but Joel had enough trouble on his hands.

He swung the door closed before facing his prisoner. "I apologize for my lack of professionalism. Normally I wouldn't lock my prisoner up before the interrogation, but it was either you or her."

"I was sore angered at you, but now I kinda feel pity," Pritchard said. "Don't expect anyone to tell you how to handle Betsy. She pretty much gets what she wants around here, but she's a good gal. There's no harm in her."

Any woman could cause harm, half the time without even meaning to.

Joel grasped the brass key ring in his hand. The ring was lighter than the one in Garber. Not as many cells, he reckoned. He opened the door and motioned Mr. Pritchard to a chair at the desk.

Pritchard flexed his wrists and wiggled his fingers. "No shackles? You ain't afraid of me now?"

"Never was." Joel dropped into his chair, licked his thumb, and flipped through the pages of the ledger. A few entries were written in faded ink, but nothing for months. "According to this record, it appears there hasn't been much trouble recently."

Pritchard snorted. "When something happens, people know not to waste their time going to the sheriff. It hasn't proven very effective."

"Well, maybe our luck will change. Or Bo Franklin's anyway. We'll see how effective we can be."

At this, Pritchard leaned back in his chair until the front legs left the floor. He turned his head to watch the trees sway through the window as Joel began his questioning.

His answers were straightforward, if not gracious, and did nothing to prove his innocence. In fact, he only verified exactly what Joel suspected. But after hearing everything and spending a few minutes with him, Joel was confident that Pritchard wasn't a danger to society, much less his own nephew. After obtaining his promise not to leave the county before he was able to appear before the judge, Joel decided to release him.

But by that time, Pritchard had begun to enjoy himself. Reciting Bo's record of thievery had thawed whatever bitterness he'd felt, and he seemed to take satisfaction in Joel's pen recording his nephew's alleged crimes. In fact, Pritchard felt good enough to offer Joel a piece of advice.

"You ain't going to keep that pony, are you?"

Joel blew the wet ink dry on the page before answering. "Do you know where I could trade it?"

Pritchard's forehead wrinkled and his long, droopy eyebrows wagged. "If you appreciate good horseflesh, Jeremiah Calhoun is who you need to see. He'll treat you fair."

Joel had heard the name before. As much as he didn't favor spending his own money for something that'd been promised him, he wouldn't get anything done until he could get a serviceable horse. No use in delaying the inevitable.

"How would a fellow meet this Jeremiah Calhoun?"

"Go out to his place. He'd welcome you." Pritchard's substantial brows met over his nose. "But you won't be able to find it on your own. I'll be back in town later this week and I'll get you a guide. You can count on me."

Joel sent up a quick prayer of thanks. What could've been a disastrous event had actually earned him a friend.

With all the nonchalance of a stage magician, Pritchard dragged the dreaded mask off the desk and headed to the door. Joel caught it by the horn. They stopped with it suspended between them.

"This stays with me," Joel said.

Pritchard shook his head in pity. "The judge isn't going to

worry one iota about me and that half-wit Bo, but you shouldn't persist in this fool notion about the Bald Knobbers."

"I don't want no trouble for you, and keeping this mask might be the best way to keep you safe," Joel said.

"But there ain't no mask that's gonna help you, Deputy," Pritchard said before he stepped into the street.

CHAPTER 12

Betsy balanced Eloise on her knee, heedless of the warm slobber the baby drooled across her left hand, and tried to pen a few more lines. It'd been a week since she'd sent in the first installment of her Dashing Deputy series. Two more submissions had followed. Naturally, the ill-tempered pony did not make an appearance. Instead it was magically transformed into a raging, strapping white steed that had never before been ridden. Only the steely-eyed lawman had been able to bend it to his will.

Betsy shivered. If only Deputy Puckett were as dashing as the man she'd created, but that was impossible. Besides, Deputy Eduardo was much more convenient. He didn't order her about, say things she didn't want to hear, or twist her words until they sounded unreasonable. She was her own boss, thank you—or at least she would be once she left Sissy's cabin. If she was in charge, she'd be more focused on writing and less focused on keeping Eloise from drooling on her paper.

She handed Eloise the rag doll that Doctor Hopkins's wife, Laurel, had made for her. If Betsy didn't know better, she'd say the doll dove headfirst into Eloise's mouth. Its rag body shook as Eloise gummed it mercilessly.

As if summoned, Sissy and Scott blustered through the door

in a swirl of leaves. Scott dumped his armload of supplies on the table. The bag of beans fell over and nearly sent a canning jar of pickled okra off the edge. He dove to catch it. The family couldn't spare a single bite of food, but by unspoken agreement, they welcomed the deputy to their table almost nightly. Uncle Fred, Scott, and Eduardo visited around the fire while the ladies cleaned the kitchen, but getting any specific news out of the deputy was as tough as scrubbing burnt potatoes out of the Dutch oven.

"Mama is home." Sissy hurried to remove her scarf and coat as if every moment she didn't have her hands on Eloise was a moment wasted.

Eloise kept her doll in her tight fist and allowed herself to fall forward into Sissy's arms. Finally, Betsy could get some work done. "Amelia is still down for her nap." She stood and gathered her pen and paper. With the family back, only the office offered the silence she needed.

"Not so fast," Sissy said. "You've been holed up in that office all week. I need you to run to Walters's store for me."

"But you just came from there," Betsy protested. "I have work to do."

"Your first priority is to help this family. Supplies are short and we've still got a long winter ahead of us. I heard Mayor Walters complaining that his back storeroom is looking full of scatterment. We might be able to trade some of your labor for more flour and coffee."

When Betsy wanted to go out, Sissy made her stay home. When she was of a mind to compose her thoughts on paper, Sissy found cause to send her out and about. Couldn't Sissy understand that if Betsy was successful, they would all profit?

"Uncle Fred asked me to get the numbers from the sale barn for his market report. I'll step out to get that—"

"—just as soon as you're finished at Walters's." Sissy had her dead to rights.

Scott shot Betsy a sympathetic look as she gathered her papers to hide in the office. As she walked away from the fire, the chill crept through her thick woolen blouse. The little stove in the office stayed lit to keep the ink from freezing, but it wasn't as warm as the family portion of the cabin. She'd better bundle up if it was that cold out.

Shutting the drawer on her dreamy hero, she hurried back into the cabin and grabbed the nearest clothes from the peg—this time it was Scott's knitted sock cap and Sissy's coat. She eased out the door with her hands shoved deep in her pockets. If Sissy knew how important her new story was . . . well, that was another reason she needed to move on out and get a place of her own.

A cold wind rolled the dead leaves down the hill to the town square. Mayor Walters's store sat to the east, the last block before the steep incline made construction impossible. At the corner, in front of the bank, Doctor Hopkins's wagon waited, full to the brim with feminine energy in the form of his youthful wife and two daughters. Laurel Hopkins and her girls waved Betsy over, barely able to contain their gossiping until she reached earshot.

"You should've seen Phoebe mooning over your cousin Scott," Anna said. "She nearly toppled Mayor Walters's canned milk display when he walked by."

Phoebe covered her face with her mittened hands.

Her mother laughed. "If you want to see more of Scott, you don't have to wait until you run into him in the store. Betsy here could come up with a reason for you to visit the Murphys."

Skinny Scott was attracting the Hopkins girls' attention? Betsy had to smile. "Come see me anytime, Phoebe. Bring taffy with you. It's his favorite."

"I'm not hankering after him," Phoebe protested. "I just forgot to look where I was going."

"Because you were looking at him," Anna howled.

Judging from Laurel's comical eye-rolling, the girls had made quite the scene. Yet poor Scott hadn't even noticed. Yes, she reckoned that the Hopkins girls would be making a call soon.

"Betsy," Laurel said, "I hear the new deputy has finally arrived. Have you met him?"

Both girls stopped their fluttering and leaned to the edge of the wagon. "Is he young? What's he look like?"

Immediately the descriptions Betsy had scribbled down came to mind. *Noble brow, intense eyes, dark*—nope. Wasn't gonna say that. "He's fairly passable, for a Texan."

Phoebe squeezed her hands into fists and squealed while Anna's eyes lit up.

"For crying aloud, girls," their mother said. "You must control yourselves." But Laurel looked as pleased as her daughters.

They tried to pry more information from her, but Betsy found that she much preferred writing about her hero than discussing him in person with other girls.

"Have you'uns been to the store?" Betsy asked.

"Yes, ma'am," Phoebe said.

Laurel squirmed in the wagon seat, as impatient as her daughters. "We brought the wagon to town to get supplies, but Mayor Walters had a matter over which he wished to consult Newton. Now we have to wait, and the good doctor probably won't even get a discount on our purchase."

Poor Doctor Hopkins. He was forever at the mercy of people seeking free medical advice. Even worse, when he was kind enough to offer it, they often contradicted him with their own preferences for the simples and charms that had already failed them.

"If Mayor Walters is keeping Doctor Hopkins, I'll put in a word for payment," she promised. "If he has enough money to buy that fine black horse, he can certainly afford to pay your husband for his time."

Waving her good-bye, Betsy dashed to the store. Inside she saw Mrs. Helspeth shopping, but no Mayor Walters. Betsy shrugged at the old mountain woman.

"He's in the back room," Mrs. Helspeth said as she continued to palm a bag of cornmeal as if estimating its weight by the ounce.

The back room. According to Sissy, that was where Betsy needed to be.

Betsy slipped behind the counter and pushed through the swinging door in the storage room. Barrels were stacked up the wall, lying on their sides, their lids forming a honeycomb pattern. Where the barrels ended, the crates started up, and after that, heavy bags of ground meal, sugar, and various beans piled up, forming a wall of burlap behind which she could just make out the top of a man's head.

"I don't know why I would be getting a bundle of switches." The words made her heart skip a beat even before she recognized Doctor Hopkins's voice. "Laurel and the girls think it's a prank, but I'm not so sure. That's why I came to town today. I told Sheriff Taney to meet me here."

The Bald Knobbers were going after Doctor Hopkins? Had the world turned upside down? Something was terribly amiss. Doctor Hopkins stayed on the right side of the law. And you didn't do yourself any favors threatening the man who might save your life someday.

"Who'd you cross?" Mayor Walters asked.

"You'd better believe I questioned the girls. They are high-spirited, but they don't mean any harm. But no one can think of any reason we'd need a warning like that. I'd think if Fowler had a bone to pick, he'd come speak to me, man-to-man."

The voices of shoppers wafted through the wall. Betsy's scalp began to itch beneath Scott's old knit cap. She should let them know she was there, but she would undoubtedly learn more if she didn't. From long practice and without conscious planning, her knees bent and she found a safer place against the crates that afforded her more protection should Doctor Hopkins glance around the sacks.

"Are those things hot yet?" Walters couldn't be seen over the mound of bags, which wasn't surprising. He was half a dollar short of fifty cents when it came to height.

"Just about," Doctor Hopkins said as he rattled something on the wood stove.

"Betsy Huckabee?" This voice came from behind her and caused her to bolt upright to her full height. "What are you up to?"

Sheriff Taney. She didn't have to turn around to know who'd caught her crouched in Walters's storeroom. Doctor Hopkins peeked his head around the bags. A grin twitched at his face. If only she'd been a more compliant child, she wouldn't incite such suspicion now. Any other lady found crouching in a storeroom wouldn't have to defend . . . well, to be honest, Betsy couldn't think of any other woman who'd be caught snooping in the storeroom.

"Don't know what you're hiding for. Might as well come on over and listen," Doctor Hopkins said. "That is, if the mayor doesn't mind."

Walters groaned. "I don't care as long as you get me out of my misery."

"You're not causing any trouble are you, Betsy?" Sheriff Taney marched forward with his arms folded across his chest.

Betsy noticed things that most people didn't. Maybe it was the way a person flinched when you approached them from the side, the way they chewed the inside of their cheek when worried, or the way they kept their face shuttered so you couldn't guess what they were ruminating on. Sheriff Taney had never been a young man in Betsy's lifetime, but he'd always been robust, able to keep up with her peers. That was until he lost Miles Bullard. Overnight he'd aged, grown more taciturn.

But this morning, he seemed energetic. He held himself tighter, more alert. There was a spark that hadn't been there before, and she was relieved. She'd wondered how the deputy's arrival would affect him. Evidently, Sheriff Taney was enjoying his reprieve.

She smiled the way old men expect young ladies to smile when being teased. "Trouble? I don't know what you're talking about."

"Spying and such."

She followed him around the barrier to join the doctor and the mayor. "There's no spying to do. Not lately."

"I can't believe you wouldn't be stalking that Texan. Seeing what he's up to," Sheriff Taney said. "Mark my words, he's hiding something. I can sense a man on the run, and he's got hounds nipping at his heels, sure as shooting."

She had to agree with his assessment. Deputy Puckett did seem to be hiding something.

"I haven't noticed anything suspicious," she said, "but I can't claim to know him overly well." But she had seen plenty of misdeeds under Sheriff Taney's watch. Funny he was so concerned with lawbreakers now.

Those shutters that sometimes closed on a person's face, they slammed shut. "I guess we owe him the chance to prove himself," Sheriff Taney said. He patted her on the shoulder as he walked toward Mayor Walters. "The fruit will bear witness."

Mayor Walters sat on a stool by the stove and cradled his right hand. His sleeve had been rolled up to his elbow. Betsy couldn't say exactly what the nature of his ailment was, but he seemed more concerned about whatever was boiling in the pot.

"Mayor Walters," she said, "Sissy said you needed help back here today. I just came to offer—"

"I can't do anything until I get this splinter out," he said.

"I told you, it'll just take a second," Doctor Hopkins said. "It's not that deep."

"It's not your hide we're talking about, either," the mayor said. Then to Betsy, "The shelves are nearly empty, and I have new shipments piled up back here that haven't been inventoried, but I won't feel like doing it today. Come back tomorrow."

"Yes, sir." She was only too happy to get shy of there. But what the sheriff said next stopped her in her tracks.

"What did you need to see me about, Doctor Hopkins?"

Betsy ground her teeth. She'd hide outside in a blizzard to hear this conversation. She wasn't about to walk away now.

CHAPTER 13

With tongs, Hopkins pulled a pair of tweezers and a large needle out from the boiling water.

"What are you doing?" Walters said. "Branding me?"

"I'm letting it cool," Doctor Hopkins said. "Relax."

Sheriff Taney looked as nervous as the mayor. "You said you wanted to talk to me. I'm of no mind to sit in on a medical procedure. . . ."

"I can talk while I do this." With a rag protecting his hand, Hopkins took the tweezers and waved them through the air to cool them. "It's about a bundle of switches I found on my porch yesterday. It's probably just a prank, unless Miles Bullard's back in town."

Now that was a worthy thought. No one had seen Bullard since summer, but that didn't mean he couldn't come back.

"Ouch!" Sweat was popping out of the mayor's forehead like a pan of popcorn over the fire.

"I haven't even touched you yet," the doctor said.

Sheriff Taney bristled. "Let me get this straight. You find the Bald Knobbers' calling card on your porch, and you want to blame their enemy, Miles Bullard?"

"I have no bone to pick with the Bald Knobbers," Hopkins said. "Why would they want to scare me?"

"Maybe because you gave Bullard shelter after he shot one of them."

True, Bullard was captured at Hopkins's place, but Betsy had never thought to blame the doctor for treating him. Neither had Katie Ellen, and Stony had been her pa. Doctor Hopkins hadn't tried to hide him or anything.

"This is going to hurt," the mayor whined.

"Put your hand up here and stop bellyaching." Doctor Hopkins dropped a cloth on the table and situated Walters's hand, palm up. Then he bent over with the needle ready. "I'm not frightened about the switches," he said. "Just wish I knew what I'm supposed to do about it. If it's a warning, I'm listening."

"I'd ask Fowler," Sheriff Taney said. "There's no one else who leaves twig bundles behind."

"Ahhh . . ." The mayor's voice rose in pitch.

"I declare," said Betsy, "you're squealing like a piglet. You'd better be planning on giving Doctor Hopkins a discount on his bill for all the fuss you're raising."

"Sure, ten percent. Just get that thing out of me."

"I've almost got it . . . almost," Doctor Hopkins said. "There! Just a splinter, that's all. See?" He winked at Betsy as he wiped his tweezers on the cloth.

In Betsy's opinion, he should've kept digging until he got a twenty percent discount.

"I'll come tomorrow to help with inventory," she told Walters. "Hopefully you'll have recovered from your amputation by then."

"Smart-mouthed girl."

Betsy didn't stay around to hear the rest. Tomorrow she'd

work for him, but she needed to get a breath of air before she went home. Who knew what chore awaited her there?

On her way through the store, she poked through the limited assortment of books the mercantile offered, but there weren't any new ones. Petting the ginger cat that lay soaking up the morning sun in the window display, she worked her way to the farm equipment—maybe Pa needed a new trowel?—but she didn't have any funds to send his way.

Betsy scratched her chin as she watched Sheriff Taney make his exit. Had anyone else noticed the change in the sheriff? One minute he seemed bitter, the next hopeful. Maybe that was just age working on him like it had Old Man Wimplegate. But other things had changed, too.

Like Widow Sanders's marital status. With the deputy's coming, Mr. Sanders had gotten overlooked, but there were many questions to be answered about his sudden appearance. Something didn't set right about the situation, and the timing with Hopkins's harassment seemed more than coincidental. Could Mr. Sanders have something against Doctor Hopkins? Could he be behind the threat? Besides the perennial ne'er-do-wells like Leland Moore and Miles Bullard, there wasn't a soul in Hart County who wouldn't give their best sow for the doctor.

Betsy had tucked her coat around her and braced for the blast of cold when she spotted Mr. Pritchard heading toward the store. She held the door open for him and stood back as he dusted the falling leaves out of his long hair.

"Glad you aren't still in jail," she said with a grin. "How long did the deputy keep you?"

Pritchard frowned. "Not long, but I have a date with the judge when he comes back in town." His nose crinkled. "Now, Betsy, you won't be saying anything about that particular association that I'm a member of, will you? We're all sworn to secrecy."

"Don't worry, Mr. Pritchard. Uncle Fred and I are circumspect about what we print. And we know how to keep a secret as well."

"I knew I could trust you, Betsy. If only that deputy . . ." He threw a glance toward the jailhouse and his eyes narrowed. "Come to think of it, he asked me if I thought you'd do him a favor."

"Me?" Betsy's hand thumped against her chest. Her heart had skipped a beat at the news. "What could he possibly want with me?"

"He needs someone to take him to the Calhouns'. Said he'd appreciate it if you could guide him, but he has to go this forenoon. He doesn't trust any of us men."

Betsy stood a little taller and almost wished she'd worn her sunbonnet instead of Scott's sock hat. Uncle Fred wanted her to go to Isaac's for the livestock market anyway. "I am headed that way. . . ." She bit her lip. Deputy Puckett did his best to ignore her every evening. Why would he ask for her help now? Very curious.

Pritchard's grin was almost ornery. If she didn't know better, she'd think he knew about the article she'd mailed to Kansas City the day before. "That's dandy. Let me run back to the jail and send him this way."

Betsy beamed. "I'll wait for him at the crossroads." For some reason she didn't want Sheriff Taney to see them headed out together. Writing romantic serials about the man for faraway audiences was one thing, but she'd never report back to Taney on the deputy. Even if the deputy wasn't cooperating with her project, it just didn't sit well.

She reached the edge of town and stepped out of sight behind a thick stand of trees. She dearly loved surprising the deputy. It was so amusing how he startled and then tried to look bored, as if her sudden appearance had no effect on him. You'd never catch Eduardo off guard, but that was one thing she liked better about Deputy Puckett. A little imperfection could be a beautiful thing.

As she waited across from Widow Sanders's house, a crash sounded. Raised voices rang out through the shuttered windows. Betsy stepped out of the woods and walked to the fence. She looked down the road, but Deputy Puckett was nowhere to be seen. She pried her fingers off the pickets and made her quiet way to the house. She surely didn't like Mr. Sanders showing up after being gone for twenty years. It was nearly indecent for him to just walk inside and take up as Widow Sanders's husband again. Seemed like someone should have given Widow Sanders a choice in the matter.

Another crash, and Betsy's concern overcame her discomfort. Her fist thudded against the door. "Mrs. Sanders, are you in there? What's going on?"

Low voices murmured and then steps sounded at the door. Betsy stepped back. What was she going to say to Mr. Sanders? Usually the Bald Knobbers took care of situations like this. She was only a lone woman, and who knew what this Sanders character was capable of?

The door creaked open so quickly that it sucked a gust of wind in around her. Widow Sanders appeared, cheeks flaming. "Betsy? What do you want?"

Peering over the widow's shoulder, all Betsy could see was an overturned kitchen chair. "I thought I heard someone call for help. Are you all right?"

The woman rolled down her sleeves. "Of course, child. Just being clumsy. That's all."

Clumsy? Like Bullard's wife? But besides being out of breath, Mrs. Sanders looked none the worse for wear.

"That Mr. Sanders, he's your husband?"

"I thought he'd died when he didn't come home from the war. Guess I was mistaken. Now, get on with you. I'm kind of busy." Widow Sanders—er, Mrs. Sanders shut the door in her face.

Betsy's heart twisted. The widow was one of the strongest women she knew. She'd managed her small house all alone throughout the war and Reconstruction. She'd taken in boarders to make ends meet and hold together. Then here came a man waltzing into the life she'd made for herself, and next thing you know her crockery was getting smashed against the log walls.

Word would get out. There were those who made it their business to right wrongs, and Betsy would see that they got the message.

Betsy stopped in her tracks. If she suspected someone was breaking the law, shouldn't she go to the deputy instead of Fowler? It stood to reason that Eduardo was the one responsible. But whom did she trust more? Fowler would come out with twenty men at his back and surround Mr. Sanders. With their masks on, they wouldn't be afraid to tell him that they knew of his evil deeds. They wouldn't have to cower like she was.

But the deputy . . . well, something told her that he wouldn't cower, either. No, he'd march up to the Sanders porch and make the exact same speech, even with no one to back him up. Even with his face uncovered and all the world knowing who he was.

She couldn't let him do that. Fowler would be the safer choice. Deputy Puckett didn't have the sense to keep himself out of danger—a charge he was likely to level against her, as well.

Joel had waited nearly a week for Pritchard to follow through on his promise. A week had been wasted with a temperamental pony not big enough for a child. Finally he would be rid of the thing.

He and the ill-tempered pony stood at the crossroads as far from each other as the stretched reins would allow. Hopefully Calhoun would let him trade in the nuisance. Otherwise he might have to buy a real horse on credit. He hadn't come to the Ozarks expecting to need that amount of finances.

His eyes traveled up and down the road, not certain from which direction his help was arriving. He'd assumed it was someone from the mountains outside of town, since they'd chosen this meeting place, but no one was on the road in that direction. Not seeing anyone, he turned back around to face a startling apparition.

It was Betsy Huckabee standing not a fishing-pole's length from him. He startled and staggered backwards, putting more distance between himself and her, moving closer to the pony.

"Stop sneaking up on me," he said. "It isn't safe."

Her eyes rolled, barely visible beneath the sock hat that was pushed down over her forehead. "Are you talking about my safety or yours?"

He took another step backwards before composing himself. "Be on your way, Miss Huckabee. I've got important business to tend to."

"Well, so do I. Like showing some tenderfoot how to get to the Calhouns' farm." She pushed her hat back so her smug expression was easily visible.

"I don't know who told you where I'm going—"

"Mr. Pritchard said you asked for my help specifically."

His head jerked to an angle. "Would that be the Mr. Pritchard I recently arrested? The one who'd be motivated to make my life miserable?" Joel crossed his arms. "I'd say he's bit off more than he can chew."

And at that moment, a sharp pain flashed through his backside, causing him to tuck tail and bolt forward, nearly landing on Betsy's toes.

With a bracing hand against his chest, she forced some space between them. "You don't scare me. Get back!"

Pushing her hand away, Joel spun around to face the mean pony whose flared nostrils and bared teeth left no question about what had happened. Joel rubbed his hindquarters, trying to chase away the sting.

"Durned horse bit me," he managed by way of explanation.

"I see that." Her laughter had everything to do with the rip he'd just located in his britches.

Seeing how keeping his back to her was now impossible, he had to face her. "Thank goodness for long drawers," he said.

Her smile would be as contagious as the chicken pox if he weren't so well practiced at keeping stern.

"I'd say you need to see Jeremiah Calhoun in the worst possible way," she said as she took the reins from him. "That is, unless you've got trousers to spare."

"This here is a Bald Knobber's pony," Joel grumbled, but even he couldn't miss the humor in the situation. Her eyes sparkled as their gazes met and held. It was . . . companionable, lacking most of the artifice that he expected from women. Night after night of sitting at her family's hearth had given him more of an appreciation for her.

All the more reason to keep his distance.

"I'm sorry for whatever Pritchard told you, but I didn't request your company today," he said.

Now the humor hardened to something a bit more challenging. "You can find the Calhouns' on your own?" she asked.

"Surely there's someone else headed that way."

With theatrical flair, she looked first one way, then the other. A week he'd waited. How much more could he afford? How many pursuits might he miss, how many arrests would he have to make? And now that he'd crossed that gang of outlaws, how many men might be hunting for him, and him stuck on a runty horse?

Evidently she took his hesitation as acceptance, for she started up the hill, dragging his pony behind her.

Her pride wouldn't let her turn around to look, but Betsy was confident the deputy was following.

Nearly confident.

Pretty sure.

Well, fiddlesticks, she might just have to peek. Under the pretense of checking on the horse, she tossed a look over her shoulder. His head was ducked, watching the uneven surface of the mountain even as they climbed higher and higher, but he was there, him and his new, stiffly starched cavalry shirt and his canvas trousers that fit snug, not like the soft, worn britches that men here favored, hanging as loose as a turkey's wattle.

He looked up and caught her watching. Betsy whirled around to face forward. If there were ever to be enough installments of her Dashing Deputy serial, she'd need more material. So far all he'd done was save a kitten from a well and arrest a middle-aged seed salesman for straightening out his own nephew. Surely he'd done something more noteworthy than that in Texas. Maybe now was a good time to find out.

She stopped in the road and waited. It seemed that he slowed down, but when he realized that she wasn't moving, he heaved himself up past the horse and joined her.

"We might as well be conversating while we walk," Betsy said.

"As long as you're not walking behind me," he answered. "I'm feeling a definite draft."

So he did have a sense of humor, despite his granite-jawed delivery. If she had the courage to look hard enough, would she catch an eye-twinkle? But he was still too wary when she paid attention to him.

"I've never been out of these mountains." Betsy lifted her chin to scan all the way up the trees that hemmed both sides of the road. "What's Texas like?"

Eduardo's chest filled and his shoulders went even straighter, if that was possible. "I can't pretend to have seen much of Texas. It's vast. You can't even imagine how big it is, and I don't figure there's anyone who's traveled the breadth of it."

"Then what's your Texas like?"

He seemed to warm to the question. His face eased into friendlier lines, making him seem almost like someone Betsy would like to get to know. "My Texas revolves around the town of Garber, which is pretty cosmopolitan as far as that goes. There's a lot of trade—markets, cattle, railroads. People come from all over. And it sits smack-dab in the middle of the largest prairie you've ever seen. All around it are ranches that cover thousands of acres. You can see for miles and miles and the sky is so big. . . ."

His deep voice drawled even slower with yearning. It was as if he'd taken her on a journey, just the two of them. Her heart skipped a beat at his tone.

Then her curiosity kicked in again. "You love it so much. Why on earth did you leave?"

He winced at her words. She'd hit a sore spot, but at the sight of the rider approaching them, all was forgotten.

CHAPTER 14

The hair on the back of his neck rose. It was that man Clive Fowler. Even alone and unmasked, he left a formidable impression. What could he want? Joel forced his brow to ease. Maybe Fowler had simply come to town for some business, but just seeing him put Joel on edge.

Never letting Fowler out of his sight, he spoke to his companion. "You might want to step aside, ma'am. This man may have dangerous intentions."

A whistle pierced the air—and his eardrum. He turned to spot Betsy with two fingers in her mouth and her free hand waving the reins of his horse overhead.

"Mr. Fowler! Over here."

"What are you doing?" Joel asked. "I don't initiate meetings with criminals when I have a woman in attendance."

"He's not a criminal. He's a law-abiding citizen." She waved again as Fowler appeared on the trail before them. "Or maybe I should say *law-enforcing citizen*, which is even better."

On that they disagreed. Either way, this meeting was fixing to happen, and he'd better get at the head of it before it took out sideways.

"Mr. Fowler," he said as soon as his foe was within earshot, "are you heading to town?"

"I'm heading to see you. It's about my friend Mr. Pritchard. I hear you got something that belongs to him." Fowler moved like a draft horse, slowly and deliberately but with a lot of power.

"Nothing he'll need again, now that I'm here."

Fowler's mouth twitched. "Is that right? You didn't stop Bo Franklin from robbing, did ya? Caesar Parrow can thank Pritchard for the return of his pelts."

"I brought Bo in, too, and took a report. When the judge gets to town—"

"The judge?" Fowler spat a stream into the brush at the side of the road. "The judge is as worthless as Sheriff Taney."

"I've dealt with crooked judges before," Joel said. "It won't be the first time."

"I said worthless, not crooked. You see, everything ain't black and white here like you make it out to be. Pritchard ain't no criminal, and he don't deserve to be treated as such."

"A criminal is one who breaks the law. Trespassing and making threats is breaking the law, and your friend Pritchard confessed to both. I don't hold to locking up good people, which is why Pritchard is free now, but he needs to know—everyone needs to know—that if they have concerns, they come to me. They don't take care of it themselves."

Fowler's eyes bored into him without mercy, but when Joel didn't waver, he nodded. "I don't think you're a bad sort, son. I just think you're in over your head. We're not enemies. You keep after those bad folks, but the people wearing those masks, they are on your side—for now."

Well, that was fair enough, Betsy thought with satisfaction. Clive was at least giving the new deputy a chance, and maybe she should, too. He'd likely want to know about the strange goings-on at the Sanders house as well as the threat to Doctor Hopkins.

"There's something you need to know." Betsy stepped forward. Deputy Puckett turned with interest evident on his handsome face. "I couldn't figure who to tell, but since you're both here, then maybe you can decide between you." She shivered as she formed the words to describe the encounter—the yelling, the crashing furniture, Widow Sanders's rumpled appearance. Both men listened intently, bristling as she finished. "And I thought that if it's not Bullard who's pulling capers on Doctor Hopkins, it could be Mr. Sanders."

"Doctor Hopkins?" Deputy Puckett said. "What's Doctor Hopkins got to do with it?"

Fowler fixed her with a steady gaze. "Is Bullard back?"

"Someone presented the doctor with a bundle of sticks on his porch, evening last," she said. "He couldn't credit what he'd made you mad over."

"Made me mad? The Bald Knobbers didn't leave those sticks. Who told you about this?" Fowler asked.

"I went looking for Mayor Walters in the storeroom, and Doctor Hopkins was there. I didn't want to interrupt them, so I waited behind the crates." She studied the dirt between them, because she was pretty sure the expressions of the two men before her weren't pleasant.

"What do you know about this?" The deputy's bandanna flapped in the wind.

"It wasn't me," Fowler said. "It wasn't my men."

"And you know the whereabouts of all your men, all the time?"

"My men are well trained. They don't act without orders." Fowler ground his heel on a dirt clod that exploded under the pressure. "And to prove I'm not behind it, I'll set a guard around his place tonight."

"No, you won't," Deputy Puckett said. "You are a prime suspect. You stay away from the doctor's place. You're more likely to cause trouble than anything."

Betsy's head was swinging from right to left so quickly she was likely stirring a breeze.

Fowler snorted. "Well, it'd pay you to keep an eye out for Miles Bullard. He might have it in his mind that Hopkins turned him in after the Watson shooting."

That was possible, but there was another suspect Betsy didn't want to escape notice. "Why would Bullard come back now? If there's a troublemaker about, my money is on Mr. Sanders. Weren't he and Doctor Hopkins in the war together? Maybe there's some bad blood left over from then."

Now she had Deputy Puckett's attention. "Is there a connection between Doctor Hopkins and Sanders?"

"Everyone here is connected," Betsy answered. "But I don't know why Sanders would hold a grudge that long. Then again, I didn't know he was alive until last week."

Fowler shrugged. "We didn't have this problem until he came back, either. He's the one who needs to find switches on his porch."

"No one needs to find switches on their porch. These juvenile warnings must stop. Maybe they did some good once, but now they're just a nuisance," said the deputy. "Y'all are hiding behind your masks. I'll speak to Sanders tonight, face-to-face, as soon as I see if Mr. Calhoun has a horse for me."

Fowler laughed. "Why? Are you tired of riding Mayor Walters's pony?"

"This is the mayor's horse?" Deputy Puckett's eyes flashed dangerously.

Betsy's mouth puckered. She wouldn't smile. She wouldn't.

"The state purchased the black horse from Calhoun. It was earmarked for the new deputy and put in Walters's care until you arrived," Fowler said. "I can't believe no one told you."

The deputy spun to glare at her.

She shrugged. "I didn't know. Honest."

"C'mon. We're headed back to town." He took the reins from Betsy and turned around.

"What happened to your britches?" Fowler called.

But Eduardo wouldn't answer that question. Instead he replied, "I'll visit Sanders today. I can't arrest him unless I have good cause, though. We need more evidence before we can do anything."

"That's exactly the problem with men like you," Fowler called. "You want everything to look good on paper, and while you're sitting with a notepad on your lap, we'll be out protecting our own." With a jerk of his head, Fowler's horse came to his side. He threw his foot into the stirrup and mounted with the grace of a mountain lion that had never missed a meal. "You go back to Pine Gap and sit in your nice, warm office. I'm going out where the danger is." And with that, he reined his horse around and took out through the thick growth over the mountain.

Betsy's ears warmed. How would her hero take that dismissal? What heroic proclamation would he utter to defend himself and restore order?

"I've got to get these britches stitched up." He held a hand against his backside as he started toward town.

It took Betsy a moment to realize she was getting left behind, and another moment to realize his torn britches would never, ever be mentioned in her story.

When the winding road broke through the trees and the neat, square log cabins became more frequent, Joel kept the pony on a tighter leash. The danger of the pony getting a second helping of his hide troubled him, but even more likely was the whole town seeing him walking down Main Street with his trousers flapping. The pony made a practical, if not willing, shield.

And so did the woman hurrying along to keep up with him.

"You aren't going to the jailhouse first?" Betsy asked. "I thought you'd want to change britches."

"I want a horse," Joel said. "That's my first priority."

"I suppose you're right," she said. "You've been patient with that animal, Eduardo."

"Eduardo?" He stopped in his tracks. What was she talking about? "Who's Eduardo?"

Despite the cold wind, her face flamed. "No one. No one real, that is. I don't know your first name and so when I was imagining—I mean, I'm not thinking of you more than I ought, of course, but it is rather cumbersome to say Deputy Puckett, even if it is just my mind talking. So I . . ."

The longer her sentence ran, the higher his eyebrows rose. She'd been thinking of him? She hadn't been satisfied only knowing him by his title?

Betsy fanned her hand before her bright cheeks. "So now I know your name isn't Eduardo. That will narrow down the options when I decide to guess again."

"It's Joel," he blurted. "Joel Puckett. And if you had asked, I would've been happy to oblige you."

It unsettled him that she had paid him particular regard. On the other hand, maybe he was pleased that someone in this town cared to know something about him beyond who he was locking up next.

He'd meant to fix her with a warning look, but his gaze softened. She'd been thinking of him.

Just as his heart kicked up a notch, he jerked his hand around behind him and held the rip in his britches closed again. "You're gonna have to walk in front of me," he said, and then in a low voice he didn't aim for her to hear, he added, "and no peeking, Betsy Huckabee."

CHAPTER 15

"I don't know that Mayor Walters is up to horse dealing today." Betsy rubbed her hand at the thought of the heated needle and tweezers. "He had Doctor Hopkins do a procedure on him just this morning."

"His health ain't my concern. His horse is."

She reckoned that Deputy Joel Puckett—Joel—had lost more skin from the horse bite than the mayor had, and he wasn't whining about it. She waited at the door as Joel hitched the pony next to the new black horse.

His chin lifted and he marched through the door like he had a whole regiment at his back.

Mayor Walters was sorting through his pinto beans, separating out the bad ones. Behind the counter, he didn't look that short, but it was on account of the ramp he'd built for times just like this, when he wanted to look his customers eye-to-eye. Or eye-to-shoulder, in this case.

"I came to get my horse." Joel's voice didn't waver. With a start, Betsy realized that Deputy Puckett was a dangerous man doing a dangerous job. He carried a lot of responsibility and deserved to be treated with respect—even if he was wearing ripped trousers.

Mayor Walters's hand dropped and scattered his pile of beans. "Are you sure? I thought since you're likely unused to these hills, a surefooted pony might be just the—"

"I'm telling you," Joel said. "Not asking. And I'd imagine that the saddle belongs to me as well."

Walters leaned across the counter top. "No use in getting testy. I didn't mean no harm. Take the horse and it'll all be water beneath the bridge." His round face was as white as the pie-dough masks Miss Abigail used to make. Leaning across the counter, Joel grasped him by the dimpled hand and gave him a hearty handshake.

Betsy covered her mouth as the mayor's knees gave way. If it weren't for the counter between them, he would've slid to the floor.

"I'm glad to know you're on my side." But Joel looked at the man with uncertainty as he squirmed to get out of Joel's grasp.

"My hand," he panted. "It hurts."

With a shrug, Joel released the mayor to collapse against the table.

"Thank you for your help, Miss Huckabee," Joel said. "I suppose I won't be needing your assistance today after all."

Betsy did want to see him on a worthy horse, but Postmaster Finley ruined her chance.

How he wanted to get in the saddle and ride, as if a few hours astride a good horse like that one could wash away all the humiliation the pony had brought.

But first the postmaster had waved at him from across the square, claiming to have mail for the both of them, so Joel and Betsy found themselves at the post office, giving everyone in town another shot at seeing his ripped britches.

"I'm glad I caught you." Postmaster Finley moved slow, as if testing his joints as he went. His soft boots scuffed against the dirt floor as he ambled to a wall covered in roughly hewn bins. "It's about time someone did something about those ruffians."

"Excuse me?" Joel asked.

"You brought Pritchard in, didn't you? It's a good start. His father stole our plow back in '47. We never caught him, mind you, but we knew it just the same. And then look at Bo. Like begets like, and that's a fact. But Pritchard rides with Fowler, so no one can touch him. Well, enough of that. It's about time you lock those Bald Knobbers up for good."

"No one is locked up. Pritchard has an appointment with the judge, but—"

"You let him go?" Finley steadied himself against the bins. "What in tarnation would make you do that?"

"The law. Can't keep a man locked up unless he's sentenced or a danger."

"What's the law got to do with it? You caught him in a mask, right?"

Joel had a perfectly good horse outside, and he had to have this conversation now? "Do you have mail for me?"

Finley wasn't pleased, but the reminder of his duty seemed to do the trick. "I've got a letter for the deputy and a telegram for you, Betsy."

Betsy stepped sideways, putting some space between them. "The deputy has important business," she said. "No use making him wait on me. Give him his first, then he can be on his way."

Finley didn't seem to hear her; he lifted a stack of envelopes from a bin and thumbed through them, licking his thumb every third one or so. Who could the letter be from? Joel sure didn't want to read it in front of Betsy.

"Here it is." Finley held a yellow slip of paper at arm's length and squinted at the letters. "This one's for Betsy, wired in from Kansas City."

Curiosity hit Joel like a barn owl hit a field mouse. "Do you have family in Kansas City?" he asked.

Betsy bit her lip. She yanked off her stocking cap and crammed the paper inside it without even looking at the return address. With a tug she pulled the cap back over her mussed hair. "It's nothing important," she said.

That girl never did do what he expected. "I'm sure people often send you unimportant telegrams," he said.

"She won't never tell me why she's writing them," Finley said. "Usually it's letters back and forth. This is the first telegram I remember." Then he leaned across the counter, close enough that Joel got a whiff of onions on his breath. "I think she's got some beau working in that office there. Someone she's sweet on. She probably writes letters like she's a fine, genteel lady and has him fooled."

Betsy's eyelashes lowered. Joel took one look at her worn dress and overlarge coat and couldn't help himself. "There's no reason to talk like that about Miss Huckabee," he said. After all, who was this postmaster to ridicule her? "I'm certain that, given the opportunity, Miss Huckabee would have improved herself considerably."

The wounded look on her face transformed so swiftly that Joel felt like he'd lost track of time and reawakened in the middle of a completely different conversation. Now her eyes were sharp and her grin, although bemused, had an edge to it. "What about Deputy Puckett's letter? Where's it?" she asked the postmaster.

Joel's neck tightened as the letter came into view. The handwriting curled in loops that no self-respecting man could form with a pen. It wasn't his mother's handwriting. Who else—

Betsy ripped the envelope out of his hand. "It's definitely from a lady. But look! The address is scratched out and over it is written: *Redirect to Pine Gap, Missouri.* Whoever is writing Deputy Puckett didn't even know he'd left Texas."

Joel grabbed her right arm. Quick as a wink she had the letter in her left hand, a whole body length away from him.

"What lady shares a familiarity with you enough to write but doesn't realize you've left town?" she asked.

"Give me the letter." He wrapped an arm around her body and was pulling her against himself before he thought better of it. That wouldn't work. The old postmaster laughed as she twisted away from him, but it wasn't a clean getaway. Joel grabbed her cap and yanked it off, telegram and all.

"Owww!" Betsy swung for her hat but missed.

Joel lifted it above his head, the crinkling sound telling him that he'd captured her secret as well. She pushed her hair out of her eyes and then made a wild swipe, but Joel held it high.

"Negotiations are on," he said. "My letter for yours."

If she knew how potentially dangerous the contents of that letter were for him, she'd give anything to read it. The contents of her message couldn't be in any way as embarrassing as his. But he had to bluff.

She twisted her mouth, hating to be bested at anything. Her eyes narrowed at her hat, and he held it higher to protect it from a desperate attempt.

"I'm sure it's fascinating reading," he said. He fished his hand into the sock cap until his fingers touched paper. "There it is."

"Fine!" She shoved his letter into his hand and snatched the cap away. "I was just fooling around."

"Glad to hear it," Finley said. "You don't want the Bald Knobbers after you for disturbing the peace."

Postmaster Finley turned away grimly, and Joel didn't find

121

the statement funny, either. If Fowler and Sheriff Taney knew what was in that letter—or at least what he suspected it contained—they'd already be celebrating that they'd rid themselves of their inconvenient deputy.

Thank goodness Betsy had a secret, too.

Chapter 16

Betsy ran home with her skirt tangled around her legs and her cap in her fist. She had to open this telegram.

The door slammed against the wall when she burst in. Sissy startled and lowered her sewing. "You're back already? Did you get Mayor Walters's storeroom organized?"

The world was filled with interesting adventures, and Sissy wanted her stuck in a storeroom. Oh, what Betsy wouldn't do for a place of her own! Perhaps the news held in this envelope could be the first step to achieving that goal.

"Is Uncle Fred in the office?" Betsy headed to the office door. "I'll see if he needs me."

"What about Mayor Walters?" Sometimes, either through distraction or plain exhaustion, Sissy let Betsy slip through without answering her questions. Today wasn't one of those days.

Betsy sighed. "I'm to help him tomorrow. He isn't feeling up to it today."

"Tomorrow? Are you sure?"

For crying aloud! Betsy was twenty-four years old, but as long as she lived under another's roof, those years didn't earn her a day of autonomy.

Betsy cracked the door open. "Tomorrow I'll work at the dry goods store. Today I'll see what Uncle Fred needs." Then, just as insurance, she called, "Uncle Fred? I'm coming."

"Come on in," he answered. "Did you get the market numbers from the sale barn?"

Betsy smiled apologetically at Sissy and then darted into the office. Uncle Fred's sleeves were rolled up to his elbows and held in place by arm garters. Today wasn't a printing day, but he claimed he wrote faster with his cuffs up. His pen flew across the pad, scratching his notes. He paused, licked his finger to rub out a word, then kept going, never lifting his eyes as Betsy answered.

"I didn't get a chance, there was so much going on." She pulled her hat off. "You won't believe what happened."

He looked up through his smudged spectacles at the envelope she produced from the cap. "What do you have there?"

"It's always been a letter before, but this is the first telegram I've received. They wouldn't do that just to tell me I'd been rejected, would they?" She probably couldn't even open it now, as clumsy as her hands felt.

Uncle Fred pulled on his ear. "So you decided to work for my competition?" But the pride in his voice was unmistakable. "Who are *they,* anyway?"

"The *Kansas City Star.* Oh, I can't open it." She crammed it into his hands but clutched at his wrist, knowing she couldn't completely let it go. "You do it. You tell me what it says."

Fred's eyes softened. "You know what, Betsy? If this is what I think it is, then you've just beat me to a dream that I've always been too fearful to try. This is your moment, and I'm not going to interfere. I'll keep Sissy busy while you get your news."

He pulled her hands off his wrist and placed the envelope in them. Then, with a kiss on the forehead, he left her standing alone to go back into the house.

Once when Betsy was little, she and her big brother, Josiah, had held a contest to see who could hold their breath the longest underwater. Determined to win, she'd wedged her arm beneath a root to anchor herself to the bottom of the river so she wouldn't float up. That did the trick until she could stand it no longer and wanted up, only then realizing her arm was hung. As she pulled against the root, nearly skinning the hide off her arm, she became aware of a pillar of fire inside her chest. She couldn't release her air, for there'd be nothing to replace it, but if she didn't expel it, she would explode.

That was how she felt right now.

She went to her cot. It squeaked as she dropped onto it, the straw tick expelling a burst of air. If they didn't want her story, she could always try again, but even being as realistic as she knew how, this was a very good sign.

Her fingers shook as she lifted the unglued flap of the envelope and pulled out the cream-colored paper. Sender was listed as the *Kansas City Star*, and the telegram read:

We will purchase your two submissions on the developing situation and request subsequent articles be sent without delay. Terms have been mailed to you and will arrive soon.

That was it? Betsy lowered the telegram to her lap. There wasn't any eloquent rhapsodizing over the exciting story where the Dashing Deputy pulled the girl out of the well? She felt slighted. But they must have liked it if they wanted to buy it, right? And they wanted her to send more.

Slowly the magnitude of what had occurred began to dawn

on her. A newspaper in Kansas City was going to publish her stories. And they were going to pay her, to boot.

If that didn't beat all.

But what did it mean, *the developing situation*? They didn't think the stories were one hundred percent true, did they? Her submission had been clear—these stories were for the ladies' section. Fictionalized serials. Not to be taken seriously. Should she say something?

Betsy held the telegram against her heart. What was the worst that could happen? Some readers in far-off Kansas City would think that a child fell down a well when it was only a kitten? What harm could that do? They'd probably be placed in the middle of the ladies' section, anyway. On the other hand, if she raised a stink about them placing her stories in the wrong column, they might not want any more. Was she willing to risk that?

More stories were already in the mail, chugging their way toward the office in Kansas City. Now that the ball was rolling, she couldn't afford to mess it up. The stories were mostly true. It wasn't her fault if they'd misunderstood.

She had to organize her hurriedly jotted notes and ideas and get the Kansas City newspaper men something else while they were interested. Hopefully Joel's interview with Mr. Sanders would make a good story. If Miles Bullard had returned to harass Doctor Hopkins, that'd fill some pages, but she didn't want anyone to get hurt. The important part was that the Dashing Deputy rode in and saved the day. That was what would sell papers.

And she wasn't using real names anyway. Not that it mattered. No one in Pine Gap or Texas would be reading that paper. Uncle Fred was the only one in town who subscribed to the Kansas City paper. She'd just have to make sure that his copy got used to wrap fish or line the rabbit cage before anyone had a chance to come in the newspaper office and borrow it.

Speaking of Uncle Fred . . .

Betsy bounded off her cot and rushed into the kitchen. As she expected, Uncle Fred was standing by the table, every bit as impatient as she was.

One look at her, and his face lifted and wrinkled into a thousand happy lines. "I didn't even know you'd sent something to them."

There were several reasons for that, but she'd start with the simplest. "I was afraid they'd say no, and then what would be the point?"

"You have to let me read what you wrote."

She shook her head. "It's nothing really. Just a story based on life here in Pine Gap. Nothing special."

"What's this?" Sissy stabbed her needle into the fabric with finality. Amelia clutched at her skirt. As Uncle Fred explained, Sissy covered Amelia's ears with her hands. "You aren't writing about the Bald Knobbers, are you? We've already got too many strangers concerning themselves with our business. We certainly don't need more."

Uncle Fred was reading the telegram for the third time. What did it say exactly? Did it mention the deputy?

Betsy knelt to flick Amelia's upturned nose. "What I'm writing is more than half concoctions of my own imagination. Uncle Fred can tell you the stories after page twelve are more sensationalized serials than true reporting."

"I still don't like it," Sissy replied.

"Pshaw!" Uncle Fred blurted. "I'm proud as punch of her. To think my own niece has been accepted by a big Kansas City paper. It's incredible."

There was nothing as sweet as an accomplishment shared

with people who only wanted what was best for you. Even though Betsy's aim was to afford her own abode, she didn't mean it as a slight to Uncle Fred. Not one bit. She'd spent as much time with Uncle Fred as with her own pa, but times were tough. She was in the way.

As hard as it'd be to say good-bye, it'd be best for everyone.

CHAPTER 17

The sun hadn't dipped behind the mountain yet, but Joel's day was feeling darker than ever. He propped his stockinged feet up against the crossbar of the cell and stretched his hands to rest behind his head on the cot.

Why was she still hounding him?

He should have ripped up Mary Blount's letter immediately and not taken a chance on anyone in Hart County reading it. How had it even reached him? Who had forwarded it? Sheriff Green? Obviously, from the address on the envelope, Miss Blount didn't know where he was or what he was doing. And from her threats, if she had known where he was, she'd ruin his life.

Again.

Joel studied the weak shadows thrown on the wall by the bars. The door to the cell stood open, but he still felt trapped. When Mary Blount first made her accusations, he'd been told the only alternative to marrying her was to go quietly. Running had given him this job, but it hadn't ended her threats. Obsessed with making him pay for her failed plans, she wanted her treacherous lies to live on. Even worse, she seemed hungry to know where he was . . . as if that knowledge in some way constituted a relationship between them. Joel shivered. What did a gentleman do against a ruthless woman? In so many ways, his hands were tied.

Swinging his legs down, he padded to the hall tree. Then, as if a sudden movement might release a dangerous plague on the town, he carefully removed the piece of paper from the pocket of his coat.

. . . no matter where you roam, you will never outrun the shame of what you put me through. I, who had your best interest at heart. I, who wanted nothing more than to bring you happiness and domestic felicity. Didn't my efforts to get you alone that night prove that I deserve you more than anyone? But how did you reward my toil? You ruined my reputation and failed to do your duty. . . .

He crumpled the paper, tossed it into the trash bin, and wished that his troubles could be thrust aside that easily. He begged God to release him from the anger, the bitterness, but most days it felt like the best he could do was to try to forget. Immersing himself in his job here helped, but always waiting at the edge of his thoughts, ready to drag him under again, was the memory of the injustice leveled against him.

"I am free," he whispered. "I am blameless." Joel spoke the truth. Surely if he repeated the words enough, even he would believe them. He waited until the roar of injustice in his head died down. He had a job to do, and it started by visiting a man who'd arrived the same night he had and who seemed to be hiding something. Just like him.

The thought of saddling up his horse raised Joel's spirits considerably. No one had read his letter. No one knew who had written it or why, and no one from Garber would tell the

Blounts where he was. The one benefit to living on the edge of civilization was that he was out of Mary's reach.

Joel sighed once he made it past the Murphys' cabin without being detected. Betsy was unlike any woman he'd ever known before. She wasn't fussy and particular like his sisters, nor was she merely concerned with roping a man. He was learning to enjoy Betsy's company, and that scared him. Had he let his guard slip? Was she safe? It was too soon to tell.

He reached the Sanderses' house at the crossroads and tied his horse at the fence. From the outside, everything looked peaceful and well kept. A knock on the door brought a bustling middle-aged lady forward. She swiped at a stray lock of hair with a quick hand and eyed him suspiciously.

"What do you want?" she asked. She reminded him of some of the ranchers' wives back in Garber—those who hadn't come into money and still worked the cattle alongside their husbands, doing a man's job of a day and then going back inside to cook dinner and clean house of an evening.

"Mrs. Sanders, I don't know if you remember me, but I'm Deputy Puckett. Is Mr. Sanders around?" If he were, Joel almost certainly would be able to see him, since there weren't too many places to hide in the tiny house.

"He is."

Boots thudded on the rough wood staircase, and step by step Mr. Sanders descended to face him.

Was he a brute? No way to know, but he did look nervous. Mr. Sanders was hiding something, that was for sure.

"Good evening, Mr. Sanders." Joel held out his hand, and Sanders took it, albeit reluctantly. "Would you mind stepping outside with me for a spell?"

"What's this about?" Mrs. Sanders stepped between them. "Is something going on that I should know about?"

Sanders's eyes shifted away from his wife. He scratched the back of his head. Whatever he might be contemplating, his wife definitely thought him capable of carrying it out from the fearful look she was giving him. Although Joel never started an encounter with a suspect without being fully ready to defend himself, the way Sanders acted gave him extra motivation to watch his back.

"Go on inside, Della. This doesn't concern you."

She was going, but she wasn't none too pleased about it. With a questioning look at her husband, she shut the door.

They moseyed into the garden, and Joel motioned Mr. Sanders onto a thick burnt stump while he took a seat on a tall-backed chair.

"You told Mrs. Sanders that what I have to speak to you about doesn't concern her." Joel rested his elbows on his knees and let his hands hang freely, looking deceptively relaxed. "Would you mind telling me who it does concern?"

Sanders's face crumpled. "I'm not sure I follow. How am I supposed to know what's on your mind?"

"How about let's start with why you are here. People in these parts have been flummoxed about why you've been gone so long."

"It's none of their business." His round nose grew redder in the brisk air.

"Perhaps not. How about what you came back for? Is that anyone's business?"

Sanders snorted. "You act like I ain't the man I'm supposed to be for staying gone so long, then you want to give me grief over coming back. Which is it, Deputy? Staying gone or coming back? Which made you afeared that I was up to no good?"

It was times like these that Joel wished he had his mother's gift of conversation.

"Then let's talk about your behavior since you returned. How have you and the missus being getting along?"

"She hasn't complained, has she?"

Which was the expected response of a wife-abuser.

"No, she hasn't."

"Then I'm not complaining, either."

Sometimes the strongest women—those who were too proud to admit they needed help—stayed silent the longest. One woman he'd come to know in Garber had survived brutal abuse. Now Anne Tillerton Lovelace had found happiness with his best friend, Nick.

"There have been reports of contention at your abode," Joel said. "Loud hollering, crashing furniture, ruckus-raising—does any of that sound familiar?"

Sanders's face set in a mask of determination. He might as well have taken an invisible key, twisted it before his lips, and thrown it over his shoulder, because obviously he wasn't going to say a blessed thing, not even a denial. He was hiding something, but was he behind the threats to Doctor Hopkins?

"Mr. Sanders, you're not going to like what I'm fixing to tell you, but I hope you'll be reasonable and hear me out." Joel flexed his fingers. "As you've probably ascertained since arriving in Pine Gap, we have a peace-keeping problem, and your behavior might be contributing to it."

"Me? I haven't done anything wrong."

"You haven't? Seems like someone around here has been misbehaving."

Sanders cut his eyes to the ground. If he was guilty, at least he did seem to be troubled over it. That was something . . . but not enough. "What I propose is that you spend some time away from your wife."

"I've been gone long enough, haven't I?"

"That wouldn't be for me to judge, but is her life better now that you're back?"

Mr. Sanders closed his eyes.

Joel pressed on. "There's another issue I'd like to talk over. Do you know Doctor Hopkins?"

"Newton Hopkins? Of course I know him. From what I hear, he sees my wife regularly."

Joel drew in a long, slow breath. Was that an innocent comment, or did it hint at a motive Mr. Sanders might have against the doctor?

Betsy was right. There was more here than met the eye.

CHAPTER 18

Uncle Fred's old work gloves kept the splinters from the rough crates out of her hands but made handling the cans awkward. It wasn't her chosen occupation, but it would provide for the family, so she couldn't refuse. And since Walters was paying her in staples, her money would go even further. Probably the biggest hardship on Betsy and her independence was that she depended on Sissy and Uncle Fred for everything. How could she refuse to help out when they clothed and fed her?

Once she'd emptied every crate and shelved every tin can, Betsy tucked the work gloves into her waistband and lifted a burlap sack from the pile in the corner. She entered the store proper to find Walters standing amid the colorful bolts of fabric, picking his teeth with a knitting needle.

"I finished organizing the shelves," she said. "How much did you say I could take?"

"I gathered you a pile there on the bar," he said, wiping the knitting needle on his pant leg. "I appreciate the help. Every time I lift those rough crates, I just know I'm begging for another splinter."

"Let me know if you need me again." She took the sack and began loading it with the sorely needed edibles.

"Well, looky here," Walters said as the door swung open and a gust of cold air swept past Betsy. "It's that lawman again."

Betsy froze with a can of sorghum in her hand. Joel would want to know what was in her telegram. Betsy didn't favor broaching that subject. One question would lead to another, and next thing you knew, the nosy man would be reading about her Dashing Deputy, and that must never, ever happen.

"Mayor Walters, I need to buy . . ." His voice trailed off. Betsy hurried to sweep the canned goods into her sack. "I'm sorry," Deputy Puckett said. "I'll come back when you're not busy."

"Don't hurry off. It's just Betsy," Walters said.

With a grunt Betsy slung the sack over her shoulder. No use pretending to be invisible now. She turned to face him. Joel lifted his eyebrows in unison with his shoulders, looking downright sheepish.

"Good afternoon, Deputy Puckett." Funny how speaking formally only made her realize how familiar he'd become.

"Good afternoon, Miss Huckabee." To hear him, you'd never guess he'd wrestled her over an envelope the day before. That hadn't been her finest moment, either, so she'd let it pass. "If Mayor Walters isn't busy, I came to ask his assistance with some wool fabric and directions to a seamstress. I find myself in need of an extra pair of trousers."

Betsy bit back a smile. Why had she wanted to hide from him in the first place?

"That wouldn't be the work of that pony, would it?" Walters rubbed his backside. "He took a hunk out of me unprovoked!"

"I am enjoying my horse. Thank you for asking," Joel said.

"Laurel Hopkins sews up a storm," Betsy said. "But she'd rather choose the material herself."

Mayor Walters nodded. "She's particular with what she sets

her needle to. Tell her what you want, and she'll whip it right up."

Joel twisted a button on his double-breasted shirt. "I appreciate the advice." His hand reached up to tip his hat but stopped at the brim. He looked at the sack Betsy had thrown over her shoulder. "Are you headed to home, ma'am?"

Wasn't he acting just like a Dashing Deputy should? She smiled. "It's not heavy."

"Mayor Walters," Joel said, "would you please round me up a sack with the same items as Miss Huckabee's?"

Walters took the knitting needle out of his mouth and put it back on the shelf. In a matter of minutes he presented Joel with a sack of equal size.

"Sorry to make you wait," Joel said to Betsy. He stepped to the side and held the door open for her. Betsy squeezed past him in the doorway. What was he doing? Had he read her serial, because he was acting like every woman's dream. Even when he snatched the sack out of her hand and tossed it over his shoulder, he was chivalrous. He didn't even wince when the tin cans thudded against his back. He untethered the horse and led it behind them.

"Are you planning on doing some cooking?" Betsy asked.

"I just realized that I need to contribute to the Murphys' larder if I'm going to continue to dine with them."

"You haven't been at the table for a few days." And definitely not since he'd got that letter.

"I'm getting hungry," he said.

"Oh, that's it." Betsy narrowed her eyes. "I should've known you weren't being friendly."

"I am friendly, just not with young, single ladies."

"I told you, I'm not young."

His cheek made some creases that looked suspiciously like

the beginning of a smile. "Beg your pardon, ma'am. I've fought against the claim that I was too young to accomplish what I set out to do, so I should know better than to paint you with the same brush. Let me revise my statement. I'm not usually friendly with single ladies who happen to be chronologically hampered despite their intelligence and experience."

She frowned. "I don't know that I favor being called experienced. Most of the time that implies—"

Out of nowhere he took up whistling.

"You interrupted me," she said.

"Looking for a change of subject." His stride was easy and relaxed.

"Did you talk to Sanders?"

He sighed. "You're right. He's hiding something."

Betsy stopped in her tracks. "I told you."

"You did. Now tell me about Mrs. Sanders. Is she the kind to be involved in unsavory activities?"

"Not unless you're talking about rigging the judging in the annual Pine Gap Pie Contest, or the Garden Club Contest, or the Quilting Bee Competition, or—well, let's just say she's competitive, but she would never condone lawlessness."

"How would she respond if her husband was whooping up on her?"

Betsy tilted her chin up and her forehead wrinkled. "I . . . I don't know. She doesn't put up with nonsense. I can't imagine her taking a beating and having nothing to say about it."

"Well, I can't arrest him with no evidence. All I can do is watch him—"

"You mean like sit outside his house at night and make sure he doesn't go after Doctor Hopkins?"

Joel shot her a sideways glance. "Actually that *is* what I had in mind. And if furniture crashes like you heard, I'll intervene."

The memory of the ruckus made her shiver. In her excitement to solve a crime, she'd forgotten that Widow Sanders was likely in mortal danger. If Mr. Sanders was a menace, she'd be very grateful for the brave man at her side.

Had she forgotten about his letter, or was she hoping he'd forgotten about hers? Joel would wager it was the second, but there wasn't any call for poking a sleeping bear. If Miss Huckabee got too nosy, he'd have to avoid her altogether, and he found that notion lacked appeal. Betsy was proving a reliable place to test his theories. Besides that, her aunt and uncle had extended an open invitation at their table. Having always lived in the same town as his doting mother, Joel had never found reason to handle a skillet. Now he was finding reason after reason to value a friendship with this independent young lady.

As they approached the Murphys' cabin, Fred came into view, hunched down against the wind. His thin frame curved inward. Between his scarf and his hat, only his eyes were exposed, and they were narrowed to slits.

"The cold hits him hard," Betsy said. "He doesn't have an ounce of extra meat on him."

Joel's eyes darted to her slender form, but he thought better of commenting. "Your uncle and aunt seem like nice folks," he said.

Betsy beamed. "The best. I helped Uncle Fred raise his boys after Aunt Doris died. My parents thought coming to town would do me some good. They live out towards the Calhouns and Hopkinses."

"I'd like to meet them someday." Saying that surprised him, but it was the truth. If Fred was any indication, he'd have nothing to lose from making their acquaintance.

"Pa comes to town fairly often. And my brother Josiah. Everyone says Scott takes after him." After a moment, she added, "Thank you for your dealings with Scott. He's convinced you're the slickest thing ever. He's about decided he wants to be a lawman, too, but Sissy doesn't want him gunning for anyone just yet."

Joel's chest warmed at her words. As a boy he'd always dreamed of wearing the badge. No one had told him how precarious the job was. How you had to dodge more than bullets.

"Scott seems like a good boy," he said. "In a few years he'll be old enough—"

Down from the hills came trouble. Clive Fowler.

Betsy stopped to wait on him. Joel lowered the sacks of supplies to the ground, just in case.

"Are you hunting us again?" Betsy asked.

"Yes, I am." The frayed seams of Fowler's coat waved in the breeze. That coat had probably been worn inside out as much as the right way. "In the spirit of cooperation, I came to report that all is well around Hopkins's place. So far there's not been a hair dropped that we don't know about."

"I told you to stay away from there." Joel felt a proclivity to get on his horse. He hated talking up to Fowler, but he had to stand his ground no matter how low it was. "You're going to mess around and get somebody shot."

"We know what we're doing," Fowler said. "We've been protecting our own since before you were born." He glanced at Betsy. "Just ask the girl. Who does she come to when she hears about trouble? It's to me."

It was a low blow. Joel wanted to believe that Betsy had intended to tell him about Doctor Hopkins receiving threats, but he couldn't quite convince himself that she wasn't looking for Fowler the whole time. Well, she'd learn to trust him. He knew how to do this right.

"I'm going to sit watch tonight," Joel said.

"At the doctor's?" Fowler asked.

"I'm watching Sanders," Joel said. "If my guess is right, he's the man."

"Would you like to bet your life on that?" Fowler asked. "Because you're asking Doc Hopkins to bet his."

"If Doctor Hopkins thinks he's in danger, he's welcome to bring his family to town," Joel said.

Betsy rocked forward. "They can stay with us. It'll be crowded, but Uncle Fred will insist."

Fowler's nostrils flared. "What if you get more than you bargained for?"

"All that's happened is that Doctor Hopkins got a bundle of sticks left on his porch. That's all. Maybe it was Sanders, maybe it was Bullard, maybe it was a prank. Or maybe it was the Bald Knobbers." Joel gave that a moment to sink in. "No one has been hurt or threatened, but if y'all keep prowling around at night, sooner or later you're gonna cross someone who doesn't understand what fine outstanding citizens you are, and there's going to be a deadly misunderstanding."

Fowler's brow looked heavy. "You want the responsibility, then it's on you. I'll tell the boys he's in your hands."

Joel felt like a load of coal had just been dumped off his back. Maybe God was listening to him. It finally looked like he might be on the road to earning their respect.

Find what Sanders was hiding. That was the key.

Chapter 19

Deputy Joel Puckett sure brightened up the supper table. True, his calm, steady manners didn't lend themselves to hilarity. He rarely cracked a smile and didn't steal the show with outlandish stories. Yet his kindness, the way he listened as they spun yarns and teased each other around the table, made him the perfect audience.

And most of the audience thought he was perfect.

Uncle Fred and Sissy had been joined by the two Hopkins girls and their mother, Laurel. Eighteen-year-old Anna's face was as fixed as a china doll's, and much to Betsy's frustration, just as pretty. She held her rosebud mouth in a perfect pout and kept her blue eyes wide open, as if blinking might mar the effect. Fourteen-year-old Phoebe jolted forward every time Joel made utterance. Keeping her hands clasped in her lap, she'd elbow her sister and lift her eyebrows before settling back against her chair. At first they'd been chagrined to learn that Scott had been sent to stay with Betsy's folks to make room for them, but finding Deputy Puckett at the table had cheered them up considerably.

Still, their mother spoke in worried tones with Sissy, airing her fears for her husband, who'd elected to keep watch over their house that night.

"I don't like it, either," Sissy said. "Those Bald Knobbers should've known their methods would come back to haunt them."

"What do you mean?" Laurel picked at the stitching on her napkin until it looked to come apart. "Haunt him like a ghost?"

Uncle Fred shook his head at his wife. "Don't be troubling her. We've got better news than that. Tell them, Betsy." He grinned, proud as punch.

Alarm had Betsy shaking her head. "Why would I do that? It doesn't concern them. Here, let me take your plates." Betsy fumbled with the dishes and landed her thumb in someone's leftover mashed potatoes.

Uncle Fred wasn't giving up. "Stars above, Betsy. You can't mean that you're going to keep this a secret?"

"You'uns haven't told anyone, have you?" Her chest pounded as she waited for his answer. From the look on his face, Joel knew good and well this pertained to the telegram she'd tried to hide from him. He was uncommonly interested, while Phoebe Hopkins yawned.

"I haven't said a word," Fred said.

"Then don't." Betsy dropped the plates in the basin and took the hot water off the stove. "It probably won't amount to anything."

Joel took that moment to start a game of pat-a-cake with Amelia. Surprised but grateful, Betsy scrubbed the dishes as the conversation resumed. Sissy and Laurel discussed their preparations for winter and the bounty or scarcity of their larders, while Uncle Fred and Joel shared stories about eventful hunting excursions they'd had. Somehow, Betsy found her ears attuned to Joel's voice. Every comment he made was amplified, every utterance clear. She found herself smiling and nodding with the conversation, even though she wasn't at the table. His voice rumbled deep as he talked with Uncle Fred, then gentled as he spoke to the youngest members of the family.

At some point Amelia had climbed onto Joel's lap, because when Betsy turned to take a peek, she saw the child lying tucked in his arm. Amelia's blond curls were pillowed against his chest as she slept contentedly.

The sight tugged a chord in Betsy's heart that had never been strummed before. Something was so right about the scene, but she couldn't define what it was. For being nothing out of the ordinary, it affected her strongly.

She didn't realize she'd stopped washing the dishes and was staring until Sissy bumped her with her hip. "It's late. The girls have already gone to the loft. Why don't you put Amelia to bed?"

Betsy nodded as she stacked the dishes and dropped the dishrag into the basin. Somehow she made it across the small room to Joel without remembering how she got there. He waited for Uncle Fred to finish before turning her way, but that gave Betsy more time to soak up the toasty warmth she was feeling. Amelia's head swayed slightly with the rise and fall of his chest. Her chubby white fingers lay atop the back of his sun-darkened hand. She looked so tiny. He looked so . . .

"Are you going to take her or not?" Uncle Fred asked.

Betsy blinked. Joel was watching her closely. What had she been thinking, stopping and staring at a man sitting in her kitchen? He wasn't doing anything special.

Joel shifted in his chair to give her a better angle. Betsy extended her arms, but for a woman who'd been tending children since she was ten years old, she found it took some thought on how exactly to extract the toddler. There was nothing to do but lean into him, slide her arms between Amelia's warm body and his . . .

He smelled good. Great stars above, he smelled good. And then, just as she got her arms around the girl and started to lift her away, he had the gall to stroke Amelia's tangled hair and whisper into Betsy's ear, "She's got your curls."

Betsy nearly dropped the poor child. Her throat stuck as he caressed the youngster's curls one last time. Even as she pulled away, his eyes followed, taking in her own loose braid and escaping locks.

She had to get away. This had never happened to her before.

Betsy sailed into Uncle Fred and Sissy's room and deposited the child into her bed. Before she'd even reached the mirror on the wall, she'd unplaited her braid and grabbed a brush. She'd worked hard all day at the dry goods store. She was tired. She was discouraged. She needed to get her head on straight. The man in there was only a man. She was getting him confused with her own *fictional* accounts of him. He wasn't the Dashing Deputy. The Dashing Deputy didn't exist. What did exist was a tiny cabin bursting at the seams with people. What did exist was a Kansas City editor who wanted more of her stories. She couldn't let mushy feelings for the deputy get in the way.

She yanked her hair into a tight, controlled braid with no soft curls escaping. Then, for good measure, she twisted it up on her head and wrapped it around in a coil. She studied her work in the mirror. Severe, no nonsense, all tidy. But the tight coif only made her blue eyes bigger. The exertion pinked her cheeks and heightened her coloring.

Her mouth tightened into a line of frustration. She might look like a love-sick, dewy-eyed miss, but her mind was sharp.

And so was her pen. She'd better get to work on another article before she lost her nerve.

When she entered the main room again, Joel was watching for her. His expression was unreadable, and she was determined not to put any thought to it. Instead she covered her mouth and faked a yawn.

"I'm tired. Good night."

If he was confused by her sudden sullenness, he didn't show it. Instead he stood and began apologizing to Uncle Fred for overstaying his welcome. Rather than standing around and listening to Uncle Fred's assurances that they didn't mind, Betsy carried a lantern into the office.

As soon as she could find a pen and her draft, she went to work. Betsy had discovered what her lawman was missing—a flaw. Every hero needed a failing. Eduardo was brave, smart, charming, and capable. He needed a weakness, and his would be . . . women.

After a moment's thought, Betsy began penning an installment in which the lovely but treacherous daughter of a moonshiner double-crossed the deputy and was nearly his undoing. It made her feel better to give Eduardo feet of clay. While Joel seemed to have integrity that would protect him from mistakes like the ones Eduardo would be making, he often came up short in the charm and dash department, and she had to remind herself of that. No one was perfect.

Deputy Pickett sat astride his massive white horse and watched the barefoot mountain lass bend over the blackberry bush. Her unbound hair fell like a curtain of silk down her back. She brushed it aside with fingers stained a rich purple. When she saw him approach, she dropped her berry basket and spilled her treasure in the deep, emerald grass. He hoped she would be strong but was fully prepared to take her into his arms as he delivered the tragic news.

Picking up the paper, Betsy blew on the ink and then, seeing it was dry, slid it beneath the blotter. On tiptoe she danced to the window and peered up and down the street. Nope, he hadn't left yet. He must still be talking to Uncle Fred. With a satisfied nod, she scurried back to the desk and slid the paper out.

The last word hadn't completely dried before she'd hid it. Now it was smeared, but she traced over the word and took up where she'd left off.

"Miss Gibson, I'm afraid I bring bad tidings."
Tears flooded her eyes, but with the courage innate to her family, she spoke. "Just tell me that you will never leave me, Eduardo. Anything else I can bear."

That was about all Betsy could write before her curiosity got the better of her and she had to look out the window again. To prevent smearing, she held the paper up to the lamp, but seeing no shining wet spots, she pushed it under the blotter on the off chance that he was at the door and decided to come inside.

This time her trip to the window was rewarded. The man in the tall cowboy hat walked down the street, but he was going the wrong way. Instead of heading to the jailhouse, he was going up the hill . . . to the Sanders cabin.

Betsy's breathing sped up. That was right. He'd said he was going to stake out Mr. Sanders's place and make sure the man didn't try to sneak away tonight.

She rubbed an ink spot on her thumb in a tiny circle as she considered her options. Spending time alone with him could muddle her thinking. On the other hand, if she started avoiding him, her stories wouldn't be authentic. And maybe the only way to keep from falling under his spell was to spend every spare minute with him—then she'd be only too familiar with his failings. Then she wouldn't be tempted to think too highly of him.

Either way, Betsy had never let fear get in the way of an adventure, and she wasn't about to start now.

Chapter 20

Joel wedged himself against the burnt stump and stretched his legs flat beneath the azalea bushes. He'd already surveyed the property. One could slip from the back door to the ravine that ran behind the house, but unless Mr. Sanders knew he was being observed, he'd have no reason to do that. Besides, with all the dry leaves on the ground and the small size of the house, Joel figured he could hear someone moving around back there anyway. Not much escaped his notice.

Or at least he thought so until he turned to find Betsy Huckabee crouched not ten feet away in the shadowy darkness beneath a cedar tree.

"What are you—?" He stopped before he got any louder and alerted the whole world to his whereabouts. Besides, he wouldn't have to raise his voice because she was scurrying closer. "You can't stay here," he whispered.

"Why not? This isn't your property." Her breath puffed in the cold. She burrowed down beside him and pushed a canteen into his hands. "It's coffee," she said. "I came prepared."

The warmth seeping through his gloves was welcome, even if she was not. "These goings-on are for bona fide lawmen only. You can't interfere."

"I'm on official journalism business. Freedom of the press and all of that."

He relaxed a bit. Betsy lived in a town full of family and friends. She didn't need him for company. But what kind of reporting did she have in mind? "I've been meaning to ask about your work for your uncle," he said. "What exactly do you do for him?"

She tugged the knit cap down over her ears. "I set the type and help him on printing days. And I'm good to gather the routine types of information. You know, prices on livestock and crops, weather reports, that sort of thing."

"When you're not hiding behind crates and eavesdropping on people?" Joel whispered.

"Usually I don't hear anything important."

"Usually?" He twisted his head to get a better look at her. "How often does this snooping occur?"

She bit her lip. "I don't set out to overhear people. They just tend to talk real loud when I'm nearby."

"Hiding."

She shrugged. "On occasion."

She made his eye twitch. Didn't she understand how dangerous this could be? "You listen here—" He had to choke down the *darling* that threatened to squeak out of his mouth. "If Mr. Sanders or anyone else comes out of that house, you will stay hunkered down. Do you understand?"

Betsy's eyes widened. "Does that mean you're letting me stay?"

"Is it up to me?"

Her grin broke wide. "Thank you."

Then her hand was on his. Joel froze, suddenly remembering how he'd been burned by a situation very similar to this. How a woman had plotted to compromise his reputation.

But Betsy merely tugged at the canteen. "The coffee," she said. "Can I have a drink? I'm cold."

He passed it to her and she took a swig, then looked at the stump behind him. "Good to see someone spending time with Lady Godiva again. She's been sadly neglected."

Joel twisted to get a better look behind him. "Are y'all so hard up for company that you name your tree stumps?"

"She used to be a statue, but she was declared guilty of inciting indecency, so they burned her. Actually that was about the only action Sheriff Taney ever took against anyone. As usual, his punishment wasn't very effective. She took the flames pretty well. If you look . . ."

The charred stump took on a very womanly form as his eyes adjusted. Joel scooted away, which placed him even closer to Betsy. Wasn't she more dangerous than the tree stump?

Then he thought of her at her cabin, surrounded by family. She didn't maneuver to be close to him. She didn't insert herself into the conversation or insist on his attention. Sure she wanted to know what was going on, but he wasn't vain enough to think that he was the primary attraction. He watched as she lifted the canteen for another drink of coffee, then wiped her mouth on the back of her glove. Betsy Huckabee had no interest in him as a beau. She couldn't hardly bring herself to take a toddler from him, while he found himself daydreaming about whether Betsy looked as sweet as the child.

Had Mary Blount warped his opinion of all women? Maybe it was time to move past that debacle. Maybe it was time to give Miss Huckabee a chance.

The leaves rustled beneath her as she shivered, but then another noise rang through the clear, cold night. A raised voice, a loud crash, and Joel sprang to his feet.

"Stay," he ordered Betsy. And with a hand to her shoulder,

he pushed her down on her backside just as she was standing. "Don't let them know you're here." Yes, he had to protect Mrs. Sanders, but protecting Betsy was part of the job, too.

He plowed through branches and bounded onto the porch. At the thud of his boots, the house went quiet. Would Mr. Sanders bolt out the back? But instead the man cracked the front door open and pushed his florid face into the gap before Joel could knock.

"I thought I heard someone out here," he said.

"Where's your wife?" Joel's fist clenched. He would intervene physically if necessary.

Sanders's eyes darted a look at something on the inside. "She don't feel like coming to the door."

"I'm coming in," said Joel.

Sanders didn't struggle as Joel shoved his way inside. In fact, because of the lack of space in the room, he tripped over the sofa in his hurry to get out of Joel's way.

"Mrs. Sanders." Joel kept the man of the house in sight but angled toward the kitchen. Spilled stew had splashed against the wall. A tin dish lay on the floor. He heard a sob, then she appeared. Her gray-streaked hair was pulled loose from her coif. Evidence of tears marred her cheeks.

She sniffed, then spoke with a wavering voice. "He was fixing to go out for the night, but I didn't think he ought to."

Joel tried to read the man who refused to look him in the eye. "Where were you going?"

"Nowhere in particular. Just needed a breath of fresh air."

The thing about lying was you always got found out, and most of the time people knew you were lying as the words left your mouth. Nobody took a walk at midnight in these mountains unless they were up to no good.

"I've got a lot of fresh air between here and the jailhouse," Joel said. "What do you say we go there and cool off?"

Sanders looked long and hard at the missus, but there was no threat in his gaze. Almost an apology. He groaned. "I guess I might as well be there as anywhere."

Mrs. Sanders pulled her shirt sleeve down over her forearm, probably hiding a mark. "You need someone here with you," Joel said. "I can send one of your neighbors—Miss Huckabee, for instance."

"Don't send anyone. I want to be alone." She lifted the dish from the floor and slid it onto the table.

"When you're ready to talk," Joel said.

She motioned to the door, but Joel wasn't leaving before Sanders. Sanders pulled on his coat, his hair getting caught beneath his collar, and slipped on some boots.

With a last scan of the room and another reassurance from Mrs. Sanders, they started to town. When Joel saw a knit cap caught in the branches of the azalea bush beneath the window, but no Betsy, he wasn't even surprised.

Chapter 21

How could Betsy sleep now? The clock on the mantel hadn't struck midnight yet, but so much had happened. Mr. Sanders brawling with his wife. Joel rushing the door and thrusting himself between them, or at least that was what she imagined. She was in the bushes, crawling her way to the window when that occurred.

And now here she was at a window again, waiting to see if he'd come back. She'd followed him and Mr. Sanders to the jail but couldn't get close enough to pick up their conversation.

If Joel didn't come back to tell her what had happened, she'd lose her mind.

A shadow made its way up the street, and her sanity was preserved.

Betsy opened the front door of the office. The light reflected off his badge, flashing in her eyes. He paused long enough for her to grab him by the sleeve and pull him inside.

"Don't you dare even think about leaving."

"It's late. I didn't know if you'd be up." Red dotted his cheeks where his beard didn't cover.

Betsy pushed the door closed behind him and motioned him

to the small stove. The light illuminated a tight circle that made the room feel smaller than it did during daylight hours. He pulled off his gloves and held his hands to the fire.

"This thing doesn't put out much heat," he said. "And you sleep in here?"

"It's not bad. I wear . . ." She had time to consider maybe talking about her nightclothes wasn't ladylike, but she didn't want him to blame her family for the hardship. "It's the best Uncle Fred and Sissy can do."

He caught her gaze, and the way he looked at her made her heart feel full. Just like when he was holding Amelia.

"I'm proud of you," he said at last.

Proud? If she were writing his lines, that wasn't what she would've chosen.

"I don't understand."

"Others might complain. Might feel slighted. But you choose to think the best of your family."

Betsy frowned. "How could I not?"

But he was done talking about it. He was plowing ahead to a new subject.

"I have a confession to make." He studied the flames. The shadows danced on his hero-worthy profile. "Here I am in Pine Gap saying how I'm going to work without prejudice, how everyone gets a clean slate, yet I'm judging you based on the actions of another member of the fair sex. I apologize."

This kind of talk, about him and her and whatever their relationship was, felt strangely exciting, but at the same time, a twinge of guilt began to form. When she'd started writing about the Texas deputy, he was a stranger. But what if Joel became her friend? Betsy looked at her desk, then breathed easier when she saw her tablet had been hidden.

"I accept your apology," she said at last. "So when you said you'd rather fall on a cactus than listen to a woman talk, you weren't speaking about me?"

"I said that?" He winced as Betsy nodded. "I've known some fairly comfortable cacti, but I'd rather converse with you than take a tumble into any of them."

That was the nicest thing anyone had said to her in a long time. Which reflected poorly on her kin, but they weren't of the sentimental ilk. She, on the other hand, was growing more sentimental by the heartbeat.

"Besides," he said, "seeing how you know everyone and everything going on, you might prove helpful to my job. That's the true benefit."

And then, just like that, he had to wipe away any notion she had that he might be partial to her. Well, if he expected her to help him with his profession, she should have no qualms about using him to further hers.

"If there's any way I can serve my community, Deputy."

"There is one other thing that concerns me, besides you being a woman and all, and that's your involvement with the newspaper. You see, my assignment here isn't generally known back home. I don't know how far your uncle's paper is distributed . . ."

"Not out of Hart County," she said. "And Uncle Fred doesn't print anything controversial." But Joel's questions only led to more questions. Who was he hiding from? Could her Dashing Deputy have a darker side? Was his name really Joel Puckett?

"So you're saying that nothing I say or do will end up in your uncle's paper?" he asked.

Betsy smiled. As much as Uncle Fred enjoyed hearing her reports, he adamantly refused to print anything of interest. That was why she'd had to send her stories all the way to Kansas City. And Kansas City was a long, long way from Pine Gap.

"The only way your name will show up in the Pine Gap newspaper would be if your pickled peppers won a prize at the fair or if you attend one of Mrs. Rinehart's teas." Betsy held up her palm in a pledge. "Besides that, your name will not grace a page printed in Pine Gap, and a page printed in Pine Gap will never reach Texas."

He drew in a deep breath. "Then I think we might be able to help each other after all."

Now he was talking. "When are you going to tell me about Mr. Sanders?" she asked. "I'm being very patient."

"He didn't speak a word all the way to the jailhouse."

"But you kept him?"

"He came willing. Seemed resigned."

The door between the office and the cabin popped open. Uncle Fred's eyebrows lowered and hid somewhere behind his spectacles. "Deputy Puckett? Isn't it late for you to be calling?"

Betsy choked down a laugh. The handsome Deputy Puckett would never come calling on her.

But Joel wasn't laughing. His face had gone grave. "I beg your pardon, Mr. Murphy. I was walking by and . . ."

What could he say? That she had rushed outside and dragged him in by the coat sleeve?

". . . I saw the light on."

Uncle Fred nodded slowly. "If it's after dark, come through the cabin, please."

"Yes, sir!" He all but saluted.

"Mrs. Sanders came looking for you, but I assured her you weren't here."

Mrs. Sanders? Betsy rushed to the outside door, flung it open, and raced to the street. "Mrs. Sanders," she called. "Mrs. Sanders!"

A small figure bundled in a blanket stopped and then turned to come back down the hill.

Betsy took a step backwards and bumped into Joel. He steadied her—and she was partial to his warm hands on her shoulders—and then he went to escort the woman the rest of the way back to their cabin.

This time he entered through the cabin side. Sissy and Laurel hadn't yet turned in for the night but were chatting quietly over steaming cups of hot tea.

Uncle Fred was all apologies. "I didn't know he was here, or I would've told you up front."

"Deputy Puckett was with Betsy?" Sissy darted a nervous glance at Laurel, who'd perked up like a bloodhound on the scent.

"I thought she'd gone to bed," Laurel said.

They might as well lock Betsy up alongside Mr. Sanders, because they were carrying on like she was guilty of a high crime. Hadn't they figured out already she wasn't going to get into any trouble with a man?

Mrs. Sanders patted Uncle Fred on the arm, and as she passed through the cabin, she couldn't help but advise Sissy on the knitting that hung on the arm of her rocking chair. "You're making it too loose," she said. "Wasting wool." She sniffed and covered her face with her handkerchief before stepping into the office.

"Stay in here, Betsy," Uncle Fred said.

"If you don't mind," Joel said, "I need her."

Betsy's heart went kerplunk. She often felt in the way, underfoot, but Joel needed her.

Before Uncle Fred could comment, she wrapped a comforting arm around Mrs. Sanders, led her to her cot, and took a seat next to her. Only over her flower beds was Mrs. Sanders's back ever bent, and even sobbing into her drenched handkerchief, her posture remained rigid.

As soon as Uncle Fred closed the door, Joel pulled a chair up and leaned forward. "What can I do for you?" he asked when there was a break between her strange hiccupped sobs.

"It's about Mr. Sanders. I didn't want to say anything . . . didn't know what you'd say . . . but I can't live with this secret any longer."

Betsy angled herself so she could better see Mrs. Sanders's face. Always a capable, strong woman, she'd aged in the time since Mr. Sanders's return. Further proof of his guilt. But now she was arranging her features for war, lining up courage in every trench of her brow.

"I knew he was alive. After the war I applied for widow benefits, and the War Department wrote back to say he hadn't died. They'd been sending his pension to California." She twisted her handkerchief with hands whose knuckles were just beginning to swell, red and angry. "I wrote him, but he didn't answer. I thought about going out to see him, but how could I? And what if he didn't want me?" Her hands tightened, the veins sitting atop sinews. "I didn't know what to do, so I just let on that he'd passed. As time went on, people started calling me Widow Sanders, and I felt like I was. Anything was better than saying that he ran off on me."

Betsy had been too young to remember the specifics. By the time she'd moved to town to help Uncle Fred, Widow Sanders was all anyone called her. For a widow, she'd been on the youngish side and tough to boot. No one wondered at a dead husband. It was common enough.

"So when he came back . . ." Mrs. Sanders drew a deep, shaky breath. She gave Betsy a half-apologetic smile. "When he came back, I wasn't too all-fired excited to see him. Where had he been? Who had he been with?"

Joel nodded. "Those are fair questions. How did he answer them?"

"He had all kinds of stories, and most of them didn't put no shine on him. But I stopped listening. All I could think of was how everyone was going to talk. How everyone would wonder. And how he had me in such a spot. What could I do but take him back? But I wasn't happy about doing it."

"When you told Mr. Sanders how you felt, is that when he turned violent?" Joel asked.

She rubbed her knuckles. "That's what I'm trying to tell you. He didn't turn violent. I did."

Joel straightened in his chair. He tucked his hands beneath his arms. "Go on."

"I lost my head, screamed, threw stuff at him. I'll be lucky if I still have a pair of matching dishes left in the kitchen. And he just took it. Told me how sorry he was for the years he wasted. Told me how he couldn't live with the guilt any longer and had to come back and take his medicine." She thumped herself on the chest. "Me. I'm the bitter medicine he has to take, I suppose?"

Joel twisted his head. "Are you telling me that he never lifted his hand to you?"

She ducked her chin. "Never, and I let him have it. Anyone who complained about a ruckus was only hearing me. I'm sorry I didn't tell you this when you came to get him. I thought he'd set you straight, but you probably didn't believe him."

"He didn't say a word." Joel scuffed his foot across the floorboards. "I asked him, but he didn't say a word."

"Not agin me?" She shook her head. "He even went to Walters's to buy me new dishes." Her tears started afresh. "Why'd he have to come back acting so nice?"

Buying her dishes and probably not threatening Hopkins. Absently, Betsy patted Mrs. Sanders's hand, but her mind was reeling. If Mr. Sanders was a penitent husband, would he be the type to harass Doctor Hopkins?

A gong sounded, paused, then resumed its clanging. Betsy hopped to her feet. "The fire bell." She and Joel bolted out the door and into the street about the same time Uncle Fred burst through the cabin side.

"Fire!" Riding bareback, Scott sped through town, spreading the alarm while Isaac Ballentine beat on the bell. "Fire up on the mountain, at Doctor Hopkins's!"

Laurel screamed. Her face contorted with agony as Uncle Fred tried to keep her from falling when her knees gave way. Betsy helped half carry her to the cabin. She'd barely got Laurel to the door when Joel came blazing around the cabin on his full-sized horse.

"Wait for me," Betsy hollered.

But he looked as stricken as Laurel. Without a word he spurred his horse toward the glow over the horizon and tore up the mountain like the flames were licking his hide.

CHAPTER 22

Another mistake.

Keeping so low that his chin brushed the horse's mane with each long stride, Joel raced along the narrow path, trying to catch up with Scott before he took a turnout and Joel lost the way. At this speed, the path turned and dropped, rose and twisted without any warning, but the horse was surefooted and Joel knew how to stick to a saddle. Good thing, because he was having a hard time seeing in the dark. A hard time seeing anything besides the anguished face of Laurel Hopkins.

His stomach twisted. What had happened? How could he face Fowler? And what about Mrs. Hopkins and her daughters? He'd let everyone down. But a man's life was at stake—much more than Joel's reputation.

The ride seemed to last forever. Joel knew that Hopkins's cabin wasn't near town, but never had he ridden so fast and felt so slow. Turn after turn, and no matter how he wished it, the next clearing never held their destination. Was Scott leading him in circles? But he remembered the young man's earnestness and set that thought aside. Scott wanted to help as much as he did.

Finally, they turned off the road. Scott lunged through thick branches, looking like he was throwing himself smack-dab into an evergreen tree, but miraculously the limbs parted and revealed a yet narrower way, no more than a rabbit trail. They scrambled up a rocky bank, sparks flying from beneath their horses' hooves lighting up the dark night.

But the dark night could hide much. What were they riding into? What evil had befallen Doctor Hopkins while Joel busied himself in persecuting an innocent man?

A cool breeze floated down the mountain and on it the scent of smoke. Through the trees shone a glow that steadily grew brighter until ringing shouts could be heard. Just to their left, the forest exploded in sound as two more men thundered over a ridge. Joel shied away before realizing that they too were set on reaching Hopkins. He didn't fail to notice a burlap sack with an oddly-shaped cone sticking out of an unlatched saddlebag. Scott only threw a look over his shoulder at the riders before continuing into the opening that marked the Hopkins homestead.

Flames engulfed the log cabin. Already men gathered, holding heavy poles and shoving against the walls. The walls needed to collapse inward lest they fall to the outside and roll down the mountain and into the men working to save the barn.

Following Scott, Joel jumped off his horse and tied the reins tightly to a tree well out of the way.

"Looks like the barn's still standing." What was Scott waiting on? For him to take charge?

Joel gulped down the self-doubt he'd been entertaining. Plenty of time for that later. There was work to be done.

The largest group of men had formed a bucket brigade to the barn, where the doors had ignited. The high stone walls wouldn't be hurt, but if the roof or the hay inside caught, they'd have no chance of saving anything. Two ladders leaned against the wall with brave men atop them. They reached down for full buckets, then dashed the water as high as they could to keep the fire from spreading. Others were trying to drench the burning doors to rescue the stock inside before the smoke overcame them.

"Where's Hopkins?" Joel shouted to the nearest bucketeer.

The man turned, sweat running in rivulets through the soot on his face. "Fine time to be worried about him," he spat. "Maybe if you'd let us do our job this wouldn't have happened."

"You can't make me feel any worse," Joel said. "But now isn't the time for laying blame. Did Hopkins get out?"

Water sloshed as the man thrust the bucket into the arms of the next man with extra force. "He's on that ladder, trying to save his animals from the foolishness of a stubborn Texas deputy."

Thank the Lord he wasn't injured. As long as Doctor Hopkins was alive, talking could wait. What Joel had to do now was save as much of his property as possible.

Among the men, one figure was easily recognized. The angry red flames silhouetted Clive Fowler's massive girth and impressive height. He stood before the burning doors with his hands on his hips. Bracing himself, Joel strode to him.

Without turning, Fowler said, "Those doors won't give yet. Not until they weaken can we open them, and by then they'll be burnt through."

The front of the barn was engulfed, obviously drenched in kerosene or some other flammable to be burning so hot. No other entry was possible through the rock walls. Someone could jump through a window, but lifting animals through was out of the question.

"Can you ax through the doors?" Joel asked.

"And send burning splinters into the haymow?"

Fowler was right. The only thing holding the doors closed was a square wooden beam that slid through the handles to keep the animals from pushing through. If only they could get close enough to the beam to slide it out.

Joel ran to his horse and grabbed his rope. He'd never worked as a cowboy, but knowing how to rope had come in handy on several posse hunts. Coming back, he eyed the beam. There wasn't much to latch onto, and it was nearly flush with the door. Maybe this wasn't such a good idea.

But it was too late. Already the buckets slowed. Heads raised, the squeaking water pump quieted. All eyes were on him. He stared at the wooden beam until his eyes burned. His hand fed the rope through the loop, going by touch to find the right length. Slowly he raised his arm and began to circle it over his head.

"Now ain't the time for your show tricks." But Fowler moved aside anyway.

The rhythm of the lasso rocked Joel all the way to his toes. He swayed with each circle until his whole body was in agreement. Only then did he let the rope fly.

It arched over the space, slapped against the barn, and slid to the ground. Joel gritted his teeth.

"Ain't that something?" Fowler sneered. "Get the buckets going," he hollered.

Joel gathered the rope. The smoldering end burned his fingers as he worked the lariat. He'd made a mistake, but he wasn't no quitter. Silently he began to rotate the rope over his head. It didn't matter if they'd lost interest. His only aim was to get those doors open before the animals inside were hurt.

This throw didn't feel any better than the last, but that was just how it fell sometimes. The lariat snagged on the back corner of the beam and balanced on the edge. With a quick flick of his wrist, Joel caught the beam more securely, then with a strong tug, the circle narrowed until it choked down.

He didn't stop to acknowledge the gaping mountain men. Instead he began pulling the beam through the handles. He'd have to hurry before the rope burnt through.

"It cleared the door," Clive hollered.

Men rushed forward to swing it open and put space between the burning wood and the inside of the barn. Joel pulled the second door open by the beam still hanging in the handle. Immediately men rushed inside and began to shoo out goats, two cows, and an ox. Others tossed water on the ground to guard against any sparks that had made it through. Lastly Scott Murphy ran out with saddle blankets thrown over the eyes of a horse and mule.

Now that the doors were swung out away from the hay, Clive took his ax and with one swing severed Joel's lariat from the door.

Joel yanked the raw end away from danger. "Thanks."

"Too bad your fancy tricks couldn't save the house," he replied. The flames reflected in his eyes. "Too bad you tied our hands so we couldn't take care of our own."

What could he say? This was on his shoulders. His humiliation was complete.

"Someone will pay," he said.

"But not Mr. Sanders? Or maybe it was Pritchard? There's another dangerous man you've locked up recently. So glad these hills are safe now that you've come."

Knowing nothing could be said in his favor, Joel strode away to face Doctor Hopkins, the true victim of the night's devilment.

It was past midnight, and no one but the babies was sleeping. Uncle Fred had saddled his horse and took out after sternly reminding Betsy that her duty was to stay with Sissy, Laurel, and the girls. Had he not instructed her to lock the door and keep the shotgun ready, she might have missed his meaning, but if there was someone out gunning for Hopkins, they could come a-calling, and Uncle Fred knew that Betsy would be ready.

Betsy crouched to throw another log on the fire. The flames revived with the fresh fuel. The dancing light mesmerized her. What was happening right now? Was Doctor Hopkins okay? Would they find him inside the cabin? She shuddered. She couldn't think such thoughts. Not when she was supposed to be a comfort to the other women.

Surely Pa and Josiah could take care of it. And Jeremiah. He'd know what to do. And Joel . . .

She covered her mouth, her fingers digging into her cheeks. Would they have been in this mess if Joel hadn't believed her about Mr. Sanders? Then again, they were both just doing the best they could with what they knew.

But that wasn't good enough.

Sissy had gone to the window. "They're here." She fumbled with the lock and swung the door open, Laurel hot on her heels.

Doctor Hopkins entered and fell into his wife's arms. She sobbed as she inspected him from his soot-covered head to his scorched feet. "Are you—are you all right? You aren't hurt anywhere, are you?"

"I'm tired as all get-out, but I'm not hurt."

Sissy's tears streamed down her face, having feared the worst for her friends. "What about the house and the barn? Did you get the fire out?"

Hopkins's eyes seemed to focus on a far-off calamity. "We saved the animals and most of the barn."

"But the house?" Laurel's hands trembled against his coat. "How much damage . . ."

"It's gone," he said. "The whole thing is gone. I didn't dare come out of hiding until I had witnesses there—too afraid he might get me after all—and by that time it was too late. No one could go inside."

His girls burst into tears. With an open arm, he welcomed them to join the tight, sad family huddle.

Betsy's eyes darted around the room. Nothing in the cabin really belonged to her, but she still couldn't imagine losing everything from the stacks of newspapers in the office to the broom she swept with.

Even over the scent of the fireplace, the men reeked of smoke. Joel stepped inside to face Laurel, although he looked like he'd rather be anywhere else.

"Mrs. Hopkins, saying I'm sorry isn't enough. We're going to catch who did this, and when I'm not hunting them down, I'll be there helping you rebuild."

But Laurel couldn't answer. With a cry she buried her face in her husband's chest again. Anna patted her mother's back, although she managed to bat watery eyes at Joel in the meantime.

Sissy squeezed Uncle Fred's hand. "I'm going to move some beds around and make room for Doc." He nodded his consent.

Betsy fell to moving the table against the wall and pulling the rag rug next to the fire. She'd offer to give up her cot if it'd help, but no one was looking to sleep in the office. She caught the opposite ends of the quilts as Sissy unfurled them and helped spread them evenly until they had a nice pad to sleep on. It was only the work of a few moments, but Doctor Hopkins already looked ready to collapse.

"I kept asking if anyone was hurt, but no one would let me tend to them. In the morning, I'm going to see Calbert. He has a nasty cut—nothing to worry about, Betsy—but someone needs to clean it."

"My ma will do it just fine," she said. "Don't worry about Pa."

"We'd better let the ladies get some rest," Uncle Fred said, since everyone was standing in the way of his pallet. That was Betsy's cue.

She said her good-nights, only then realizing that Joel had already fled. With her brows knit, she picked up a lamp and went into the office. The poor man. She was the first one to suggest Mr. Sanders was the culprit. Joel had listened to her and bore the blame. In a way he had it worse than the Hopkins family. Everyone would help them. Everyone would rush to their aid, while the whole town would hear how Joel had failed. He'd be reviled, ridiculed, and disrespected. Doc and Laurel had each other and their family. Joel had no one. He was all alone.

Betsy was impulsive in every area save one. Where men were concerned, she'd never ventured anything. Let others wear their hearts on their sleeves; let others chase after masculine attention. Betsy had more interesting pursuits.

But maybe, just maybe, there was a man who needed someone to bolster him tonight. What if he rejected her company? What if he thought her too forward? Was he worth the risk?

Making her decision, Betsy pulled a shawl over her shoulders, snuffed out the lamp, and slipped out the door.

Chapter 23

"No hard feelings." Mr. Sanders gathered his coat and hat. "Don't judge my wife too harshly. I should've told you up front."

"You had your reasons." Joel dropped his hat on the desk. He wished he could assure Sanders that it was fine, but Joel had nothing left to give. He was spent.

"You'll get through this," Sanders said. "If Della can forgive me, then people will give you another chance."

But he hadn't earned it. They had no reason to trust him. He'd let them down. Joel dropped to his chair. "It's late."

"Sometimes God can only work with us after we've come to the end of our own efforts," Sanders said. "You didn't expect this blow, but if it's gonna knock you down, make sure you fall toward God, not away."

Joel had already been leaning on God, hadn't he? What did another failure teach him?

Sanders didn't move, just stood, looking him over. Was Joel going to have to throw him out? Finally, with a sigh, Sanders scuffed out of the building, leaving Joel alone in the dark.

He could close his eyes and still see the light of the flames burning inside his eyelids. The house would be standing yet if it weren't for his bullheadedness. He'd come in here so proud that he'd show these people a thing or two. A firm hand was all they needed. Just be tough and they'd straighten up.

Instead he'd caused an innocent man to get his house destroyed and nearly got him killed. Joel dropped his head to his desk. What could he have done differently? Wasn't the law to be respected? Wasn't he hired to stop the Bald Knobbers, not to give them permission to play army? He'd followed his orders, but how could he face everyone tomorrow? How could he recover the ground he'd gained?

He huffed a bitter laugh. Ground gained? Before this, they'd just as soon feed him a bowl of poison ivy as greens. They cared even less now.

A knock sounded on the door. Joel lifted his head. Couldn't they wait until morning to scorn him? Why couldn't they let him be for at least one night? The hinges creaked, but he didn't move, too worn down to even care if he was in danger.

Then Betsy peeked around the corner. Never one to get all womanly about his emotions, Joel would've had a hard time pinpointing exactly what he was feeling at the sight of her pert face—embarrassment that he'd let her down, aggravation that he couldn't wallow alone, warmth that she cared enough to come.

Without saying a word, she entered and then gently pressed the palm of her hand flat against the door and eased it closed. Removing her shawl, she hung it on the hall tree. The only light was what streamed through the window, but it was enough to see the concern in her eyes.

"You're covered in soot," she said.

He didn't know where to begin. An apology? An excuse? A promise to do better? No words seemed to matter compared to the gravity of what had occurred.

From somewhere she produced a rag and began dusting off

his hat. Specks of ash floated in the moonlight, light and airy, unlike the destruction that had produced them.

"You shouldn't be here," he said. "It's late, and we're alone." Going by his rules, he should send her away immediately. The standards he'd sworn by before he arrived had no room for a lady friend, especially one who would come to check on him long after everyone else had turned in for the night. But even when he went with his convictions, he seemed to always disappoint. Somehow doing what he thought was right never worked out.

"What are you going to do tomorrow?" Now she was dusting off his coat, little caring that it was throwing ash onto her shawl hanging next to it.

"Tomorrow? I really can't see past tonight."

"That's because it's dark. Tomorrow there'll be light. Don't you worry."

And what would the light bring? The smoldering scene at the Hopkins homestead?

"You know," Betsy said, "this sort of thing has been going on for generations. You didn't cause it."

"But I'm supposed to prevent it, and I failed." He shook his head. "Not that anyone here expected me to succeed."

"Maybe I did."

He looked up. "Sorry to disappoint you."

She caught his gaze for just a moment before turning away. "Sorry is what you're feeling for yourself. We need you. You've got to get past this."

"Do you think everyone else will be as forgiving?" he asked.

"Of course not. Clive is going to wear you out with scorn. Every Bald Knobber in Hart County is telling his wife how pigheaded you are, and every child is listening at the knothole, laughing at your stupidity."

Joel groaned. "You have a way with words."

"What I'm saying is that you thought this would be easy. It's not. You know that now. You're at the bottom, and only God can lift you up from here. That means He's getting ready to do something."

Just what Sanders had said. They couldn't both be wrong. When he'd been shamed in Garber, he'd thought that was the end of his career, but then this job in Missouri came open. If this door closed, could he trust that God had yet another journey ahead of him? He was so tired. What if he didn't have another fresh start in him? Could he weather another excuse and a sad letter back home explaining to his folks that he'd failed again?

Betsy took his canteen off his desk and pulled her own handkerchief out of her pocket. Water gurgled as she poured it into the handkerchief. A spark of interest was all he could muster. The rest of him was too burdened to care. She hooked a chair with her foot and pulled it directly in front of him, so close that when she sat their knees bumped.

The handkerchief cooled a wide swath on his brow. His eyes focused. Leaning forward, Betsy passed it again across his forehead, easing the tension and the burning guilt of failure. Joel suddenly became aware of her proximity. Her lithe, active body swayed gently even as she folded and refolded the rag to find a clean spot.

He was falling in love with her. Against all his resolve, he was falling in love with her and her tough, determined spirit, her sweet, protective nature. Betsy Huckabee had stolen his heart, and he knew he'd never be the same. He knew it with the same sad certainty that told him he'd soon be looking for another place to try his luck. His chance at success in Missouri had slipped through his fingers before he'd ever got a grip on the reins.

She tipped the canteen onto the handkerchief again, moving

it to the side so the excess water spilled out on the wood floor as she wrung it. He took the canteen from her hand. Her eyes caught the moonlight. She watched as he set it to his lips and took a long draw from it, then smacked in satisfaction, wiping his mouth with the back of his hand.

"Oh, your hands," she said.

Sure enough, they were as black as shoe polish. He splashed some water on them and wiped them on his pant leg before realizing he should've let her do that. But her mouth quirked as she studied him.

With as much care as if she were fixing to stroke a rattlesnake, she lifted the handkerchief to his face, but this time she was paying particular attention. She started mid-cheek and slowly stroked down. She'd moved even closer, one hand on his knee to steady herself as she followed his cheekbone, then his jaw to his chin, going back to catch a spot of soot she'd missed.

The lines of worry that had creased her brow back at the cabin had melted. Now her face was flushed, her lips fuller than he'd noticed before. She looked away as she dampened the handkerchief again. He wadded fistfuls of pant leg in both hands to keep himself under control for what he knew was coming next.

Had it been any woman besides Betsy, he would've thrown her out on her tailbone, but Betsy was different. She didn't look at him as if he were her prize ticket to a happily ever after. No, he trusted Betsy. Whatever happened was between the two of them. No outside agenda. No friends to impress. She wasn't thinking of her ambitions. She was thinking of him, and he loved her for it.

"You're still a mess," she said.

"Fix me," he answered. "Please." Was it wrong of him to accept her care? To take the comfort she offered? He'd been wrong so many times already, but this didn't feel wrong. It felt more like healing.

This time, as she leaned forward, her hand rested on his. With the freshly rinsed handkerchief wadded in her other hand, she began the slow work of scrubbing the soot out of his cropped beard, then the area above his top lip. She took his chin in hand and turned him toward the window to catch what moonlight she could. Her thick lashes lowered as she contemplated her work. The handkerchief traced his mouth, coming back for a second scrub at the side.

He could hear her breathing now, could feel it against his damp skin, and these were no lazy draws. Her heart must be pounding as strong as his.

The cloth slipped, and it was her finger touching him. His eyes slowly closed at the contact. Hesitating, then more boldly, she followed the soft skin of his lips until she'd touched every spot.

He opened his eyes. She was there, the question so plainly etched on her face. He laid his hand against the bare skin of her neck and urged her forward until their lips met. Just a touch. A sweet taste that was not nearly enough but was more than he deserved.

He released her. Betsy returned primly to her seat and faced him. She folded the wet handkerchief and smoothed it against her knee.

He shook his head, clearing the warm fog that had overtaken him. "I know what you're doing, Betsy. You're kissing a miserable excuse of a man just to cheer him up."

She scrunched her nose. "I'm very particular with my kissing. Not just any man, I'll have you know." She stood and reached for her shawl.

He didn't want her to go, but he got to his feet to help her with her wrap. "So I'm one of the lucky few? One of a dozen? A score?"

"You're one of one," she said, her face full of promise. "The only one. But don't think that means anything. It'd take more than that to sweep me off my feet."

Then, with a saucy wink, she was gone.

CHAPTER 24

Betsy had always been a romantic. Even as a little child, nothing made her feel better than seeing her parents embrace. She understood the bright shine in her mother's eyes when her pa brought her wildflowers, and Betsy danced with delight when he remembered to pick some for her, too. Over the years she'd watched various courtships in the neighborhood: Jeremiah and Abigail, Wyatt and Miranda, and her own brother Josiah and Katie Ellen—although she still didn't understand what Katie Ellen saw in him. Over the years she began to realize that she wouldn't meet the man of her dreams in Pine Gap. She'd already met every man within three days' walking distance, and it was highly unlikely that someone would move in.

But someone had.

She put the final touches on her latest Dashing Deputy column. Funny how different Joel was in real life than she'd first imagined him. Heroic, yes, but humble, caring, and a host of other attributes that Eduardo Pickett didn't have time for—not when he was leaving behind as many broken hearts as captured criminals. Thank goodness Joel had more of a conscience.

She paused with the three pages of her latest story in hand. Joel wouldn't like this. He was careful around her, careful around all women. Any similarities between Eduardo and him would trouble him greatly. She knew that now, but what was she supposed to do? Try to make Eduardo more like Joel so he wouldn't be offended, or make the differences greater so he wouldn't see the resemblance? If it wasn't her job, her opportunity for independence, then maybe she'd do him a favor and quit, but she couldn't afford to. Not yet. She was just getting started.

And she wouldn't write anything that might hurt Joel. She wouldn't write about him mistakenly allowing the Hopkinses' house to burn. What kind of hero did that? Instead she had him rushing out to single-handedly save the house and barn, and she did include the bit about the lasso and the door. Josiah must have told that story three times yesterday at church. And then about her going to the jail afterward . . . well, maybe it was the Dashing Deputy who comforted the distraught young woman instead of the other way around, but it made for a good story, all the same.

After reading it over one last time, she carefully creased the paper and slid it into an envelope. She wasn't naïve enough to think that she held Joel's heart. That kiss hadn't changed anything. He was still apt to come talk to her, of course, but only if he had a compelling reason. Reasons like to tell her about his day—who he'd talked to, where he'd ridden to, what he suspected. But that didn't mean he was sweet on her. For all she knew, he might board the next train to Texas and she'd never see him again. In the long run, her best bet would be these stories. She couldn't count on siphoning off support from her family indefinitely.

Today was Monday—auction day. Isaac Ballentine would start the auctioneering in an hour or so. Uncle Fred would exchange his trays of type for an account book and help in the auction house office, and folks from all over the hills would come to trade their stock and share their news. Monday was always a busy day for Betsy, but she had to take care of her business first.

Knowing that no one must catch her with an outgoing envelope, she scurried to the post office as soon as she saw Postmaster Finley up and about that morning. He had just dumped the water bucket from yesterday into the flower bed and was pumping fresh water when she approached. He pulled a kerchief from his back pocket and dried his hands before taking her envelope. Then he whistled the same whistle he always did when she had a submission.

"Still stringing along that same beau?" He waved the envelope back and forth like a tipsy hypnotist.

Betsy forced a smile. How she'd love to tell him she'd sold a story, but no one could know. "I try to keep it quiet."

"Or maybe you're trying to be a writer like your uncle?" He slapped his knee. "Wouldn't that be something? I'll tell you what, if you sold something to a big city paper, you'd better believe I'm sending something in the next week. If they like you, then they'd be tickled pink to get my thoughts on the matter."

"Why don't you do that?" If that anger warming her neck was pride, she'd best get to talking to God about it, because it was running over her something fierce. Although why should she be mad? She always carried on like she was an irresponsible, untamable youth. She shouldn't be so surprised when someone treated her like one.

"Betsy, I nearly forgot. Your uncle's papers came in with the train last night—the whole mess of them." With a toss of his head, Finley motioned her inside the post office. Betsy could barely stand still, waiting for him to pull the bundle of papers from beneath the cabinet. As soon as she could reach them, she snatched them from his hands.

"And a letter, too," he called.

She found room for the letter in her waistband, because she needed both hands to flip through the newspapers. The *St. Louis Post and Dispatch*, the *Philadelphia Record*, the *Boston Globe* . . . the *Kansas City Star*! There it was.

Sticking the rest beneath her arm, she unfolded the paper and held it wide as she hurried toward the newspaper office. Nothing on the first page, of course, nor would there be anything in the news section. She flipped the paper over and greedily scanned the columns on the back page. Usually the women's articles and the serial stories were near the back, and that was where she hoped to see her story, but it wasn't there. Had it come out in this edition? She opened the back page and began to work her way forward. Nothing, nothing. Then there it was, on page two! And it had her pen name right there: E. M. Buckahee. So they'd decided to run it with the real news after all?

Whack! She ran smack-dab into a wall of iron. No, it wasn't a wall of iron, it was a bona fide Dashing Deputy, but he felt every bit as solid as a piece of foundry. Quick as a wink, Betsy closed the paper, wadded it together, and shoved it behind her back.

"What's the news?" he asked. Only then did she see Leland Moore swaying next to him.

"Leland, you've hit the jug already?" she asked. "It's still forenoon."

"He's on his way to a dry cot so he can sober up and not interrupt the auction," Joel said. "What was so engrossing about the paper that you didn't see me coming?"

"You ran into me."

"No, I just stopped in front of you."

"Why?"

He rolled his eyes in masculine exasperation. "Never mind. I want to tell Doctor Hopkins that I've telegraphed around asking about Bullard. We'll see if he's been in trouble with the law in another county. Might be able to track him down."

"He's a wanted man. Don't you reckon Sheriff Taney sent out word when he went missing?" Now it was Betsy's turn to roll her eyes. "He didn't, did he?"

"Must have slipped his mind," Joel replied. "Are you going to be around town today?"

Betsy dimpled. "It's quite possible." She dug her toe into the ground as her skirt swayed around her ankles.

"Maybe we'll run into each other again." And he almost sounded like he was looking forward to it.

"For the love of Pete," Leland cried, "would you stop your flirting and get me somewhere quiet where I can lay my head?"

"Come on, then." The strict deputy had returned. There'd be no dalliances while he was carrying out his duties. Then over his shoulder he called as he walked off, "Watch where you're going."

Easy for him to say. If he knew what was in that paper, he'd be walking into people, too.

She hurried to the office where she could spread the paper out unobserved. Reverently she smoothed her hand across the words that she'd composed right at that very desk. They'd been written there but printed in far-off Kansas City, and now people she didn't even know were reading about the handsome lawman come to help the little Missouri town. While she hoped everyone far away was reading it, no one in Pine Gap could. She rummaged in Uncle Fred's desk for scissors and then clipped out the evidence. It really was too bad it was on the second page, because someone was sure to notice that the paper had been diced up.

Hastily she arranged the other papers to take up most of the drying rack. Sometimes Uncle Fred might actually sell one of the papers, but for the most part they came for his enjoyment and for his guests to have something to peruse while waiting on him to do an interview about their latest tomato crop. No one would miss it if the Kansas City paper wasn't available.

With one last fond look she tucked the clipping into her journal and her journal into her desk. Only then did she remember the letter she'd gotten.

It too was from Kansas City. Looking around the room guiltily, she made her way to her cot and opened the envelope. In it was a check. Made out to her. Betsy held it to her nose, trying to catch a scent from the busy office in far-off Kansas City where this check had been signed. She'd open a bank account. That was what she'd do. And she'd put this in it so that soon she'd have enough to start out on her own. Finding steady employment in Pine Gap was a challenge, but if she could write her stories and mail them in, then she'd have the best of both worlds.

The letter contained congratulations and repeated their desire that she would continue to send her column. No mention was made that it'd been printed as a news item. Instead there was a line about syndication and how they currently had many newspapers interested in running it.

Betsy's swinging feet thudded against the floor. More than Kansas City? That was what she wanted, right? But she was already walking a fine line with Joel.

She held the paper lightly between her fingers. She knew what she'd do. She'd write those Kansas City people and let them know not to publish her stories in Texas. She didn't know what that exclusion would cost her, and Joel wouldn't ever know what a favor she was doing for him, but she felt better knowing his people wouldn't read her stories.

The last thing she needed was him hearing about the Byronic

fantasies she'd penned and thinking that she was head over heels for him. It'd puff him up like a tom turkey strutting around the barnyard. Especially since she'd kissed him. She'd never hear the end of it.

She sighed as she stuffed the letter into the envelope. She already spent too much time thinking about him. He probably didn't spend half that time bothering with thoughts of her. Certainly he wasn't making her the heroine of some romantic plot.

Once again fixing to head to the sale barn, Betsy opened the door only to come belly to belly with her overtly pregnant sister-in-law, Katie Ellen.

"Where's your brother?" Katie Ellen grimaced with one hand clutching her stomach and the other propped up on the doorframe.

"It's Monday morning. He should be at the sale barn."

"Well, he ain't. I told him my time was coming, and he took out just like every other time."

"Where are the rest of the kids?"

"With your parents. But I'm having this baby now, and for once I want my husband to be around when it happens."

Katie Ellen could be powerfully stubborn once she set her mind to something.

Betsy gazed at her cot with regret. "Wait here. I'll find Josiah and Doctor Hopkins. Sissy and Laurel can tend to you while I'm gone."

"I don't need a doctor; I need my husband." Katie Ellen gasped. Her hand tightened over her abdomen, which was bigger than a watermelon and looked ready to burst. "I told him it'd be today, but he wouldn't stay home, so I just climbed in the wagon with him. If I wasn't laboring before, that rocky road sure done the trick. My waters broke coming over the hill, but he still found somewhere else to be."

Betsy would wring his neck. "You're in no condition to be hunting him down. I'll have him back—"

"Well, if he ain't here, then I'm going to find him, even if it means having this baby in the middle of the road."

"Katie Ellen, you're distraught. You ain't thinking straight. You gotta do what's right for the baby."

"The baby wants its pa." Katie Ellen lumbered back to the road and headed toward the square.

"Lands sakes alive," Betsy murmured. Katie Ellen was going to make a spectacle of herself, and it was Betsy's job to protect the family honor. Couldn't have a new nephew or niece making their appearance in the street. She chased after her sister-in-law. "Josiah's at the sale barn."

"He's not. I looked."

"Where do you think you're going?"

"I'm not thinking. I'm just . . ." Katie Ellen paused, bowing over.

"We have to get Doctor Hopkins." Betsy scanned the square for the best option for a birthing bed. The jail had a cot. That was all she knew. "Head to the jail." She took Katie Ellen and dragged her forward. "If Josiah isn't there, we'll send the deputy after him."

When they burst through the door, Joel couldn't have looked more startled. One glance at Katie Ellen and he started sputtering. "No—no—this isn't the place . . ."

"You were hunting for Doctor Hopkins," Betsy said. "He should be at the sale barn. And get that low-down brother of mine while you're at it. We can't let him skip out on all the fun."

"Yes, ma'am." He spun on his boot.

Leland Moore shook the bars of his cell. "You can't leave me here. Have mercy."

Joel grabbed the keys and opened the cell door. "No more

whiskey today, you hear? Now get out of here and leave the women to their business."

Katie Ellen was more than happy to collapse onto the cot. "I wouldn't enter this building if Sheriff Taney had anything to do with it. That worthless—" She stood again and started pacing.

"I can't believe my brother's child is going to be born behind bars," Betsy said, "but I shouldn't be surprised." She needed the doctor, she needed Josiah, she needed linens, and most of all, she needed her sister-in-law to simmer down.

That wasn't too much to ask, was it?

CHAPTER 25

He couldn't keep the criminals in the cells, and he couldn't keep the women out of them. Joel strode to the sale barn, fully aware of the contemptuous glares thrown his way. He hadn't given up on catching the culprit, even if it was a Bald Knobber, but they had to give him time. Anyone could hide in the forest for a few days. Sooner or later they would slip up, and when they did, they'd find that they'd messed with the wrong county.

Until then, Joel had to find a reluctant father. He entered the wide doors of the sale barn and marched through the clusters of people into an arena of sorts. With the pen in the middle and the stands around it, it reminded him of a miniature indoor rodeo arena. But no way anyone could race or rope in such a small pen. Isaac Ballentine sat on the platform with an old scale in front of him and a new gavel in his hand. He met Joel's gaze, then quickly looked away. Guilt, or just disgust that a fine fellow like the doctor had lost his house? Undeterred, Joel waded through the crowd and marched right up to the gate around the arena.

"I'm looking for Josiah Huckabee." He was speaking to Isaac, but the crowd hushed.

"Is he another dangerous criminal you're going to arrest?"

The anonymous heckler had plenty of admirers, judging from the guffaws.

"First Mr. Pritchard, then Leland Moore. No wonder Josiah's in trouble, running with such a dangerous crowd."

Leland stepped inside, grinning drunkenly and waving at the mention of his name.

Isaac's sad eyes looked troubled. "Josiah should be out back, Deputy. Cut through the door here on the side and you'll see him."

Another heckler. "Bet he won't see him. He couldn't see a buzzard if it landed square on his nose."

Joel unlatched the gate to the arena to get to the outside door. The latch pin jammed, requiring him to turn around and purposefully reset it, much to the amusement of the crowd.

He prayed for patience. Hopkins's house had burned to the ground, and that was on him, but it didn't make it any easier to endure their scorn and ridicule. He just hoped that some of them would entertain the possibility that they might could work together, else what hope had he for bringing the arsonist in?

Once outside, he scanned the pens and saw Josiah absently tapping the backs of calves that had nowhere to go. Just as Betsy had suspected, he was hiding out.

Joel was able to get pretty close to Josiah before he was spotted. Guilt crossed a face that seemed just as easily animated as his little sister's, but he didn't make a run for it.

"Do you know why I'm looking for you?"

"I know better than to offer a reason when a lawman asks that question."

"Don't worry about me locking you up. The jailhouse is full of women at this moment, and one of them isn't getting along too well."

Josiah tugged on the brim of his hat. "I told her to stay home."

"She wanted to be with you."

"She doesn't need me. This is our third young'un, and she'll do just fine without me."

Although he'd never sat behind the bench, Joel was a fairly good judge of people. Josiah came from good stock. He just needed a push in the right direction.

"I've seen you with your young'uns, and I know a proud papa when I see one."

Josiah nodded. "I'd do anything for them, but this here, it's women's work. I don't know why she's so downright insistent on making me be there."

"How does your wife usually act when she's scared?"

"Scared? Katie Ellen's never scared, really. Sometimes she gets where she's all underfoot and can't leave me alone. Times she should be scared, instead she's just hanging around . . ."

"Afraid to let you out of her sight?"

Josiah's foot, which had been propped up on a rail, dropped to the ground. "She's never said she was afraid."

"Would she?"

"Not for all the zinc in Joplin."

Joel watched as Josiah sorted through the problem. Sometimes those closest to you were the hardest to understand, but Josiah was making a fair attempt.

"She's at the jail, you said?" Josiah chewed his lip and absently tapped his whip along the calves' backs. "If you really think she's scared, then I should be there, shouldn't I? Nothing wrong with a father helping with the birth of his child." He shrugged. "I do it for my cows, anyway."

"Then do it for your wife," Joel said.

Josiah nodded, then took out for the jailhouse. It felt good to get something right occasionally, but not everyone saw it that way.

"Did you let another one get away from you?" There was the old sheriff, watching the whole exchange. "You might want to take after that Josiah. He ain't a real outlaw, so you might stand a chance of tracking him."

Joel ignored the jab. "Is there something I can help you with?"

"I doubt it. Unless we throw a carnival and need a trick rider or roper, then you might come in handy. But as far as real men's work . . ."

So Sheriff Taney had heard about his roping at the fire? He should've known that whoever told the story wouldn't have painted him with a fair brush. "The investigation is ongoing—" Then he saw the man of the hour approaching. "Doctor Hopkins," he called. Hopkins came over, looking aged and worn.

"I don't think the doctor wants to talk to you," Sheriff Taney said. "Not after you let his house turn to ashes."

A woman scorned? Hell hath no fury like a former sheriff, more like.

"Deputy Puckett isn't responsible for my house." Doctor Hopkins balanced his medical bag atop the fence. "He can't be everywhere at once."

"I know who's responsible." Fowler rode up on the gathering, sitting tall astride his powerful horse. The stripes on his shirt bowed on their trek across his hefty body. His buttons took the strain as he gathered a breath for his announcement. "It's Miles Bullard."

Sheriff Taney waved a hand before his face, chasing away the stink of the very suggestion. "What does Miles Bullard have agin Doctor Hopkins?"

"He's not coming back to Hart County," said the doctor, "not with a murder charge against him. But he's not the only one

I've made angry. Caesar Parrow got mad when I couldn't revive his goat that'd fallen in a sinkhole, so I've got my enemies."

"Caesar isn't your enemy. Bullard is the one to come after you," Fowler said.

"Then why would he leave the bundle of switches? That doesn't make sense."

"Mark my words, Doctor," Sheriff Taney said. "There's only one group that does that. You know who's responsible." Then, with a glare at Fowler, he was gone.

So the sheriff thought the outlaw was Fowler, Fowler thought it was Bullard, and Hopkins thought it might be retribution over a goat in a sinkhole. In the meantime, Joel's office had turned into a birthing chamber.

"Doctor Hopkins," said Joel, "if you'd go to the jailhouse—"

"You want to question me?" Doctor Hopkins said.

"No, it's Mrs. Josiah Huckabee. She could use your assistance."

"At the jail?" The doctor's eyes took a mischievous gleam. "I'm on my way."

"And don't bother telling the deputy your troubles," Fowler said. "I'll find who burned your house, and I'll do something about it."

Joel waited until Doctor Hopkins had left before correcting Fowler. "You can't do that."

"I'm not asking permission. I'm just pointing out the obvious, since you seem to be a tad slow. We tried it your way. We held back and nearly got a man killed. You can't ask us to do that again. While you've been playing hide-and-seek, we've been collecting information, and we think we know where Bullard's been hiding. And out of the goodness of my heart, I'm going to make you an offer you can't refuse. You can ride with the Bald Knobbers and be there when we bring him to justice."

Joel's jaw worked. If there were no law on the books, if there were no governor to whom he was accountable, if the only consideration for making decisions was doing what was expedient, then he'd do it in a heartbeat. Most likely, these men would capture the culprit and possibly even produce enough evidence to convict him. The offer would allow him to save face, and in that respect, it was generous. But he couldn't do it without breaking his convictions. What if they didn't bring the suspect in alive? What if some of the gang got out of control?

"You aren't the law, and Miles Bullard hasn't stood trial."

Fowler threw his head back and laughed. "You say some funny stuff, Deputy, but you and me both know that if I leave it up to the law, Bullard won't ever stand trial. The Hopkins family will have to stay in hiding or leave permanently."

If anyone knew how much leaving one's home hurt, it was Joel. "I have rules I have to follow, Clive. They might not be expedient, and they might keep me from succeeding, but if I break those rules, then I've failed. While I think your offer was generous and made in good faith, I can't accept. Doing so would be a greater failure than having a house burned down."

"Fine words, sir. Let's just hope your lofty morals don't get someone killed."

"I'm praying that with every breath," he admitted. "But I'm not the only one who could compromise. If you know where Bullard is, I'd leave this second to find him." Why hadn't he heard back from his telegraphed inquiries? He hated going about this blind.

"But you wouldn't find him. Have you considered that this might not be a one-man job?"

Joel filled his lungs. He had to stop the Bald Knobbers, especially if the possibility existed that they might be behind the outrage, as Sheriff Taney claimed. "Bringing peace to this place will require the whole community's cooperation, that's true. But I won't ask anyone to put themselves in danger."

"We've lived in danger since before the war. Since before you were old enough to shine those pretty pistols. It'll always be dangerous here, and the only way to deal with it is to attack first. Why don't you keep Leland and other drunks off the streets here in town and leave the mountains to us?"

With that he turned his horse and walked it sedately to a group of men who'd been watching the exchange with more than disinterested curiosity.

Feeling like a little boy left behind when the men went hunting, Joel climbed over the fence and headed back to town. Maybe that was all he was good for—policing family feuds, incarcerating tipsy citizens, and finding missing husbands for overwrought wives. In Texas he'd hunted down hardened criminals, so he knew he could face the challenge, but in Texas you knew who the bad guys were. In Garber, people didn't get dressed up and go out threatening each other at night. This was more complicated than facing bad guys. It was like trying to unravel five different spools of fishing line that'd been knotted, spliced, and retied together. All while getting shot at.

But if the Bald Knobbers were on the move, then they must have information. He'd trail them—that was what he'd do. After dark he'd wait in the woods and follow one of the gang members who wasn't very alert. Mr. Pritchard, for example.

He'd about reached the jail before he remembered that he might be waltzing into a rather embarrassing scenario. How long would this birthing take? Joel scratched his chin. Was he going to be exiled from his own office all day? Through the iron bars on the windows, he could see people moving, then a light as the back door was opened. Deciding that it might be his only chance to get news, he hoofed it around to the back and found

Betsy at the water pump. The way her eyes shined up at him made him forget all the abuse he'd endured at Fowler's hands.

"How in the world did you get Josiah to come?" Her words were chopped short by her vigorous working of the pump handle. "He marched right up to Katie Ellen just like a hero."

"The only difference between your average man and a hero is that the hero figures out what to do before it's too late." He nudged her aside and, with a few more pulls, filled her bucket. "Then he has the nerve to go on and do it."

Betsy leaned back as if she was trying to get a complete view of him from head to toe. "Is that all it takes to make a good hero?"

"One more thing. A hero always comes back for his lady." Joel picked up the bucket, pleased to see her spunky smile. If he could only see one friendly face, it'd be hers. "How's your sister-in-law?"

"Should be better any minute now. Doctor Hopkins sent me for more water, and I'm guessing that you don't want to carry it in for me."

His eyes traveled to the bucket, then back up to her ornery grin. "I don't think you need my help."

"Now that Josiah's here, we're all fine."

A primal growl sounded from inside the building. Joel grimaced. "Would you mind bringing out my gun belt, saddlebag, and rifle? I'm pretty sure I have no business going inside."

"You loading up?" Betsy raised a lone eyebrow. "What's going on?"

"Now that Sanders is cleared, Fowler insists Bullard must be in the area. They're riding tonight." He cast a nervous glance toward the jail and lowered his voice. "I'm going to see if I can find out something more. I might not be back for supper."

"Can I come with you?"

"Together there'd be more chance of them seeing us. I'll tell you everything tomorrow, I promise."

She bit her lip. That lip had pressed against his for a split second once upon a time. But she was a nice lady, and he couldn't just go kissing her every time he thought about it. Because he was thinking about it now—getting quite warm thinking about it. Maybe just another quick peck. After all, he was going into a dangerous situation—

A baby cried.

Betsy's eyes shone. She took the bucket from him, their fingers getting tied up together for a few precious moments. "I'll bring your stuff out to you. Do be careful."

He nearly bowed his agreement. "Congratulations on your new kin," he said. "Give the baby a kiss from me."

From the mischievous look she threw him, she'd been thinking about him, too.

After squalling through his bath, the baby had finally calmed at the breast of his mother, who'd quite taken over the jailhouse as her rightful domain.

"This place is so disorganized," Katie Ellen fretted. "As soon as this baby falls asleep, I'm going to purge this building of every last trace of that lousy Taney. The lawbooks are thrown on the shelf willy-nilly, and the cobwebs are more likely to keep someone from climbing out the windows than the bars are. What must Deputy Puckett think of us?"

Betsy stripped the dirty sheets off the cot to carry home and launder. What did Deputy Puckett think of them . . . of her in particular? He had repented from his early claim that he couldn't abide to converse with women. Or at least he'd decided that she didn't fit in that category. Betsy gathered the sheets up into a loose bundle while humming a song. Joel Puckett definitely thought of her as a woman, and for the first time in her life she was appreciating the attention.

Time to go home. Sissy and Laurel would want to see Katie Ellen's baby, but that meant Betsy would have to sit with the girls, which wasn't a bad idea. Betsy wouldn't mind resting during their nap time. By the time the sun set, she'd just be getting started tonight. No way was she going to sleep when the Bald Knobbers were riding.

Joel was probably right. They couldn't go together. She'd rather be undercover—be in on the action firsthand. Just think how much she'd have to write about. A few more stories, and she might have enough money to rent a cabin for a spell. It'd be a start. Besides, she might learn something that could help Joel. She wasn't just thinking about herself. She was putting others first, like she ought. Doing nothing out of selfish ambition, but esteeming others as more important. She was a walking Sunday sermon.

Joel needed her help; she needed a story. Everyone would win.

But if anyone saw her, they'd send her right home. She needed a disguise. Unobserved by the family behind her, she loosened the corners of the sheets as she lugged the bundle toward Joel's desk and the heavy chest sitting beside it. She'd seen Pritchard's hood the day that Joel arrested him, and she had every reason to believe it was still here.

With her back to the wall, Betsy faced the cot where Katie Ellen fed her new babe while Josiah smoothed her hair, muttering words of appreciation. Bending at the knees, Betsy wedged her fingers beneath the lid of the chest and eased it open. Hinges creaked, but no one noted it. Light cleared the shadows, and she spotted the terrifying hood of black with cork horns and white painted mouth. In one smooth motion, she dropped it into the bundle, lowered the lid of the chest, and gathered the sheets around it.

Nervously she approached the cot to make her farewells, but Josiah and Katie Ellen weren't the least bit concerned. With mixed excitement and dread, Betsy hurried out and headed toward home. Uncle Fred's coat, worn inside out, would serve well. Scott wasn't home, so she could borrow a pair of his trousers and he'd be none the wiser. A horse from the sale barn, and all was set.

She'd always wanted to ride with the gang. Tonight was her chance.

CHAPTER 26

It hadn't been as easy as he'd thought. If the Bald Knobbers had designated a time to meet, they surely didn't break their necks being punctual. Instead, every few minutes a man left town, making it hard to follow for fear that someone was coming up right behind him.

But the trees did serve a purpose. On the prairie you were as noticeable as a tick on a hairless dog, but here you could hide in the dark if you just stood still anywhere besides the trail. But then, so could everyone else.

So far no one had ridden out of town with their peculiar costume, which meant that everyone would be stopping somewhere in the woods to take up their disguise. He wished they'd hurry. It'd be easier to know who to trail if they were all decked out.

A stocky man rode through town on a mule, not in a hurry, just trotting along like he was headed to work. Joel eased out of the trees at the crossing with his horse's reins in hand. Let the man get just a little farther along, then Joel would step in behind him, but first he had to make sure there were no other latecomers to catch him. Looking both ways, he spotted yet another figure darting through the shadows. He froze. The others had ridden down the road with no concerns, but this man didn't want to be seen, and he was headed toward the auction house.

Praying that his horse wouldn't give away his location, Joel pulled the reins and eased off the road to follow the path of the loner. Once he reached the clearing around the sale barn, he stopped. Where had the man gone? To step into the opening before knowing was foolhardy, and Joel had already made enough mistakes. A gate crashed closed, hooves sounded, and right before him dashed a hooded figure on one of the horses that'd been left in the pens. Before he could reckon who in town didn't have a horse, who might have access to any stray livestock at the barn, he realized that the figure now wore the hated Bald Knobber mask and that the mask was familiar.

Joel's horse whinnied. He barred his arm against its muzzle, but the rider hadn't heard. He was too busy trying to keep his light bones from bouncing out of the saddle. Joel didn't recognize the man, but he did recognize the mask. He hadn't thought to look for it before he left, but someone had lifted Pritchard's hood right from beneath his nose. And the man on that horse wasn't Pritchard.

It had to be Josiah Huckabee. Joel swung into the saddle and chucked to his mount, setting off at a safe distance behind the rider. Josiah had plenty of opportunity to run across the hood while his wife delivered their baby. And he worked at the sale barn, so it only made sense that he'd keep a mount there. While Joel would've expected a livestock dealer to be able to ride better, maybe the shadows were playing tricks on him. Had Josiah managed to have his wife give birth at the jailhouse as part of his plan? Joel wouldn't think they'd go that far just to get Pritchard's hood, but stranger things had happened. Especially here.

The moon had risen, but the clouds meant that light wasn't constant. Joel only hoped he wasn't discovered before they led him to Bullard's supposed hiding place. In silence he followed Josiah for what seemed like winding miles. Once the man stopped suddenly and cocked his head, the horns of his hood swinging from side to side. Had he heard something? But surprisingly enough, Josiah seemed to consider the bend ahead and then reversed direction. Joel barely had time to rein his horse into a thicket before Josiah was facing his way. He rode toward Joel a few lengths, then plunged off the trail into a gulley. Could it be that Josiah didn't know the way to the meeting place? Joel pondered this as he eased down the treacherous drop. Maybe Josiah wasn't part of the gang. If he were, wouldn't he have a hood of his own? But why join up now? Why on the very day he had a new baby?

Because of Katie Ellen's pa. If Bullard was back, naturally Josiah would want a part in capturing him. And if he found another neighbor responsible for sheltering Bullard, what would happen then?

Joel had been warned how knotted the allegiances were. Postmaster Finley hated the Pritchards. Katie Ellen and her family blamed Taney for Bullard's escape. And someone carried ill will toward Doc Hopkins. The tangled roots of family trees determined which side of a feud one was on, and the seeds from those trees kept the feuds sprouting up year after year. Joel had been very judgmental and more than a little naïve when he'd come, thinking that these people were all troublemakers who hated the law. He tried to put himself in their position. What if someone had killed his pa or some kin of his? Wouldn't he go after the perpetrators, badge or none?

The trees thinned out. They'd reached the bald knob—the

hilltop void of any covering—and the purpose of meeting here was only too clear. While Josiah broke through the forest and trotted to the gathering at the center, Joel was relegated to waiting in the trees. He tethered his horse away from the path they'd come in on, wary of more stragglers, and inched his way as close to the edge of the cover as he dared.

Twenty to thirty men, all in disguise, circled up on the hill. From opposite his position, another two rode out to join them in the moonlight. The giant leader waved them forward, but Fowler was the only one easily recognized. Joel tried to place some of the horses, but knowing they'd been rubbed with soot, all he could do was guess. Well, he wasn't interested in unmasking them, only in intervening before they could carry out their vigilante plans.

But someone was unmasked. From the other side of the mountain, Scott Murphy appeared with his coat turned inside out. He hesitated until he spotted Fowler, then trotted forward. Did his aunt and uncle know he'd slipped away from them? If so, they'd be sick with worry. But the lure of adventure and heroism was too strong a draw on a young man. Joel understood only too well.

"What do you think you're doing here?" Fowler bellowed.

The riders fanned out to face him, but Scott didn't cower. "I've come to do my part. I'm riding with you tonight."

Joel looked for Josiah. Would he intervene? But he'd gotten lost among the other black hoods.

"You've already done your part, son." Fowler's words rang out clear through the burlap hood. "It's thanks to you that we found his hideout."

"And you were supposed to tell the deputy," Scott answered. "You promised you wouldn't go out for Bullard alone."

Scott knew where Bullard was? Scott was one person Joel

hadn't thought to ask. And the one person who believed in him . . . besides Betsy, that was.

"The deputy was invited. It was his decision to stay on the porch instead of running with the pack. You've put your faith in the wrong man."

"That may be, but I'm still going to make Bullard accountable for what he did to Doctor Hopkins and Stony Watson. They're my neighbors, too."

It looked like Scott might get his way, but then the men began to murmur. Finally, a man with rough, homemade britches and a coat that had more holes than material spoke up. "Scott, we're all your neighbors and your pa's, too. We don't aim to make an enemy of Fred, but if we let you ride with us, that's what's going to happen. He'll be hot at you, but we'd all share blame." Hoods nodded in agreement. "Go on home, Scott, until you're older. It'd be a favor to us not to have to explain to your folks."

The murmurs grew in strength, until it was clear that Scott had lost his bid. With slumped shoulders and head hanging low, he didn't seem to even notice the men who rode near to slap him on the back or give him a word of encouragement. Did he know who was talking to him? Joel yearned to know, but that wasn't his first concern. His first concern was getting to this Bullard man before they could mete out their own punishment, and Scott might just be his answer. If he hurried, Joel should be able to circle the hill and catch up with Scott on the south side. He just had to get to his horse.

Joel turned, right into the double barrel of a shotgun.

"Hey, fellers," the masked man called. "Looky what I caught."

How did they wear these masks in the summer? Even with the cool air, the thick burlap trapped her breath until Betsy felt liable to suffocate. Or maybe it was the racing of her heart that was depleting the oxygen. Scott's appearance hadn't helped any. No matter what story she jeopardized, Betsy could not allow Scott to ride with the Bald Knobbers. Even if it meant disclosing her identity, she'd do it to make sure her cousin was protected. Thankfully that hadn't been necessary.

Scott had just disappeared into the trees when a shout from the other side of the clearing was raised. Another straggler? Betsy tugged her hood into place so she could see better. So much for the secret location. Seemed like everyone in the county knew where to find them.

But when she saw the man walking at the business end of a shotgun in his pointy boots and with his hands raised, her heart sank. Good thing they hadn't come together.

Fowler separated from the group to meet the man being prodded toward him. "Deputy Puckett, you decided to join us after all?"

"If by *join* you mean break the law, then the answer is no." Even if she hadn't recognized the tenor of his voice, Joel's profile was unmistakable—his cowboy hat set firmly on his brow, his legs braced apart like a gunslinger. Remembering how fast he'd drawn when practicing, she believed he'd still be able to get a shot or two off if he needed, and she wondered if Clive had any idea how dangerous Joel was.

Of course Clive knew, and that scared her.

"And yet here you be, snooping on us. We don't admire spies in these parts."

Betsy's hands tightened on the reins as she seesawed between her choices. She'd plead his case if needed, but would it help? Or maybe another chance to help him would present itself if she waited. She wished Joel knew that he had a friend there, but maybe he did. Time and again he glanced her way, almost as if he were speaking to her.

"You know my title, and with that title goes a responsibility. I can't turn a blind eye to this, even if I wanted to. Now, I've been fair to all of you, even thought I could call you friend"—and here there was no doubt that he'd singled her out—"but friend or foe, the law is the law, and I'm honor-bound to enforce it."

All eyes went to Clive. His men would follow him implicitly. Was Joel's offense going to earn him a licking?

"Tie him up." Clive motioned to a leafless maple at the rim of the clearing. "When we're done doing his job for him, some of you'uns can come back and let him go if you have the mind to."

Fighting wouldn't accomplish a blamed thing, so Joel submitted to being bound to the closest maple tree amid the jeers of the crowd. Really brave, the things they were threatening, especially while wearing masks. Somehow he figured they wouldn't have the courage to repeat them standing face-to-face, but he'd keep such thoughts to himself for the time being.

The ropes caught on his wrists beneath the cuff of his leather gloves, and then rope was wrapped around his body until he was trussed up like a roasting pig. Of the two men doing the tying, one smelled strongly of some sort of sour homemade brew. Hopefully his handiwork would be as impaired as his crooning—Ol' Dan Tucker couldn't be that fine a man—but his partner was cold sober. The ropes held.

Back at the crest of the hill, Fowler conducted the meeting like a trail boss adjusting his drovers. While not close enough to hear every word, clearly a few men had been scouting out the place and were giving advice about how they'd approach. Hands rose volunteering for assignments. Groups formed and departed, taking slightly different routes, but all with the same coyote yelping that Joel had heard that first night at the train station, as if the noise could summon up whatever courage was lacking. What would it be like to have that many men on hand? Back in Garber, Sheriff Green had formed posses, but it was only in response to an emergency.

The cold rose up from the ground to chill Joel's hindquarters. What was the difference between forming a posse and joining the gang tonight? If Clive would let Joel lead, wouldn't it be the same thing? But a posse was bound by rules and laws. These men made it up as they went.

Fowler turned in his demented black hood for one last look at Joel. If only Joel could read his thoughts. What did he have in mind for Bullard? Was Fowler capable of a cold-blooded execution? Joel prayed not. If a death occurred tonight, he'd have to bring in half the men of the county on murder charges.

Instead of threats, he'd be better off trying to convince Fowler that they were on the same side. "Don't do anything you'd regret tomorrow," Joel said. "The law is the law."

"Sit tight for a spell and we can debate the law once the job is done." Fowler jabbed his heels into his horse's side, and they streaked across the clearing to be swallowed whole by the dark forest.

The sounds faded quickly. Evidently the yelping got stopped before they got within earshot of their quarry. Give them an hour, and if it started up again, Joel would know they were successful. But he wasn't going to wait around for an hour. He had to get loose.

Pulling off his gloves, he stretched his hands in every direction, searching for the knots that held his body tight against a knothole inconveniently situated against his shoulder blade. Nothing he could reach. He pressed his body against the tree trunk, knothole and all, but the ropes didn't slack enough to mention. He was held fast while lawlessness ran amok in the hills.

His body tensed before he realized why. Someone was standing just to his left, watching him. Several unfavorable possibilities occurred to him. Had Fowler talked nice in front of witnesses but sent a lackey around to finish Joel off? Or was this man a rogue looking for revenge against some lawman in his past?

Pretending that he'd seen his visitor much earlier, Joel finally said, "They're gone now. What are you waiting for?"

The man came to stand in front of him. With a glance at his hood, Joel eased up a bit. Josiah. But now that he got a good look at him off his horse, Joel realized it couldn't be. This was a youngster, definitely not filled out to a full-sized man yet, but hopefully he had the convictions of a mature Christian. Joel figured he was about to find out.

The man crouched next to Joel's outstretched legs. Joel squinted to see into the eye holes of the mask, but it was too dark. "I'd like to at least face my captor," he said at last.

"It's blazing hot under this stinking hood, so I don't mind if I do."

Joel's eyes widened. That voice was no man's.

With a flourish, the hood was ripped away and golden hair spilled out in every direction. "I should've washed this thing," Betsy said. "That Pritchard better not have lice, or I'm going to kill him."

Hair stuck to her damp forehead and beneath her chin. Joel made to move it before realizing that he was still bound. And then he realized that it was Betsy who'd stolen that hood from him. Of all the cotton-picking, thieving vixens.

But now wasn't the time for a comeuppance.

"You're a sight for sore eyes." He smiled in a way that the ladies had always claimed was irresistible. "I didn't know how I was going to get out of here."

"Excuse me?" Betsy wedged her finger beneath the ropes and against his chest. "I might prefer you tied up."

CHAPTER 27

Joel's face might sport a smile, but he was definitely holding something back. Betsy didn't have time to learn his secret. Rescuing him might cause her to miss the action and lose the best story of her life. With a tug, she tested the tension of the ropes around his chest.

"I didn't think Bo could tie that well tipsy."

"That was Bo Franklin?" Joel looked away. "I thought he was in trouble with the gang."

"When you arrested his uncle, he felt really bad. Now they have a common enemy. You." She smiled a charming smile, and he looked charmed, sure enough.

"It's a pity I'm all tied up," he said. "I just thought of something I'd like to do." His eyes traveled to her lips, and somehow his expression became that of a starving man sitting just inches from food he couldn't eat.

For crying aloud, they had Bald Knobbers on the hunt. She couldn't stay here and make calf eyes at him all night, as much as she might want to. "Where's your knife? I'll cut you loose."

"Left boot."

She fished her hand inside his boot, then pulled the knife out of its sheath. Putting it to the coil on his chest, she was about to start sawing when he protested.

"Don't cut it there. Do it at my hands."

"What do you care?"

"I've got my reasons. And it's a good rope."

Oh yeah. The lasso. She leaned forward to reach around him. Her cheek fit into the space by his neck. She took a long draw of his scent and wanted nothing more than to nuzzle into his warm skin. He had stilled, sparking with the same awareness, but from this angle she'd peel the hide right off his hands with the knife. Regretfully, she stood and walked around the tree, then squatted to cut through the rope around his wrist.

"I didn't expect you to show up," she said.

"Showing up wasn't in my plans." The ropes fell away. With hands now free, Joel unwrapped the coils. "I would have preferred to stay hidden."

"Me too. Nobody looked twice at me," she said. "Reckon everyone's so worried about their own disguise that they don't look too hard at anyone else."

Joel stood and pulled on the rope until he'd disentangled it completely from the tree. He wasn't kidding when he said he admired the rope. Looked like he was going to take it with him.

Betsy bent to pick up her mask. "Let's get going. They're headed to Parrow's cave. Scott thinks Bullard might have a hideout there. It's an old bushwhacker camp. I can get you there quick."

Joel caught her by the wrist. That bothersome longing had returned. It was so hard to stay focused when he was around.

"I told you there was something I wanted to do," he said.

Betsy waved a hand his direction. "You were just trying to sweet-talk me into untying you. Thanks for the thought, but it really isn't necessary. We need to hurry."

"You risked a lot to save me, Betsy. And we can't go until I say thank you."

His deep, gray eyes were mesmerizing. Kissing him had been nice, but she was pretty sure there were stronger words than nice that he could evoke. A whole thesaurus full, if given half a chance.

"They'll be finished before we get—" But he closed the space between them, and Betsy couldn't think of any reason she shouldn't be in the arms of the best-looking lawman in the country.

With one hand he gathered her hair off her shoulders, bunching it to cushion her head against the tree trunk, but beyond that, he didn't seem to know exactly what to do. He paused, his eyes on her lips. Evidently he was determined, just not practiced. He leaned forward and brushed his mouth against hers. Betsy hummed as the warmth in her chest rushed through her veins and chased the cold out of her fingertips. It was a good start, but they had to go. There was too much going on to stand around and—

He kissed her again, and she had to hand it to him, he was a quick learner. She plumb forgot anything else besides the feel of him holding her—his strength, his tenderness. He kissed her like he was a man on a mission, and if his mission was to make her head spin 'til she wasn't sure which direction the mountain was slanted, he was doing a fine job.

He groaned like something was troubling him. She tried to pull him closer, but that rope kept getting between them, and no matter how she wiggled, she couldn't get him to drop it. He released her hair and wrapped both of his arms behind her. Good thing for the tree, or she might not be able to take this standing. Her legs were as stable as soaked white oak splits on basket-making day, too weak to hold her up. Her arms rested heavily on his shoulders.

His hands moved to her shoulders and skimmed up her arms until he had her wrists. His kisses slowed as he brought her hands behind the tree and held them there. Gradually, Betsy became very aware of the contours of her body and how they fit against him, but two other thoughts niggled at her brain.

One, no matter how good of a man he was, she really didn't like the vulnerability of her position, hands pinned behind her, especially considering that they were alone.

And two, that blamed rope really seemed to be getting in her way.

He wasn't kissing her anymore, but looking over her shoulder as he fiddled with something.

It was the rope, and it was wrapped around her wrists.

"Are you trying to tie me up?" She started to step forward but found herself securely held against the tree.

"Not trying, my dear. Succeeding."

"What?!" Her heart was already racing, so it didn't take long for her to get worked up. She struggled to get her hands free from his grasp, but with them pinned behind her back, they had no strength. Before she knew it, they were bound tight—tighter than a gentleman ought to bind a lady, in her opinion.

"We don't have time for this," she said. "I told you we have to hurry if we want to catch them."

"*We* aren't going anywhere, and if I thought you'd listen to me and go back to town, then this wouldn't be necessary."

"You did this on purpose?"

Of course he did. From the time she'd knelt beside him, he'd known what he was doing. Those smoldering looks, those white-hot kisses—he'd fooled her and fooled her good. Strapped across her belly and rumpling her already bulky overcoat were three lengths of the rope. If only she could get her hands free, she'd slap the handsome clean off his face.

"You should be ashamed of yourself."

His eyes glinted and a dangerous smile emerged. "I might feel really bad if it weren't for this." He held Pritchard's hood before her eyes. "You went through my things and stole this, didn't you?"

"Technically it belongs to the City of Pine Gap. If it was obtained during official—"

"No excuses. I've already wasted too much time."

"Wasted?!" She stretched against the ropes, praying for the strength of Samson to break the ties and rip this man in two. Regrettably, God did not honor her request. Instead He let the blackguard wander off in the woods and return on horseback.

"Stop thrashing about."

How dare he sit up there so proud! If it weren't for her help, he'd still be trussed up, looking like a fool. Like she was now.

"Remember, a hero always comes back for his lady," he said.

"Don't bother." She turned her face away to let him know the conversation was over, but when he rode off without another word, she found more to say. "Don't bother because I might just catch pneumonia, get frostbite, die, and get eaten by non-hibernating bears, all because you left me."

He wasn't coming back. She stomped her foot, the only other option of protest being to bang her head against the tree. He was a tight-hearted, conniving pig, and she was portraying him so graciously that half the women of Kansas City were probably in bed dreaming of him at that very moment.

If they only knew.

CHAPTER 28

"Should've known not to trust Bo to do anything while intoxicated. It's embarrassing you got out so fast," said a masked man.

Joel wasn't about to admit how he escaped. For the first time, he worried what they might do to Betsy if they found out. Or more likely, what they'd think. He didn't want to be held responsible for another woman's sullied reputation.

"Where is he?" Joel angled his horse across the opening of the cave.

Fowler stepped out into the moonlight with a gasoline tin in hand. "He's back, sure enough." Fowler's sweat-soaked hair stuck to his head like a wet rug thrown over a stump. "He must've heard we were coming and took out, but he left his gear behind."

Joel walked his horse closer. "All I see is a bunch of Bald Knobber members in possession of incendiary devices not far from Hopkins's homestead. Seems suspicious the way you're so eager to name a culprit."

Fowler spat and threw the tin down the hill. "I gave you my word. That should be enough." The tin clanged and rattled until it came to rest against some tree. "Bullard's a guilty man, else why'd he run away instead of facing his accusers?"

The sentiment burned more than Joel liked to admit.

"You don't think he might have reason to be afraid, with this group hunting for him?" Joel asked.

"There ain't nothing wrong with straightening a man out when he needs it."

"But the law tells us when he needs it and just how much straightening is just."

"You and your ever-loving law. Someday you're going to realize that no matter what's written in some books at the courthouse, there comes a day when a fellow has to take care of himself. He can't rely on some government man to fight his battles for him."

While Joel had more sympathy for that position than he had before he came to Missouri, he still knew there was a better way. "But sometimes it backfires and an innocent man's house is burnt to the ground because he wasn't prepared for the consequences."

Fowler's brow drew lower. "We were prepared, but you assured us that you would take care of him. If you hadn't gotten involved—"

Joel lifted his hand to interrupt. "And maybe I would've caught the outlaw if you hadn't tied me up."

"We didn't hurt you." But Fowler's voice had lost some of its swagger.

Pressing his advantage, Joel continued, "But you interfered with the duties of an officer. That crime carries jail time, and if I thought you'd do it again, I'd have to bring you in."

Long seconds passed. Joel could almost feel the heat burning off Fowler into the cold air. Finally, his shoulders relaxed.

"I ain't your enemy, Deputy," Fowler said. "The only reason I did that was because I was afeared that you'd help him escape." To Joel's protest, he continued. "I know you wouldn't have meant to, but just the same, you would've been in the way. Surely you can agree that I'm not on the side of lawbreakers."

"But you are breaking the law."

"Breaking the law to enforce the law? Then maybe the law needs to change." Fowler looked up at the moon. "It's getting late. I'm to home and to bed. Have yourself a good night."

Joel moved aside and watched as Fowler and the other Bald Knobbers headed down the mountain. Why did Fowler have to be so reasonable? Why did he have to sound so noble? It almost made Joel feel petty with his nit-picking regulations. *Don't catch bad guys because you don't have a certain piece of metal that authorizes you?*

And what did that piece of metal mean? In Joel's case, it meant that he came from a good family and his parents had friends who could recommend him for the job. That was what it meant. It also meant that the word of a young lady could un-authorize you and all the good words from your parents' friends suddenly amounted to nothing. Had Sheriff Green not glossed over the situation in his recommendation and the governor of Missouri not been desperate for impartial lawmen, Joel would have the same rank as Fowler, which was nothing. What would he do in Fowler's shoes?

Praying that no one would return to the mountaintop before him, Joel continued upward, yawning freely along the way. The air nipped at his cheeks. Good thing Betsy had that coat on or she'd be chilly. The thought of taking her into his arms chased the frost from his limbs. Maybe they could warm up together, but she wouldn't be favorable to that idea. He'd treated her wrong, and if she was half the woman he suspected her to be, he'd pay dearly for it.

When he arrived, he hugged the perimeter of the clearing, still wary of troublemakers looking to correct his freedom, but there was no one to be seen. No one except an adorable woman shivering and fuming.

"You could have at least put my hood back on so as to keep my head warm." Her brows formed a line so straight he could've balanced a marble on them without it rolling off.

"I did it for your own good."

"Not only did you curtail my freedom, but now you're insinuating that I'm so simpleminded that doing so was the only recourse to keep me from injuring myself. You attack my person and my intelligence?"

"Where'd you learn to talk like that?" he asked as he dismounted. "Do you always throw out ten-cent words when you're riled?"

"I'm particularly incensed, three notches past riled. And you deserve to be doused with the very dredges of my vocabulary."

Despite her florid speech, she rested against the tree as if the ropes were of no consequence. Maybe she'd spent herself straining against them already, but he had the feeling that removing them would restore her vitality.

He stepped around the tree and untied the knot. Gently he unwound the rope from her wrist, wincing at the marks it'd made against her delicate skin. "I'm really sorry, Betsy." How he wanted to rub them away, but doing so would probably smart. "I'll make it up to you."

Reaching around her, he removed the rope, and as soon as it loosened, she bolted from the tree. Joel flinched, fully expecting a hearty slap. But instead she sped past him and climbed on his horse.

The only thing he could predict about Betsy was that she'd do the unpredictable.

A split-second later and he wouldn't have been able to snag the reins. "Where are you going?"

"Let go. You have no right to stop me."

He tightened his grip on the reins and grabbed the bridle with his other hand. "You're on my horse. Why not get on your own horse?"

"Because yours is faster and I don't want you to catch me."

But he had caught her, and he wasn't about to let go. "Betsy, I'm sorry I had to tie you up, but you need to understand something. For us to be friends, you have to respect my authority. How can I trust you if you take evidence out of my possession? How can we get along if you're conspiring behind my back?"

Were her eyes red because of the cold, or was he to blame?

"I thought you wanted to kiss me, but instead—" She turned her face. "I reckon it's not important." Although her tone told him the opposite. "What's important is that I find out who fired the gun on the other side of the mountain."

Was she kidding? She wiped at her nose with the back of her coat sleeve. Was it all a ruse to pay him back?

"Very funny," he said. "Now give me my horse."

With a sigh, she dismounted. "But I'm not joking. I heard gunfire."

He dropped the rope into his saddlebag. "You're safe, nothing hurt you, so don't turn this into some revenge—"

"I'm not joking, Joel." And lands sakes alive if she didn't look serious. "About thirty minutes ago over towards my folks' place."

His blood pounded in his ears. Thirty minutes ago? They'd all gathered in the opposite direction, hadn't they? "Is Hopkins's place out toward there?"

She didn't answer, just took off running.

"Where are you—?" But she was going for a horse, and he'd better, too.

They took off together, her clumsy horsemanship and farm

horse no match for his, but she could find her way through ravines he'd thought impassable. They barreled down a bluff, loose gravel crashing below them with every stride, and jumped over a creek, Betsy nearly bouncing out of her saddle, then followed the narrow valley until they crossed the railroad tracks. Seeing the tracks helped Joel with his bearings. Nothing ever felt so confusing as the endless curving paths of the mountains. Nothing ran true north, south, east, or west, but snaked around until you'd swear you'd crossed your own path already.

Finally, they joined a larger trail that led to an honest-to-goodness road. Even a wagon could cross here. Down they went to the riverbed. Their horses' hooves echoed hollowly on a wooden bridge, and once across, Betsy paused.

The air had grown frosty. Her breath clouded before her with every puff. "I can't be sure where it was," she said. The road branched on this side of the river, winding its way around the hill in opposite directions. She paced her horse from one path to the other, peering into the darkness. "We could split up."

"Not on your life. I'd come closer to tying you up here and keeping you out of harm's way."

"I'd say this is pert near the middle of harm's way." She tugged on the bulky coat that had begun to rise up under her chin, and then she chose a direction.

The road narrowed again, and branches tried to snag Joel's coat but couldn't find purchase. A fallen tree barred their path, branches throwing a barrier as big as a barn. Dismounting, they left the trail and were picking their way along a narrow ridge when he noticed prints off the road.

"This tree hasn't been down long, but there are tracks that have come through here before us."

Betsy shivered.

He loosened his gun, no longer feeling the cold. "Are you sure . . . ?"

"You aren't leaving me behind."

"Where's this road lead to?"

"It goes through Fowler's land and comes out around the back of Hopkins's place."

"If you're right on the time, I had just reached Fowler when the gun was shot."

She shivered again. "Maybe someone was just coon hunting." But they both knew no one would be out piddling around on a night that the Bald Knobbers were riding.

They made their way more carefully now, watching both sides of the road, sometimes stopping for Joel to investigate a hollow or sinkhole.

"The woods aren't usually this quiet," Betsy said.

"It's nearly morning."

No light had appeared yet, but there was enough moonlight to throw a shadow—the shadow of a riderless horse.

CHAPTER 29

Instinctively, Betsy stepped closer to Joel, easing behind him just a tad. The muscles of his arm jolted beneath her hand, but he stayed planted.

"Hello?" he called.

The horse stepped forward. Moonlight falling through bare branches showed that its saddle was empty. Its reins dangled as it nickered softly.

"Is anybody here?" His voice echoed off some rocky bluff unseen in the night, but no one answered. "Do you recognize the horse?"

Betsy's fingers tightened, putting a crease in his coat deep enough to feel the solid mass beneath. "It looks familiar, but I can't place it."

"Stay here." He covered her hand with his own before removing it from his arm and taking up his pistol.

Stay behind? Was he crazy? Then, remembering the hour she'd spent bound, she decided to postpone that debate for the time being. She could stay put for a bit.

Slowly he approached the frightened horse. Even in the shadow of the trees, its eyes reflected how scared it was. "Shhh . . . there." With an outstretched hand, he eased forward until he caught its bridle. Holstering his gun, Joel ran his hand down its wet neck. "This horse has been pushed," he said. "Someone was in a hurry."

Betsy couldn't help glancing over her shoulder. If someone had wanted to get away, they could be here still—crouched behind any tree or hunkered down behind any rock. But as dangerous as it was, she'd rather be here than anywhere else.

Joel bent next to the horse and filled his nostrils with the same wet dirt smell that she was smelling. Or had he found something else? "Betsy," he said, "get in my saddlebag and find the matches."

Rushing through the buckles, Betsy dug her hand inside and fumbled past a bag of jerky, a compass, and a sheathed knife until she felt the waterproof canister of sulphur matches. Taking the knife out of the sheath, she quickly sawed a dead limb off a nearby evergreen tree. She kicked some pine needles together, and cupping her hand around the match, brought the flame to life. Gently she added pinecones, and once they were coaxed into fire, she held the dried branch to the young flames. Soon she had a torch twice as bright as Mrs. Rinehart's candelabra.

Cautiously, she approached Joel. His figure appeared to shift in the darting light. He motioned her closer then caught hold of her arm and held it low.

In one area, wet leaves stuck to the rock surface beneath their feet, while all the other dead leaves blew loose and dry. "What is it?" she asked.

They squatted for a better look, and when Joel ran his finger over the rock and held it to the light, there was no mistaking the deep red color.

Her stomach knotted. Normally she'd tell Fowler about anything suspicious, but in this case everyone was a suspect, and that left only her and Joel to rely on each other.

"May I?" he asked.

She handed him the torch. After securing the horses' reins in the crook of a bare crabapple tree, she followed Joel, careful not to step on anything that might be evidence. The clouds rolled in front of the moon again, and the darkness reclaimed every spot not touched by the torchlight.

Joel bent over and walked slowly, pausing every few feet to swing the torch in a wide arc just above the ground. Occasionally he stopped, squatted, and rubbed the ground. The piney smell revived her senses, but the brightness from the torch hurt her tired eyes. She looked away, but she continued to see the glare of the torch blinking through the darkness.

Having searched the clearing, Joel went to the edge of the bluff. There he knelt and brought the torch to the ground. His head bobbed gravely, as if answering a question she hadn't voiced. Then he extended his arm over the void, throwing light on the rocks below.

Betsy's curiosity could be denied no longer. She picked her way to him and stopped a good foot from the edge. Even if they didn't have crumbling rocks in Texas, she was too familiar with the danger of putting your toes in the air.

"What do you see?" she asked.

"Nothing," he said. "There should be something there, but I don't see anything." Was it her imagination or did he sound disappointed? "I'm going down to get a better look."

He tested the stability of the ledge with his boot heel, but a low groan from somewhere nearby had both him and Betsy stepping back into the shadows.

"It's down the trail," Betsy said. "Just a little farther."

Forgetting the ravine, Joel moved silently ahead.

Another groan sounded, and Betsy stopped. This was one time she was content to wait behind. She'd let her Dashing Deputy handle this part alone.

No more leaves rustled. Only stillness. Should she call for Joel? Make sure he was all right? Before she could decide, he spoke.

"There's a man here, and he's hurt. I don't want to move him alone. I need you to go to town and bring back some men. Some good men who are trustworthy."

Betsy shivered. Good men who were trustworthy? Did she even know who that was anymore?

Her feet were rooted to the spot. Was it Bullard, or had Bullard shot someone else? The memories of Stony Watson's funeral came flooding back. Who would be in the casket this time?

"Who is it?" she asked. "I have to know before I go."

Even from a distance she could hear Joel's troubled breathing. "I don't want you to worry."

She'd commenced worrying when she heard the gunshot. Why couldn't he just answer the question?

Joel appeared out of the shadows, went to the horses to grab a canteen from his saddle, and returned to Betsy. He looked at her face, then took her by the arm. "Betsy?" he said. Another jostle and her focus came back. "I need you, Betsy. Can you do this?"

"I have to know. I'll be sick fretting over—"

"It's the sheriff. He's been shot, and he's more dead than alive. That's why you have to go."

The sheriff? Betsy's mouth opened, but there were no words. Just disappointment in the men she'd trusted. And anger. Burning anger.

"I'll bring help. Town is too far. My pa, Jeremiah, Caesar— their farms are close."

"Then go there. And stay with the ladies if you'd rather. This will be gruesome business."

It'd be near daylight before she could get everyone rounded up and back here. Sheriff Taney needed help before that. She'd stop by Jeremiah's and let him go after her pa while she raced to town and Doctor Hopkins. Thank goodness he was staying in Uncle Fred's cabin.

As her horse picked up speed, her thoughts slowed. Hopkins working on the man who'd let Bullard escape? Would his hands be steady enough? Could he still practice his vocation?

And what about her? The exciting danger that had spelled intrigue in her stories was no longer a harmless threat. Even if she obscured the details, she didn't have the heart to dress this story up for entertainment. It was more serious than that. Would her Dashing Deputy be up to the challenge?

CHAPTER 30

The next morning found Betsy anxious and conflicted. The Bald Knobbers had always represented excitement and freedom to her. They claimed to be fighting for justice, and she'd wanted to believe them, even as she knew the complaints of those they'd disciplined. But those complaints seemed paltry now. Sheriff Taney had been shot. Doctor Hopkins's house had been burned. Those switches on his porch were no empty threat after all.

But who had made the threat? And who shot Sheriff Taney? Was Bullard the culprit, or had a well-meaning vigilante mistaken the sheriff for the criminal? If only Taney would come to and tell them what happened.

Before Aunt Sissy called her to breakfast, Betsy had already put the finishing touches on the story. Unlike the earlier articles, this one bulged with dark injustice and frustration—the same frustration that she'd seen on Jeremiah's face as he'd saddled his horse, the grimness of Doctor Hopkins as he jumped on bareback and rode to help Sheriff Taney, the sadness in Uncle Fred's eyes as he lit the candle and told Aunt Sissy to go back to bed. Someone's life teetered on the brink, and another man had stained his hands with blood.

And unlike her earlier stories, this one contained the truth

224

about her Dashing Deputy. He was still Eduardo Pickett—no use in changing the name at this point—but he was facing real problems instead of single-handedly capturing bad guys and wooing women. He was more like the deputy she knew, and she found the realistic description of him even more endearing than the counterfeit.

Betsy folded the manuscript into thirds and then halved it again before stuffing it into an envelope. But what about her promises to Joel? Betsy tucked the envelope into her waistband and entered the cabin, where Aunt Sissy was dishing out porridge while Uncle Fred slept. Technically she'd kept her promises. Joel's name wasn't in the article, and the article wouldn't reach Pine Gap, but she knew he would object. Why wouldn't he want his heroics to be known? She didn't understand, but somehow sending this article felt like a betrayal. And yet this one was important. It was the truth.

"I just don't understand these men." Aunt Sissy pushed a bowl of porridge in front of Betsy. "I've never seen such selfish behavior."

"Selfish?" Betsy blinked. "Why would you say that?"

"They act like they're trying to help people, but really they're just looking for excitement. They want to make a name for themselves instead of letting the authorities handle the mess."

The paper in Betsy's waistband crinkled as she leaned forward. *Do nothing out of selfish ambition. . . .* But she wasn't being selfish. If she had a job, it would help her family. Already they were short on space, short on food, and it'd only get worse as the children got bigger. And now—now she wanted to publish a serious piece that would put words to the sadness she felt. She wanted everyone to know how she felt living among people who did not value life. These people played with justice like it was a game between two teams, but as everyone kept score by their own reckoning, a clear winner would never be declared.

But would her story help or hurt? And what about Joel?

Before daylight that morning, Sheriff Taney had been delivered to his own personal cell. No reason to cart the old bachelor to his remote cabin when he'd be better served and better guarded in town.

Betsy hadn't talked to Joel since but figured she'd be better able to cope after catching some shut-eye. While tied to the tree, she wanted nothing more than to leave Joel afoot with a pack of wolves on his trail. She also wanted to be warm in his arms and get more of that mighty fine kissing he'd been doing lately, but he perturbed her, just arbitrarily decreeing when she was allowed to go with him. Maybe he really did worry about her getting hurt. If so, then someday she might forgive him. Truthfully, if she had to be tied up, getting smooched into submission wasn't an all-out horrible method.

Betsy walked outside, envelope now in hand. The sun glowed a weak gray from behind the thick clouds. She pulled her coat tight and hurried to the post office.

Deputy Puckett had certainly changed his tune about her. He'd gone from rude and hateful to acting like he might learn to care for her. In the time they'd been together, he was always protecting her, always sheltering her, rushing to share the latest event, talking over his plans with her. And she could tell this was something new for him. Not as if he regularly admitted women into the inner sanctum of his company.

Would that change if he knew about her articles? The envelope creased in her hand. At what point did she become beholden to him? At what point did she stand to lose more than she could gain?

She meandered to the post office with the fatigue from the

night before dragging at her limbs. A year from now, what did she imagine her life would be like? She wanted her own home. She wanted to spread her wings and get out from under the shadow of her aunt, her uncle, and all the people who would continue treating her like a child. But did she want Joel? Could it be possible that her future involved a strikingly handsome deputy? Could his feelings for her be genuine? Or did he, like Eduardo, have a lady friend in every town?

Postmaster Finley lowered his cup of coffee when she entered and rapped his swollen knuckles against the counter top. "My, you're up early this morning. Seems like everyone else is sleeping in. Must have been a busy night." She looked for the red rim around his eyes that went with riding on clandestine missions, but found none. Of course not. Wasn't Bullard his cousin? Then he wouldn't be fond of the gang.

She forced a bright smile, hoping he wouldn't notice her own bloodshot eyes. "I've got another letter." No use in changing course now. Joel would never know, anyway.

He took it, held it at arm's length, and squinted. "Another one to the Kansas City newspaper? Aren't you writing them right often?"

Before she could come up with a good excuse for her frequent letters, he cut in.

"You *do* have a city beau up there working in that office, don't you?" He waggled his curly eyebrows. "Your uncle introduced you to a real reporter and now is playing Cupid?"

"You know me, Mr. Finley. Been chasing the boys since I could walk."

"Now you're just pulling my leg."

Before he could continue, she hurried outside. She'd just stepped onto the road when she heard her name called.

"Betsy! Yoo-hoo, Betsy!" Phoebe Hopkins waved with one

227

hand over her head as she sat astride her mule. "You slept so late we gave up waiting on you."

Betsy had to look twice because either she was seeing things or Phoebe had two heads. She really should go back to the house and get some sleep. But upon second look, she could make out Anna riding behind Phoebe with her head on her sister's shoulder and her arms around her waist.

"Have you seen him this morning?"

Betsy came closer and straightened their lunch pail so it wouldn't tip over as it rode strapped to the mule's saddle. "Seen who?"

"Eduardo."

Her heart faltered. She didn't remember calling him that in front of the sisters. "Are you talking about Deputy Puckett?"

Phoebe turned to share a smile with Anna, who bounced in the saddle, making the mule's ears go flat. "Mr. Murphy said that while we were staying with you'uns, we could read his newspapers for free. And you won't believe what we found!"

Betsy's throat tightened and her already burning eyes went even drier. "What?"

"The most engaging article. Mother was reading to us from the Fayetteville paper after supper last night, and she came across a story that, if I didn't know better, sounded just like Deputy Puckett. It was even set in Pine Gap. Just imagine!"

This couldn't be. "Fayetteville? Are you sure it wasn't the Kansas City paper?"

"We wanted to read the Kansas City paper, but someone had gone and cut it to shreds, so we took up the Fayetteville one. Besides, it had to be Fayetteville, because how would they know about the darkly handsome Texas deputy Eduardo Pickett all the way in Kansas City?" Anna squealed. "Pickett? Can you believe even their names are so close?"

"What is our deputy's first name, anyway?" Phoebe asked. "Do you know?"

"Why would you think it's him?" Betsy caught the bridle of their mule to hold them still. "He hasn't saved a child from the well, has he? It can't be him."

Anna piped up from over her sister's shoulder. "Your uncle is a better writer than I thought. The way he describes the Dashing Deputy, I can just see him riding that white horse—"

"Deputy Puckett's horse is black," Betsy interrupted.

"And wearing that big hat and boots and the shiny belt with all the bullets around his waist. And the way he smiles . . ." She frowned. "I can't imagine him smiling like that for your uncle Fred, though."

This was a disaster. Sure, Betsy knew what syndication was, but she hadn't counted on the article showing up in any of the other papers her uncle got. Was her uncle the only one in Pine Gap who got that paper? She tried to remember who else had family from Arkansas. Who else would have reason to stay informed?

"We'd better get to school," Anna said.

"Yeah, maybe at recess we'll see him outside. See you later, Betsy," Phoebe said. "If you see Eduardo, tell him we send our best."

Betsy covered her forehead with a tired hand. What had she done? By dinnertime the schoolyard would be full of giggling girls all swept off their feet by the charming man she'd created. She'd made a mistake, but was it too late to keep herself from making another?

Finding her second wind, Betsy strode back to the post office. It was the work of a minute to convince Postmaster Finley to dig her envelope from the outgoing mailbag. It might be the work of an hour to get him to return it.

"Looks like you've had a change of heart," he said. The envelope dangled from his fingers, just out of grasp. Act impatient and he'd be bound to take his time handing it over. Instead of reaching for it, she rubbed the back of her neck.

"I just can't make up my mind," she replied.

"That's precisely what's ailing you, Betsy. If'n you would act a bit more interested in the fellows, you might catch yourself a husband. There's still Cross-Eyed Carl—"

As he was gesturing out toward Carl's farm, the letter swept in front of her. Quick as a rattler, she snatched it out of his hand and eased away from the counter. "Thank you, Mr. Finley. I'm beholden to you."

Not appreciating that he'd been bested by a woman, Finley swiped his bare hand over his counter with a petulant pout. "Just as well. That Kansas City beau was probably having second thoughts about you, too."

Betsy was having second thoughts about everything—mostly about her own culpability in regards to Joel's story.

Who else knew?

CHAPTER 31

Joel stood at the door of the jailhouse, hands folded before him, as Josiah walked out of the building, babe in arm, and helped Katie Ellen into the wagon.

"Don't mean to run you off," Joel said, "but having an injured man in the nursery can't be pleasant."

Josiah wrinkled his nose in an expression that recalled his sister. "Have you had any word from Fowler?"

"Not this morning. How about you? Have you heard from him?"

The weightiness of the question wasn't lost on Josiah. "I was here all night, Deputy. Here with my wife and my baby. And there's no way I'd go out toward home while leaving my ma in charge of the young'uns. If she found out I'd left her to tend them while I was gallivanting around, she'd skin me alive."

"You didn't answer my question." Someone was guilty, and Joel couldn't let family connections get in the way of his investigation.

"You're wasting your time." Josiah looked up the road toward his uncle's house. "Does Betsy know about Sheriff Taney?"

Holding his baby with its fragile little hand gripped around his pinky finger, Josiah was the picture of innocence. Joel would take it for what it was worth and assume that Josiah didn't know about his sister's nocturnal ramblings, either.

"She knows. I'm going to check on her this morning."

"Why does Betsy need checking on?"

Joel met his gaze and realized some weak excuse about his job wouldn't cut it. His greatest fear was being accused of acting ungentlemanly toward a woman. After his antics the night before, he needed some accountability. "My intentions are honorable," he said.

Josiah whistled. "Intentions for Betsy?" He shot a glance at Katie Ellen, who was making herself comfortable on the wagon seat, then whispered conspiratorially, "I have to applaud you, Deputy. You sure don't shy away from lost causes." Then he grew more serious. "But this investigation, you might not like the answer you find."

"My wishes have nothing to do with it. I can't let a criminal go free."

"Josiah, it's getting cold." Katie Ellen rocked as she inched the blanket higher over her shoulders. "Give me that baby."

Josiah handed the baby over, hopped into the wagon, took up the reins, and released the brake. "I'm praying for you, Deputy—that you'll put an end to this violence and that you'll put a nice beginning on that other quest of yours."

"Praying is the best thing you can do," Joel said and then walked inside the jailhouse. Catching the men responsible for this outrage would go far in vindicating him. If he didn't succeed here, he'd have no good recommendation to fall back on. This could be his last chance.

"He's coming to," Doctor Hopkins said from the side of the cell cot.

Joel rushed forward. Sheriff Taney's skin had bleached

overnight, leaving it an unnatural, bluish shade. He groaned and tried to roll to his side, but Doctor Hopkins held him down.

"Don't get up, Sheriff. You're hurt. Stay still," Hopkins instructed.

Taney fell flat against the cot. Sweat beaded on his forehead. "I'm at the jail?" He licked his lips. Joel passed Hopkins a dipper of water.

"You were shot," Joel said as Hopkins gave him a drink. "We're keeping you here for protection." To the doctor, he said, "Doesn't look like getting winged in the shoulder would've set him back this far."

"He's covered with scrapes and bruises. Looks like he took a beating, too. Did you see that knot on his head? It must've knocked him senseless," Doctor Hopkins said. "Otherwise he would've been able to get on his horse and ride for help instead of lying there bleeding out."

After a few swallows, Sheriff Taney pushed away the dipper. He lay so still that Joel figured they'd lost him again, but when his eyes opened and fixed Joel with a cold glare, Joel knew he was feeling strong enough.

Maybe he could remember after all.

"Do you know what happened, Sheriff Taney?" Joel asked. "Did you get a look at the man who shot you?" It'd been dark last night, clouds and all, but there was a chance.

"I saw," said Sheriff Taney. "It was Fowler. Him and his .38."

Joel recoiled as if he'd been punched in the jaw. His gut hadn't twisted like that since Mr. Blount had showed up and demanded his badge from Sheriff Green in Garber.

"That's the concussion talking," Doctor Hopkins said. "We might never know for sure—"

"Did you find the bullet?" Joel asked.

Doctor Hopkins nodded. "He's right about the caliber."

"And I'm right about the shooter," Sheriff Taney growled. "And this deputy didn't do anything to stop him."

Hopkins shot Joel a nervous glance. Again he held the dipper to Sheriff Taney's mouth, but Taney was done. His scratched, weathered face eased. His mouth drooped open, and his breathing slowed.

"That's right," Hopkins was saying. "More sleep will do you good." One more look at the bandage covering the sheriff's shoulder, then he turned to Joel. "Don't put any stock in what he's saying. After a head injury like that, he probably doesn't remember at all."

Fowler wouldn't have shot the sheriff. He had character that went beyond that. Besides, Fowler couldn't have shot the sheriff. Joel had been with him and his gang on the other mountain when Betsy claimed to have heard the shot.

From what Joel could tell, the sheriff hadn't done anything to oppose Fowler or his gang. He hadn't done anything to oppose anyone, actually. Joel left the cell to stand before the window and study the mountains just beyond the bars. Could Fowler be responsible for burning Doctor Hopkins's house and the sheriff had evidence to prove it?

"Find Fowler and see what he has to say," Doctor Hopkins suggested. "But Sheriff's thinking is muddled. Don't let it trouble you."

Finding Fowler was good advice, but Joel believed Taney to be as clear-thinking as he ever was. He had the gun caliber right. If Sheriff Taney could remember the size of the bullet that shot him, it seemed that he could remember the man who pulled the trigger.

"Does Bullard resemble Fowler?" Joel asked.

Hopkins shook his head. "Not even on a dark night."

"If only I knew where Bullard was. I haven't heard back from any of the wires I sent."

"You telegraphed out for information on Bullard?" Hopkins scratched the back of his head. "I hate to tell you, but Postmaster Finley is Bullard's kin. I'd be surprised if those telegraphs ever made it to the line."

Another hostile townsperson to deal with. Joel grabbed his Stetson off the desk. Finley deserved a visit and Fowler needed questioning, but first Joel would see Betsy. No lady should have to confront the aftereffects of violence like she had. He wanted to carry that burden for her. Then there was the fact that he'd left her tied to a tree in the middle of the night. That might take some sweet-talking to overcome, but mostly he just wanted to know there was someone in this place who cared about him. Someone he could trust when everyone from the postmaster to the mayor was against him.

He walked past the schoolyard as the teacher rang the bell. Racing boys curved their paths to the open door. Little girls cradling corn-husk dolls tucked them into their coats, and the big girls whispered behind their hands as he approached. All eyes darted to a tall, dark-haired beauty, one who'd been spending her time at the Murphys' lately. Hopkins's daughter gathered her courage like a soldier gathers his camp gear and marched directly at him. Exactly the kind of woman he'd learned to avoid.

"Good morning, Deputy Eduardo," she said.

Where had he heard that name before? Seemed like someone else had called him that once. Still, he wasn't fool enough to encourage her banter. "It's Deputy Puckett. May I help you?"

The girls at the schoolhouse steps giggled as she threw a triumphant glance toward them. "Deputy Puckett, we wanted to know when you stopped riding your white horse. Did you leave it in Texas?"

His blood chilled. What did they know about Texas? Had he said something over dinner when talking to Fred and Betsy that would make them suspicious? The only connection he could find was that Miss Hopkins seemed cut of the same cloth as Mary Blount. All the more reason to cut this encounter short. He had more important matters to attend to.

"I don't own a white horse." He tipped his hat. "Good day, ma'am."

Her face crumpled into annoyance at his dismissal, but she mastered it before she turned to her friends. "Good day, ma'am," she crowed, as if it were the most profound utterance since the Gettysburg Address. They exploded in laughter, causing Joel to stop altogether and stare. Didn't they know something terrible had happened last night?

Girls. Women. Females of all ages. His Betsy was the exception.

When had she become *his* Betsy? Probably when she made that trek to the jailhouse the night of the fire. He'd needed a friend. She fit that bill and proved she could be so much more. Never before had he met a woman who made him want to settle down and make his mother's dreams come true, but Betsy had him thinking along those lines. If he could lose his bachelor status, then those silly encounters with the girls would peter out soon enough.

The white siding of the newspaper office shone through the tree trunks. Just as Joel was reaching the path to the door, Betsy strolled around the corner of the building. Upon seeing him, her face went white as a Sunday slice of bread. She hid her hands behind her back, but not before he caught sight of another letter.

She looked sorely put upon, but no wonder. Over the last sleepless night, she'd ridden through the mountains, been tied and left in the elements, tracked a bad guy, and then heard a wounded man moaning in agony. How he wanted to gather

her into his arms and ease her exhaustion. Was it right to feel that way? He'd talked to God about base temptations before, but this was something more. Something stronger. He realized he wouldn't be satisfied until she admitted that she felt something special for him, too. And he shouldn't have to tie her up to hear it.

He stepped forward to intercept her. She slowed, then stopped altogether. Her eyes remained lowered, her hands hidden.

"How are you doing?" he asked.

"It was a rough night. And you?"

"Today isn't going to be any better." Especially with their one witness proving unreliable. "The good news is that the sheriff is improving. Doctor Hopkins said he'll survive."

"And did he tell you who shot him?" Betsy pinned him with a searing gaze. "He did, didn't he? Who? Who shot him?"

Joel shook his head. "You've got to give me some room, Betsy. Give me some time, and I'll let you know when I can."

"You said you liked my company, that I was an asset. Then let me come with you."

"Letting you come with me could put you in danger. It'd be irresponsible."

"I'm responsible for myself." She barred her arms across her chest, and Joel saw the letter again. More secrets? But he had enough on his mind today.

"Betsy, we're in this together," he said, "but we have different roles. You've got to respect the boundaries I'm setting, or else you're really not helping. You're just doing what you want to do with no regard for my position."

"I know you're a deputy, but I'm not breaking the law. You can't force me to stay home."

"The stakes are too high and it's too dangerous. If you'll respect my leadership in this, then there'll be other adventures we'll have together." He bent to catch a glimpse of her down-turned face. "Other much more enticing adventures."

The letter crinkled in her hand. "That sounds just fine for you. You're not the one confined to another woman's cabin, caring for another woman's family. I need more than that." Then with a shake of her head, she said, "I didn't sleep last night. Normally I wouldn't be this tetchy." Her chin dropped. "I'm sorry."

He took her hand, the one not holding the secret envelope. "You're fine. Get some rest and you'll feel better."

She squeezed his hand before leaving. Funny how being able to offer her rest made him feel more rested. And what a paradox to find that because you loved someone, you had to send them away. But as soon as he got this settled, he'd be back.

Because a hero always came back for his lady.

CHAPTER 32

Since dawn the wind had picked up. Joel buttoned the lower buttons of his coat to cut down on the draft, but on second thought he decided he might want quicker access to his guns. After another night in the mountains, even he could sense that the mood in town had changed. He was tired, his horse was tired, but there didn't seem to be any rest ahead of them.

Finley hadn't sent the wires. Only under the threat of arrest yesterday did he finally carry out his duties. Not that Joel expected to hear news of Bullard, but he could leave no stone unturned.

With the perpetual malefactor Bullard unaccounted for, the unease in town was palpable. Sheriff Taney's accusations against Fowler didn't help, either. Fowler hadn't come to town, so either he was lying low or he hadn't heard that he'd been named. For all Joel knew, half the town might have witnessed the crime. They'd never tell.

In fact, they might all be hiding, because it was nearly noon, and the only people he saw out and about were two strangers waiting for him at the jailhouse. City men, from the looks of them.

The bruiser standing by the door was as thick as a dam and

just as solid. He removed his cap and clasped it in front of him. The badge on his vest reflected dully as he came to meet Joel, who dismounted.

"I'm Officer Harrison, sent from Governor Marmaduke's office. Are you Deputy Puckett?" The cuffs of his new police coat clung tightly to his broad hands. He must have to squeeze his jacket on.

"I am," Joel said. "Would you like to come inside?"

"We tried to enter earlier, but the doctor refused us," Officer Harrison said.

Telling Doctor Hopkins to keep everyone out was more for Sheriff Taney's protection than anything else, but Joel was glad to hear that someone was listening to him. "He was just following orders."

"Detective Cleveland," the man seated on the bench said by way of introduction as he got to his feet. He possibly had more years on him than the officer, but he wore them better. Although not overly slim, he looked like the kind of guy who could walk through a rainstorm and not get wet. Like he knew where the next strike would fall and was quick enough to avoid it. And he hadn't stopped taking Joel's measure since he'd first ridden into sight. As the officer droned on with small talk about their trip from Jefferson City, the detective studied him.

Joel didn't like being judged without knowing what the charges were. He ushered the men into the jailhouse and interrupted the officer by saying, "Have a seat." He didn't know what they'd come for, but he didn't cotton to finding out before he'd sent Doctor Hopkins on his way. "I'll sit with him for a spell," he told the doctor, nodding at Sheriff Taney's sleeping figure. "You go home, er . . ." Not home. Hopkins didn't have a home anymore thanks to him. "Go to Fred's and get some rest."

Keeping his head down as if trying to avoid witnessing something unpleasant, Doctor Hopkins closed his bag, buckled it up, and headed straight for the door.

Joel motioned the men to the two chairs in front of his desk, hoping that what they'd come to converse on wouldn't wake Taney.

Officer Harrison leaned forward in his chair, anxious to get started. Detective Cleveland seemed content to sit back and observe.

Joel didn't have time to waste. "I doubt y'all made this trip to sit and gawk at me. What can I do for you?"

"Just a bit of paperwork we're after," said Officer Harrison. "It's been brought to our attention that we missed some information when we hired you. Need to get it ironed out, that's all."

The casualness of his words didn't match the effort of their actions. Coming all the way from the state capitol to have him sign a form? The hair lifted on the back of Joel's neck. Something smelled fishy.

And the detective recognized Joel's concern. In fact, he was watching for it. Joel eased back in his chair and reached for a pencil, feigning a nonchalance he didn't possess. "Time's a-wasting. Let's see these forms."

But instead of pulling out a document, Officer Harrison threaded his fingers together on his knee. "You come from Garber, Texas. Is that right, Deputy Puckett?"

"It is." Joel's whole scalp was tingling now. "You have the recommendation of my superior, Sheriff Green, in my file."

"We do. That's what makes this so puzzling. You see, we were contacted by a man in Garber who claims that you are unfit to hold office. He claims that you were relieved of your duty because of misconduct. Is that true?"

The words echoed in Joel's ears. *Relieved of duty. Miscon-*

duct. His heart sank like he'd been dropped in the lake with a millstone tied to him. This couldn't be happening.

"Deputy Puckett?" Officer Harrison slanted his head.

Joel lifted his. "Yes," he answered. Yes, he'd been relieved of duty. Yes, he'd been accused of misconduct. Yes, he'd been found unworthy.

The detective and officer exchanged glances. "Deputy Puckett, can you explain why Sheriff Green would recommend you to a post when you were no longer welcome to serve with him?"

"Why?" Joel asked. "Why would Mr. Blount contact you?"

Something sparked in Detective Cleveland's face. Joel knew instantly. They hadn't told him who had filed the complaint.

"Mr. Blount was under the impression that you would never work as a lawman again. When he heard reports of a deputy named Puckett from Texas serving in Pine Gap, Missouri, he contacted us to see if it was true."

How? Had his parents told? Joel had been very clear with them what would happen if they let it slip that he was still working. Who else knew? He'd completely cut ties with the folks back home. The only people he'd seen on his way out of Garber were his friends Nick and Anne Lovelace, but he trusted them with his life.

"It is true," Joel said. "I was relieved of duty, but it was because of the false accusations of Mr. Blount's daughter. The sheriff was facing an election year and didn't want the controversy. It was easier on him if I just went away."

"Yet he expected us to take you in."

"False accusations," Joel repeated. "He knew why I'd spent the night with Miss Blount."

Detective Cleveland's eyebrows rose. "So you did spend the night with her?"

"And I didn't lay a finger on her," Joel said.

"You had to realize that your actions could've destroyed her reputation." Detective Cleveland's voice had a whine that set Joel's teeth on edge.

"They weren't my actions. They were all hers."

"But you understand our concern," Officer Harrison said. "We hired you because we needed an honorable man to clean this place up. If you aren't who you portrayed yourself to be—"

Joel stood. He held his hands out to his sides. "This is who I am. Stay here in Pine Gap. Follow me around. I'd be glad for the help. Make your own judgment of me, but please don't send me away based on a ruthless falsehood. I've already lost everything in Texas without a trial, without a hearing, with nothing. Don't take Missouri away from me, too."

He couldn't leave. Not now. Not when he'd just found Betsy.

Officer Harrison looked at Detective Cleveland. Cleveland nodded. Harrison cleared his throat. "We're taking you up on your offer, Deputy Puckett. Show us how you're succeeding in Pine Gap, and we'll consider keeping you on. We want to be impressed."

Impress them while he had the former sheriff bleeding in the cell behind them and a doctor's house in cinders? Joel had some work to do.

CHAPTER 33

The doctor and his family still lived under the Murphys' roof, and Scott was still banished to Betsy's childhood home. Betsy had expected to see him in town more often, but she supposed Pa was keeping him busy on the farm—a decent trade, since she helped Uncle Fred. Sheriff Taney convalesced in the jail, and two new lawmen from the government had been sent to lend a hand. At least, that was what she supposed, since they'd been identified by Doctor Hopkins as officers and they were seen riding with Joel.

All of this information Betsy had gathered on her own, because until that very night at dinner, Deputy Puckett hadn't told her a blessed thing.

Betsy sat and watched him eat. She was as tense as a fly waiting on a spider web, still not convinced that letting him make the rules was something she could abide. She'd always enjoyed freedom when it came to her comings and goings, unencumbered by boundaries. As long as her chores were done and she did her part, no one cared where she went.

But he cared.

And so Betsy had done what he'd asked. She stayed in town, didn't poke around the jail, and didn't get too nosy. She'd had a scare with the Hopkins girls reading that stray article and didn't want to push her luck.

She waited while Joel carried on with Uncle Fred and Doctor Hopkins, discussing the job and the news. Normally hearing this would have been enough, but now she wanted to hear something only for her. Something about her. Something about him. Something that wasn't casual talk over the supper table.

"What are they here for, again?" Uncle Fred asked. "They don't trust the job you're doing?"

Again the talk had turned to their visitors, now residing with Mr. and Mrs. Sanders. The two men hadn't gone out of their way to make any friends—just shadowed Joel around like the grim reaper waiting on Methuselah.

"They don't know me," Joel said, "so they've got no reason to trust me. I've got to prove myself."

But why bother now? And if they didn't think he could do the job, why'd they hire him?

"Any word on Bullard?" The question was asked every time someone stepped foot inside the cabin, this time by Uncle Fred over a piece of fried parsnip.

"Nothing on Bullard yet. If that was him hunkered down in the cave, he's on the run again."

"What does Fowler say?" Uncle Fred asked.

"Fowler didn't burn my house." Doctor Hopkins stopped with his fork mid-air. "He has naught against me. He's supposed to be by tomorrow to help with the rebuilding."

"But Sheriff Taney says Fowler shot him." Laurel looked around the room. "Then again, the sheriff came near to dying. Maybe he's confused."

"I'll talk to Fowler tomorrow," Joel said. "Maybe he'll know something further."

Aunt Sissy stood, ready to leave the room any time controversy was introduced. "Girls, would you like to play cat's cradle? I've got some yarn in the bedroom."

She handed Betsy the baby and took Amelia by the hand. Phoebe and Anna, who hadn't given up on trying to get Joel's attention over dinner, didn't budge until a stern look from their father forced them to leave the room to the adults.

Betsy looked up to find Joel watching her again. She felt her face growing warm. Slowly Joel dragged himself away to face her uncle, who had noticed the exchange and widened his eyes at her in speculation.

Uncle Fred and Doctor Hopkins's discussion continued as Betsy cleaned the table with her free hand. Drumming his fingernails gently against his tin cup, Joel answered what he could but left much unsaid, particularly when it came to his two new assistants. Once the babe's eyes had closed, Betsy laid her in the crib and tucked a warm wool fleece over her little body to stave off the cold that seeped through the log walls.

Betsy returned to see Laurel hang up the dishtowel and untie her apron. "Sounds like Sissy and the girls are having fun in there. I'm grateful to you, Fred, for putting us up. Tell Scott we're beholden to him for giving us his room."

Joel rose to his feet. "I know it's getting late, but do you mind if I visit with Betsy for a spell?" he asked Uncle Fred.

Finally. She'd been waiting all day, every hour dragging by until she could talk to him again.

Uncle Fred leaned back in his chair and threaded his fingers over his gaunt belly. "Is this concerning official law-enforcing business?"

"No." Joel's throat bounced, but he faced Uncle Fred full-on. "This visit concerns my growing admiration for your niece."

Betsy's jaw dropped. Had the fire suddenly blazed? Because the room felt toasty.

Her uncle had the nerve to laugh. "Be sure and leave at a decent hour, then."

Joel pushed open the door to the office and stood aside to usher Betsy through. What had prompted him to say that in front of her family?

"I don't see a rope, or did you have other methods in mind to make me stay?" she asked.

"You're not still mad at me for that," he said. "Come on." With a hand at her arm, Joel deftly steered her on through to the office before closing the door behind them.

He admired her and told her uncle so? Unforgivable! Inconsiderate! Irresistible!

If Joel was careful around the ladies before, he would be even more so now with Detective Cleveland and Officer Harrison watching his every move. That was why it was better to go on and tell Betsy's uncle, her brother, her pa, and any other man exactly where he stood in regards to Betsy. And maybe even tell her, if she'd allow him.

"Why do you think I want to talk to you?" Betsy said. "You haven't made much account of yourself recently. Just another hungry mouth to feed at suppertime, and then you won't tell me anything interesting."

"I contribute to the meal. More than my share. Besides, it's not the food I'm after. It's the delicious company." If the people of Garber could see how he acted with Betsy, no one could accuse him of being in love with Mary Blount. As different as night and day.

Betsy bloomed a fetching pink while forcing her mouth into

a pout. "If it's my company you're after, you should know that I'm pacing in this room nearly every hour of the day, fighting cabin fever. No reason to wait until suppertime."

"Actually it wasn't *your* company I had a hankering after. It's those Hopkins sisters. They're the real reason—"

But he didn't finish before Betsy slugged him in the chest— just as he'd hoped, for it gave him an excuse to catch her by the waist and pull her to himself.

Silently they embraced, basking in the companionship, the possibility that just maybe they'd found someone who belonged solely to them. Betsy snuggled into his arms as if she didn't want for anything else the world had to offer, and Joel prayed he'd be enough for her. She had ambition. She craved excitement. Would she be willing to sacrifice some of that for him? For a family?

She drew a long, contented breath and nearly purred. "I thought maybe you'd changed your mind and decided you didn't need me after all."

His arms tightened. "I need you. I need you here for me to come home to. I can't imagine ending my day without seeing you."

Betsy looked up, puzzled by his urgency. "But you've been here."

"Not *here*." He planted a kiss on her forehead. "Thank you for staying out of this mess. More like than not it's going to involve people you know. I don't want to see you hurt."

"Don't forget," she said, "I know how to take care of myself."

"How about you let me take care of you?" Then, before she could rekindle the debate, he lifted a finger. "I told you that I need you, and with the sheriff talking, Fowler coming in, and the hunt for Bullard on, we might be close to a breakthrough."

She stepped out of his arms. "Now that it's just the two of us, why don't you tell me why those men are here?"

Joel's boots suddenly felt like they were pinching his toes. "Those men? I told you, they're checking up on me."

"But why? If they were concerned, why didn't they come sooner, like when you arrived? Did they hear about Sheriff Taney getting shot?"

Joel turned and began to fiddle with the newspaper rack. "No. They hadn't heard until they got here."

"Did someone send for them?" she asked.

Joel's chest squeezed tight. *Oh, Betsy.* He didn't want to tell her. He couldn't tell her. The shame would be too great. Without thinking, he picked up an out-of-state paper and set about tidying it. Someday she had to know. He just hadn't figured on how to say it. Would she understand?

"What's wrong, Joel? There's something you're not telling me."

Betsy reached for the paper he held, but before he could hand it over, something caught his eye. It was his name, printed on an inner page that had slipped out of place. He pulled the paper away from her. A quick scan revealed his name repeatedly in the column, but it wasn't his name. Not exactly.

"Deputy Eduardo Pickett?" he asked.

Betsy's lips went tight. Her blue eyes snapped with—what was it, fear? "What? Why would you say that?"

Joel scanned the column, not believing his eyes. "Deputy Eduardo Pickett of Pine Gap, Missouri." He blinked, but the names didn't change. "And it says here that Deputy Pickett is from Texas."

"In the New Orleans paper?" Betsy's hands were shaking as she wiped them against her skirt. "How odd."

The lines of print wavered, and his voice sounded far away. "According to this, Deputy Pickett spends his time tracking a gang called the Bald Knobbers."

"Obviously it's not you," Betsy said.

"'. . . *a dark Adonis breathing fire that inflamed the heart of any lady who witnessed his approach . . .*'" Joel's neck was red. His face was red. His mood was black. "'. . . *the envy of every man and the dream of every woman.*'"

"Look how dark it is." Betsy moved to the window. "When did it get so late?"

His supper soured his stomach. "When I first got here, you called me Eduardo, didn't you? You made up some excuse, but that's what you called me."

She shrugged. "It's a common enough name."

"And then yesterday I was stopped by the girls at the schoolhouse, and I have a sneaking suspicion that they've read this."

Her eyes darted to the cabin, where the Hopkins sisters were staying. "I don't think they know how to read," she said. "And I know they don't get the New Orleans paper."

"But they heard it somewhere. Is this why Mrs. Sanders asked me if I'd pulled a little girl from the well?"

But wait. This was the New Orleans paper. Would anyone in Garber get the New Orleans paper? The clock struck ten, chiming for each hour, while he stared at Betsy. Then with that quick-draw movement he'd practiced for so many years, he snatched the Fort Worth paper off the rack. Betsy dove for it, too, but she was no match for him. He held the paper over his head and out of her reach. The paper crackled as he paged through it. He did a double take before his mouth set in grim lines.

"What do you know? Another article by E. M. Buckahee. Would you happen to know this woman? Isn't Betsy short for Elizabeth?"

He didn't hear her answer because he was too sickened by the next lines he read:

She cried into her pillow every night, bemoaning the stolen future she'd planned for herself and the dashing deputy who'd stolen her heart. Little did she know that a lady of her steady temperament could never hold him. She could only be grateful for the time they'd had together.

He was going to be ill. "What . . . what is this?" The paper crumpled in his fist. "Is this what you think of me?"

"No, not at all." Her face blanched. "That's not you. It's just a character I made up."

"A character that has my job, my description, and most of my name? Did you not think of the consequences? This ran in the Fort Worth paper. Do you not understand?"

From the puzzlement on her face, she didn't, but the situation was becoming only too clear to him.

"I told them not to print it in Texas, but it was too late," she said. "And I stopped writing them once I got to know you."

"You stopped?"

He wanted to believe her, but then he saw something—evidence—he couldn't ignore. How he wished he could turn his back and leave—just walk away and save what shreds of friendship might remain, but he had to know the truth.

"Betsy"—his voice lowered with dangerous control—"there's an envelope on your desk. It's got a stamp. It's got an address. I can't read the address from here, but would you mind if I looked at it?"

Tears filled her eyes before splashing down her cheek. "Don't, please," she said finally.

His arms dropped. "I actually felt bad asking you to stay behind. I didn't want to hurt you, but you had your own agenda, didn't you? You needed me so you could twist everything around and make me look like a fool." He shook his head. "I should've known not to trust a woman. Didn't I say that when I first arrived?"

But he had trusted her, and look at the trouble it'd brought him.

"I thought you were different," he said as he stormed outside, a gust of cold air blasting through his coat and chilling his heart.

CHAPTER 34

"He knows. He knows all about the articles." Betsy laid the tray of type down in front of her. The individual type blocks blurred before her gritty eyes. "When I started this, he was just a stranger."

Her brother might not be the most sympathetic soul, but she didn't deserve sympathy. She needed someone to listen as she told them how sorry she'd treated Joel. She wanted someone who would agree that she'd made a mess of things and help her figure out how to earn Joel's forgiveness.

Josiah hopped up to sit on the high table. His boots swung in the air like he was splashing in the swimming hole back home. "How'd you keep this under your lid? Getting published all over the country, and you don't tell your own brother? I bet you were about to bust."

"I would've told you, but I thought I'd keep it a secret until Deputy Puckett left town—then we'd all have a good laugh about it. But Joel didn't laugh."

Josiah grinned that annoying big-brother-knows-everything smile. "And somewhere along the way Deputy Puckett became Joel to you. Kinda hard to explain to a friend why you'd be using their story to make money, especially when they specifically made you promise not to publish anything about them."

"And he acted like I'd gotten him into trouble somehow, as if my article had hurt him."

"But he didn't say how?" Josiah asked.

"Just that there were consequences. That's all." But her statement couldn't adequately describe how disappointed he'd looked, or how sorry she felt.

"Boy howdy, Betsy. Won't Ma chew you out over this one? And Pa won't know what to think."

Her parents would read the articles? Betsy dropped her head into her hands. Ma would not approve. Not the way Betsy had carried on about the deputy.

"I can't face Pa," she said. "He and Scott came by and got Uncle Fred just a bit ago, and I stayed scarce. I don't know what they came to town for, but I hope he doesn't hear. He'll probably make me go back to the farm."

"Now that you mention it, when I rode in just now I thought I saw Pa's horse down at the jailhouse." Josiah shrugged. "I just figured he was arranging a shotgun wedding, seeing how his daughter has publicly humiliated herself over the new deputy."

Had she not possessed her great store of maturity, she would've thrown the composing tray at her brother, enjoying each stinging metal block that pelted him. Shotgun wedding? It'd take a shotgun to force Joel anywhere near her again. Tears started stinging her eyes again.

"Buck up, Betsy," Josiah said. "So he's mad at you. What's it matter? After this mess with Sheriff Taney, he'll probably have to pack his bags and head back to Texas anyway. Who cares what he thinks?"

But what her brother meant as comfort only stung more.

Joel tossed the burnt remains of his breakfast out the back of the jailhouse. No morning meal with the Murphys this morning. It would be more than he could bear.

He dropped the charred skillet on the stove and leaned his forehead against the bars of the cell. The cold iron felt soothing after the burning thoughts he'd wrestled with all night. He really did need to find a place to board. With the sheriff convalescing in one cell, Joel would have to sleep in his chair if they found Bullard.

Joel ran his hands through his hair and scruffed it up good, wishing he could rough all thoughts of Betsy out of his mind. Thinking on her had kept him up half the night, and now he was dragging around this morning. She was interfering with his work, even though she was nowhere near.

What was she thinking, writing about him like that? He reached beneath his hat on his desk and dragged the papers out now that it was light enough to read again. Where did she get her ideas? Turning the cat rescue into saving a child? Under her pen, Pritchard became a dangerous bushwhacker that he alone could rein in. And Fowler . . . well, she didn't have to exaggerate about him any. He was a rival for any man. But surely she was mocking Joel. Knowing Betsy and her sarcasm, he could only imagine how she must have laughed while writing his supposed exploits.

The only things she got right were her descriptions of him— dark hair, brooding eyes, strong jaw. Although how could she make out his jawline from beneath his beard? The paper rustled as he tossed it back on his desk and made his way to the mirror above the washbasin. Joel ran his hand along his jaw. It'd probably be even more noticeable if he kept his beard trimmed shorter.

He jerked his hand away. Why was he standing around gawk-ing at the same face that met him in the mirror every morning? He couldn't let his vanity get the best of him.

His blood started boiling again. Why did she have to ruin everything? Maybe someday he'd forgive her, but he couldn't trust her. If he got to keep his job, he'd have to keep her away. Maybe it was time for him to move on after all.

Bending over, he dunked into the basin and then shook his head, flinging water on the mirror. He scrubbed the water into his hair, enjoying the bracing cold on his scalp. He'd felt sorry for Betsy, a woman of her energy living with her uncle's family, obviously longing for something more. He should be proud of her. With her writing, she'd achieved something remarkable.

In the beginning she'd assured him that matrimony wasn't her aim. At least she'd told the truth then, but where did that leave him? If she didn't have a story to write, would she want to spend time with him? Were her smiles really for him, or were they for Eduardo? And just as important, if they *were* to marry, what outlandish names would she come up with for their children? Eduardo? Really?

He'd better get moving before Sheriff Taney awoke and needed tending or before those detectives appeared. But be-fore he'd finished, he heard voices. Brushing the water droplets from his shoulder, he buttoned up the bib on his cavalry shirt and stepped outside. Detective Cleveland and Officer Harrison came down the hill from the Sanderses' boardinghouse, and just behind them was a small group of horsemen that included some friends of his.

"Good morning, Deputy," Officer Harrison said. "Looks like you got company coming."

Saddle leather creaked as Fred and Scott Murphy dismounted. Joel didn't know Scott was back in town, or why Fred needed to be on horseback when he lived just down the street, but he looked like he'd ridden a piece already that morning. They conferenced with the rough mountaineer who'd arrived with them before coming up the steps.

Scott looked small between the two men, as if he'd shrunk inside himself since the last time Joel had seen him. He looked about as excited as a condemned man looking at a noose. Another look at Fred's grim face, and Joel knew this wasn't just a youngster being moody. The three of them stood before him, Fred with his hand on his son's shoulder. The lines around his eyes had darkened, and his face looked like it'd weathered a storm overnight. Scott's face had bleached as white as bones in the desert.

Fred avoided eye contact with Detective Cleveland and Officer Harrison. "Deputy Puckett, is there somewhere we can go to speak in private?"

The detective's eyes narrowed. Officer Harrison harrumphed. "We are officers of the law, sir. We are obliged to listen to any dealings with this deputy."

But Joel recognized stubborn, especially stubborn from the Murphy and Huckabee lines. Fred wouldn't be doing any talking with these men present. Just last night Joel had declared himself a suitor for Betsy. Even if things had changed, he could draw on that connection to give Fred the time he sought.

"Gentlemen," said Joel, "this conversation is of a personal nature. The lady I'm courting, Miss Betsy Huckabee, is of this family. This here is her uncle and her cousin." Then he pointed at the grizzled mountain man who was giving him the stink eye. "And this gentleman is . . ."

"Betsy's pa," he growled, startling blue eyes pinning Joel from beneath a black floppy hat.

Joel shrank back a step. Maybe claiming kinship with the

Murphys wasn't such a good idea. "Yes, this is Betsy's pa, so this is a family discussion."

But at the detective's surprised look, Joel realized that an unexpected visit from a stern father might not swing their opinion in his favor. Come to think of it, what if Mr. Huckabee was here to dress him down over something Betsy had told him? Well, Joel would just have to take it, but not in front of the government men.

The detective sidled up to Joel. "You say this Miss Huckabee is a friend of yours? Where could we find her?"

No way in the world was Joel about to give up Betsy's location, especially considering three of her blood kin were staring him down.

The detective took in the general attitude of the crew and motioned to Officer Harrison. "I think we'll do fine on our own. Let's go."

Mr. Huckabee and Fred stepped aside to let them pass, and once they were gone, Fred nudged Scott forward. Scott walked like a hundred-year-old man, probably the only time Joel had ever seen Scott not excited to see him.

"I'm here, Deputy Puckett, to turn myself in." Scott fiddled with a rough kerchief tied around his neck. "For killing a Bald Knobber."

CHAPTER 35

"Here comes the constables," Josiah said. "Don't we have enough trouble on our hands?"

And they were turning in at the printing office. Josiah swung the door open before the men could knock, giving Betsy little time to compose herself.

"Good morning, fellas. How can I help you?" Josiah asked.

The stout officer in front sized Josiah up, but his partner looked right past him to Betsy. Why hadn't she gone inside the cabin? She was in no mood to visit with another lawman at the moment.

"I'm Officer Harrison. I understand this is the newspaper office." He stood with one broad shoulder angled into the door, as if ready to hold it open should Josiah decide to close it in his face. And his face looked like it might have had many doors slammed on it already.

Josiah looked pointedly at the printing press, the trays of type, and the newspaper racks. "What do you know? It is the newspaper office," he exclaimed. Her brother was a born antagonist, and the years had only strengthened the inclination.

Holding her skirts tight to her knees and making herself as small as possible, Betsy edged to the wall as the other man introduced himself as Detective Cleveland. He hadn't over-looked her like the officer had. As the officer droned on with small talk about the weather, the detective watched her. From her mussed hair, to her inky apron, to her blackened fingers, then to her desk—he'd placed her. He seemed to have already figured out what no one else in Pine Gap had—that Betsy did more than report to Uncle Fred and set type.

Why hadn't she dived into the cabin while she still had the chance?

The detective raised his hand and silenced Officer Harrison. When he spoke it was to Josiah, although he kept his eyes on her. "You wouldn't know a Miss E. M. Buckahee, would you?"

Josiah's mouth twisted, and the bluffing face he always wore when dared to do the impossible slipped on. "I don't know anyone of that name. Honest. There are no Buckahees in Pine Gap." But that story would only buy them a little time. No use in delaying the inevitable.

Gripping her apron, Betsy spoke up. "There are no Bucka-hees here, but I am a Huckabee. You must be referring to my pen name."

"She's not done anything wrong." Josiah stepped between them. "If you hadn't wanted us to poke fun at that deputy, then you shouldn't have sent him here. He's a fish out of water—"

"Miss Huckabee is in no trouble. Actually we're very im-pressed with her work and want to know more. Much more." The detective pulled a stool out and set it in front of Betsy. Sitting with one boot heel hooked on the brace and his arms crossed in front of his chest, he shifted a bit to find a comfortable spot before asking, "So tell me, Miss Huckabee, how much of your stories are true?"

Her throat jogged. "My stories? Well, I didn't put them on

the second page of the Kansas City paper. I submitted them for the serial portion, which is fiction."

"Kansas City? I'm sure the Kansas City readers are impressed, but it's the out-of-state readers who've rattled our chain."

"Rattled? What do you mean?"

"Your articles have brought a dangerous situation to our attention," the officer said. "We came here to investigate, and I'm sorry to say, we find it even worse than you described."

Betsy's eyes slid closed. They were here because of what she'd written. No wonder Joel was so angry.

"You think this is bad?" Josiah asked. "Things are better now than they've been in years."

"I understand the difficulties," Detective Cleveland said, "but the people of Missouri, and in fact people from around the nation, do not understand. After reading Miss Huckabee's compelling account of a deputy named Pickett, we have to ask if that's an accurate reflection of the behavior of Deputy Puckett."

"No," Betsy said. "Deputy Pickett only exists on paper."

"There are remarkable similarities," Detective Cleveland said. "Enough to catch notice of people who knew Deputy Puckett in Texas."

The Fort Worth paper? Betsy wanted to crawl beneath her cot and never come out again.

"It's not Deputy Puckett," she said. "If you spend any time with him, you'll realize—"

"But you did spend time with him, and we've read your description."

She knew she was in trouble when even her rotten big brother looked worried.

"They shouldn't believe everything they read," she said.

"Our mistake was that we didn't check into his past before hiring him. It appears that Deputy Puckett was reprimanded for dishonoring a lady. He didn't come to Pine Gap by choice. He was run out of Texas."

The room tilted. Betsy's bones jarred as she dropped too hard into a chair. Joel and another lady? The thought made her sick. Was Joel capable of taking advantage of a woman?

"I'm sure there's a mistake," she said.

"No mistake. He confessed to being relieved of duty on those charges. What we need to know is whether he's offended again."

They were watching her, and she didn't have the fortitude to hide her devastation. Could it be true of Joel? If womanizing was his aim, he was fishing with the right bait—his brooding looks, his commanding presence, how he poured on the charm for the convenience of tying her to a tree and leaving her. Twice now he'd taken liberties—well, at the jail he couldn't be blamed entirely—but Betsy thought she was someone special, that she'd broken through his general dislike of women and proved herself an acceptable example of womanhood. Was it a ruse? What kind of man enjoyed playing games like that?

A proud, arrogant man. A man who pretended to eschew feminine company in order to avoid suspicion. A man who had no intention of staying, so he ate his seed corn and didn't worry about the next season.

Was that the kind of man she'd fallen in love with?

"If my sister has nothing else to say on the matter, then I advise you'uns to go." Josiah held the door open.

She knew she should respond, should stop making a fool of herself and finish the conversation, but she lacked the will. Every bit of strength had been drained out of her, along with her confidence that she knew Joel Puckett.

Her mind in a whirl, she barely noticed as the door closed. Hadn't she wondered from the onset why he'd take such a thankless position? The way he talked about Texas and how he loved it, hadn't Betsy questioned him about why he'd left? If he was discharged, there had to be witnesses. Surely he wouldn't lose his job based on a groundless accusation. Had he forced his attentions on a lady? She clutched at her stomach. It was too awful to consider. What would cause him to do such a despicable thing?

Josiah squatted before her. "Stop and think, Betsy. Does that sound like the man you know?"

"I don't want it to be him," she said. "How can I decide what is true when I can't stand to know?"

"You *can* stand it. You *must* stand it," he said. "You're a smart girl. You can think through this. Is it true or not?"

Did it matter? Joel would never speak to her again, either way. But Josiah was right. She had to know the truth. Still hugging her waist, Betsy began to list the evidence. "He misses home, acts like he regrets leaving. I don't think he left by choice."

Josiah nodded. "Good. Keep talking."

"He said from the beginning that I couldn't use his name in the paper. He didn't want stories about him to get back to Texas."

Josiah winced, but he kept his voice steady. "If it's true, you need to know. Think through everything."

"And then there's how he acted when he first came. He told me to stay away from him. I told him I wasn't worried about my reputation, but he said he didn't want his reputation to suffer."

"Then I'd say that Deputy Puckett has had a run-in with scandal. The question is, was he guilty?"

But she couldn't think in those terms, because with accusations that horrid, he'd never be freed from suspicion.

CHAPTER 36

"You've got my attention." Joel's ears rang, he was listening so close. Kill a Bald Knobber? Why would Scott do that? "Come on inside, and let's hear what you have to say for yourself."

Fred nodded and motioned the boy inside. Once they'd stepped across the threshold, Joel closed the door and came around to sit on his desk in front of them.

Scott looked over his shoulder for his pa and shivered. He crammed one fist into his pocket and stood with a shoulder raised while he scuffed his foot. After what seemed to Joel an eternity, his voice squalled. "I didn't mean to kill him."

"Kill who?" Joel blurted.

"I don't know," Scott answered.

A hundred questions buzzed in Joel's head, but they would wait. He needed to hear how the boy told the story without any prompting.

"Go on," he said.

"I wanted to help Fowler. I wanted to ride with the Bald Knobbers, but they sent me home. They didn't think I could be any help." He tossed another pleading look over his shoulder and this time met his uncle's unwavering gaze. "I went back to Uncle Calbert's, but I took the long way around. I figured that if Bullard knew they were hunting for him, he wouldn't stick to the main roads, so I took the trail. I didn't have a single notion what I was going to do with him when I found him. Just thought it'd be exciting to be involved." His chest caved. "I should've realized when I came upon the tree that I'd walked into a trap. I had to get off my horse, and that should've warned me, but I was too fired up about finding someone. I just wanted to get past there and ride hard again. I never thought about a Bald Knobber being in the thicket until he had me by the coat."

"Wait," Joel said. "Are you talking about the night that the Bald Knobbers rode? The night I saw you up on Dewey Bald?"

"That's it," Calbert Huckabee said. "He came home telling me what'd happened. We weren't sure what to make of his story, but it sounded like something that needed to be told, so here we are."

"Days later. If it was important, don't you think you should've come sooner?"

"He was hurt, and we had some thinking to do," Calbert said.

Fred studied the ground. "I didn't know until this morning."

There'd be no apologizing from Calbert, Joel could see that right off. He'd done what was right eventually, and any person who couldn't understand why he had to agonize over his choice didn't deserve an apology.

Joel's mouth tightened. "He had you by the coat . . ."

"He had me by the coat, and I just laughed. Why would I have anything to fear from a Bald Knobber? I haven't run afoul of them."

"How'd you know he was a member of the gang?"

"He had a mask," Scott said. "Kinda hard to miss that clue."

Was it Bullard? Joel paused long enough to let the thought grow. Bullard disguised as a Bald Knobber, committing crimes that would incriminate his old foes? The theory had some merit.

"Your attacker had you by the coat," Joel said. "And then what happened?"

"I thought he was fooling around. I said, 'Did you find Bullard?' But he brought out a knife. That's when I started thinking hard. I mean, I'd just left the gang back on the mountain. How did this fellow get ahead of me? Once he put that knife to my throat, I knew I was in trouble. At first I just went limp. I let him push me to the edge of the drop-off because I was so afraid. He said, 'Are they behind you, boy? Are they coming this way? Well, you ain't gonna have a story to tell if they are.'

"My neck was stinging and I could feel the warmth running down to my shirt. Then I knew what he had in mind. No matter how I tried talking sense to him, he was going to kill me. Being afraid of him wasn't going to save my life. So I pulled out my pistol, just like a real deputy. I pulled it out fast and shot him in the chest." His face paled and contorted. He closed his mouth, then with a shake of his head, he continued. "His eyes. I could see them through the mask. Suddenly he was more afraid than I was. He was still holding onto my coat, but he'd dropped the knife and was holding his chest. The blood coming through his fingers . . ." Scott dropped his chin. "He started yanking to get his mask off, and then he disappeared. Down the cliff."

Happy shouts from the schoolyard could be heard as Scott's peers waited for their instruction to begin. Joel finally swallowed the lump that'd been caught in his throat ever since they'd arrived. He wanted to believe Scott, but his story wasn't adding up with what they already knew.

"You mean to say you were on the trail where the pine tree had been hacked down? That's where Sheriff Taney was attacked, too. And he says that it was Fowler who attacked him."

"It wasn't Fowler that had my boy," said Fred.

"Do you think the boy could get a shot off if Fowler had him by the neck?" said Calbert Huckabee.

"Let me see your neck," Joel said.

With awkward tugs, Scott loosened the scarf that shielded his throat. Beneath it was a bandage. He fumbled with the knot, but it stayed secure. Joel reached for his own knife, but at the sight of it, Scott recoiled. Sweat beaded on his lip along with the beginnings of thin whiskers. Leaning backwards, he held out both hands.

"It's okay, son." Fred put a steadying hand on his shoulder. "He's got to cut the bandage off."

Joel should've thought before he pulled the knife, but if he needed any proof that Scott had been scared for his life, it was standing right before him. "Do you want your pa to do it?"

"You can."

Separating one layer and slicing through the bandage was the work of a few seconds, but from the way Scott expelled his breath, you'd think that it was a year-long ordeal. Finally able to act, Scott unwrapped the bandage, which showed red after the first few layers. The final round found it stuck to his neck. He grimaced as he tugged it free.

It wasn't deep. Couldn't be if the boy was still alive, but it sure enough had the length and width consistent with a sharp blade being held against vulnerable skin for a lengthy conversation. Not a swipe, not a jab, but a slow sawing meant to subdue the victim with fear.

Joel looked Scott deep in the eyes. Getting a first response could only happen once. If Scott was going to falter, it'd be this time, so he had to see it.

"Is there any chance that you did this to yourself?"

Scott drew back like he'd been socked in the jaw. "What? Cut my own throat? Why would I do that?" Such confusion would be hard to fake. Joel studied Fred and Calbert to see if their reaction matched. Neither of them had even considered staging the injury.

Calbert stood and pulled a wrapped bundle from his vest pocket. "I went back to where it happened, and sure enough, I found this knife in the ravine."

Joel took it, unwrapped the handkerchief, and flipped the knife blade in his palm. It wasn't a man's knife—not really. Too small. You wouldn't skin an animal or saw through a rope with it. He tested the blade with the rough part of his thumb. Razor sharp. Surgical, even.

"If there's nothing else you need . . ." Calbert looked to the door.

"Sit," Joel said, and then because of Mr. Huckabee's age and partially because he happened to be Betsy's pa, added, "Please, sir."

Joel turned to Scott. "Are you sure the man you shot fell into the ravine?"

"Yes, sir. I saw him lying at the bottom before I lit out for home."

"But I didn't find no one," Calbert said. "Only the knife."

Joel stood and paced to the back door, trying to figure a chain of events that made sense. A man attacked Sheriff Taney, left him for dead, and then jumped Scott when he came along? Had Bullard, disguised as a Bald Knobber, tried to frame his enemies with the death of the sheriff, but Scott walked into his trap? Either way, the culprit had escaped, leaving a frightened boy and a wounded lawman behind.

He studied the three men sitting before him, each sharing the same concern but expressing it by different measure. Poor Fred looked like he'd been milked dry of his last drop of blood. Calbert sat stonily, and Scott trembled in waves.

"I'm not a judge, you understand." Joel had heard Sheriff

Green back in Blackstone County give this speech several times, but he hadn't counted on doing it this soon. "I have to present the evidence to the district attorney, and he'll make the call on whether or not you are tried. But the good news is, there's no evidence of murder."

At the word, Scott flinched. "It was self-defense. He had a knife to my throat." He gestured to the bloody gap, his eyes wild with fear.

Joel continued. "But there hasn't been a body found. No body, no murder. But I'm obliged to go look again."

"What if you find a body this time?" Fred leaned forward.

"With Scott's injury, it'd be hard to prove that his life wasn't in danger."

"So what's that mean?" Calbert asked.

"It means that Scott needs to write out a statement telling exactly what happened. Any other evidence that you possess"—he stared pointedly at Calbert—"needs to be turned in, including the gun."

"I . . . I dropped the gun," Scott said. "I left it there."

"I found it when I went back," Calbert said and then, at Scott and Joel's shocked expressions, "At least I didn't give it back to the boy."

"Well, it needs to be in my possession." At least Joel knew the culprit hadn't turned around and used the .22 that Scott dropped to leave a .38 wound in the sheriff. "I'll present all of this to the authorities, and we'll see what they say."

Scott squirmed on the bench. "Until we hear back from the district attorney . . . ?"

Joel pulled his desk drawer open and produced a bound leather journal. "Considering that you came in of your own volition, I think we can trust you to stay in the area should we need to question you further."

"You mean I can go home?" Scott's eyes filled with tears as his mouth twisted. His chin wobbled as he tried to make his words clear. "I've been so scared. I thought the worst was when that man laid ahold of me, but ever since then, nothing has been right. No matter what I did that night, it's like he still was going to make me pay."

Gone was the boy eager for excitement and vengeance. His desire to help people had cost him, but hopefully he'd be a stronger man for it.

"Which is exactly why your pa and Miss Sissy didn't want you riding with the Bald Knobbers," Joel said. "And why Fowler sent you home that night. Some burdens weren't meant to be borne by one as young as you."

Calbert raised his head. The light caught the silver streaks at his temple as he regarded Joel with sage-like gravity. "How old are you again?" he asked.

Feeling half his twenty-four years, Joel pushed the book toward Scott. "Write what happened in your own words. Consider yourself under oath, too, because should this go to court, it'll be presented as evidence."

"Will there be a court case?" Fred asked.

"If we keep everything out in the open at the beginning, we shouldn't have any questions. Just tell the truth and everything will work out."

But it hadn't for him, had it? He'd told Sheriff Green the truth when he was accused, but the sheriff really hadn't cared. The election was more important. He'd rather sacrifice Joel.

Thankfully, Joel was the one in charge here, and Scott wouldn't face the same fate.

Chapter 37

Scott and his kinsfolk had left, headed back to Calbert's place over the mountain. Fowler had promised to come in to face the accusations, and Sheriff Taney's wounds had healed well enough for him to travel. Despite the obvious entertainment it'd provide, Joel couldn't interview Fowler with Taney in a cell behind them. Thankfully, Mr. and Mrs. Sanders had volunteered to look after the sheriff, the mister going as far as bunking down with Taney until he was back on his feet.

Which he was struggling with at that moment. Groaning, Taney sat up, holding his shoulder, while Mrs. Sanders gathered the various poultices and bandages strewn around his area. Taney swayed, and Mr. Sanders rushed to his side. With the sheriff supported between the two of them, they made their way to the door.

"We'll keep you posted, Deputy," Mr. Sanders said. "Hopefully he'll get his strength back soon."

What Joel was really hoping for was that he'd get his memory back, and that the memory would include a better description of the man who'd shot him. Not Fowler.

As luck would have it, Detective Cleveland and Officer Harrison returned at the same time Fowler arrived, all three men eying each other suspiciously as they approached the jailhouse. Joel tossed the dirty water out of the basin onto the street, his last task in tidying up the cell that Sheriff Taney had evacuated. He greeted Fowler first. Fowler grunted in return and marched past him to take the biggest chair in front of his desk.

"Come on and ask me questions," Fowler said. "We all know I didn't burn down Hopkins's house and then shoot Taney. Taney got his skull cracked. That's all."

And Joel was inclined to agree, but he had to investigate, especially with the oversight of the two men standing behind his desk.

"Are you saying that you were nowhere near that ravine that night?" Joel asked.

"You know where I was," Fowler said. "I was tying you to a tree and then going to search through Parrow's cave. I have plenty of witnesses."

"Just a minute." Officer Harrison walked around the desk to stand over Fowler. "Did you say you tied Deputy Puckett up?"

Detective Cleveland took a seat, pulled out a pad of paper, and starting taking notes.

Joel would like nothing so much as the freedom to cuff Fowler upside the head at that moment. "We'll deal with that later. Right now I just want to see if the sheriff's charge has any merit."

"It doesn't," said Fowler. "I have thirty witnesses who were with me until late that night. I didn't shoot him."

"Give me a list of your alibis," Joel said.

"I'm afeared that's a problem," Fowler admitted. "I'm not handing over the identities of my brothers-at-arms to the federals."

Joel tapped his pencil against the desk. "Name one."

Fowler leaned back and crossed his arms over his chest. "You're fishing with no bait, Deputy. Let me help you with your investigation. Do you have any witnesses?"

"Just the sheriff, and he says you did it."

"What about tracks?" Fowler asked. "Did you get any tracks on the shooter?"

"Only tracks we could identify belonged to the sheriff's horse."

"What caliber of gun was he shot with?"

".38."

Fowler waved a beefy hand like he was shooing a pesky fly. "Lots of people carry .38s."

"Remove your shirt," Joel said.

Fowler's head drew back. "I don't know how you conduct interviews in Texas, but we prefer to remain clothed."

"I'm looking for an injury," Joel said. "You got any unexplained wounds?"

Without blinking, Fowler commenced the arduous process of removing his many layers. He didn't move like an injured man, but when he stripped off his outer shirt and final layer, Joel was surprised by the scars that pocked his chest and back.

"I told you," Fowler said, holding his arms out to the sides, "things used to be rough out here. These marks were taken for our town, and I'm as proud of them as any soldier is of the medals on his uniform."

Joel's neckband took that moment to dig into his throat. He didn't long for those kinds of awards on himself, but he hoped he'd carry them as well.

"What's this about?" Detective Cleveland asked. "Did the sheriff wing the outlaw?"

"We have another report of a crime," Joel said. "Scott

Murphy came in this morning to report that he'd been attacked that same night, in the same location. He claims to have shot his attacker."

Fowler's eyes narrowed. "Scott got attacked by the same man?"

"Sounds like it. Dropped him in the gully. But Scott has a .22, not a .38."

"You're wrong there, Deputy," Fowler said. "He had his uncle's .38 that night when he came to meet us. I saw it stuck in his belt. I wish I hadn't, but . . ."

Officer Harrison clapped his hands together. "This Murphy fella confessed to shooting someone, and we have an injured sheriff? Seems like our job is done. That man wasn't attacked. He was out hunting for bad guys and got jumpy."

"He's not a man, he's a boy," Fowler said. "And don't forget, Miles Bullard, a known murderer, is still on the loose."

Detective Cleveland angled his way between Joel and Fowler and found a corner of the desk to sit on. His pinstripe pants stretched tight over his knee as he swung his foot. "I've got another theory, Deputy Puckett." He studied Fowler for a long moment.

"Spit it out," Fowler growled.

"I think Scott Murphy and Mr. Fowler are in cahoots. You'll notice that Mr. Fowler didn't turn himself in until Murphy had time to come in with his story. He wants us to believe that it's not Mr. Fowler who shot the sheriff, it's another bandit . . . one who is now injured and on the run. But where is that man? He's nowhere to be found."

"Scott Murphy has no reason to confess to a shooting on my behalf," Fowler said. "I turned him down when he wanted to join us."

"And this is the way he can earn your favor," said the detective.

"Throw some doubt into what happened, muddy Taney's testimony, take the fall if necessary. If he's just a boy, the jury would probably go easy on him."

Fowler fumed. Officer Harrison and Joel both got ready to intervene if necessary.

"I did not go after Sheriff Taney," Fowler said. "I didn't shoot him, and I know nothing whatsoever about what happened to Scott Murphy. I don't hide behind children. I answer for myself."

"Besides," Joel said, "Fowler was with me."

"There's another scenario to explore," Detective Cleveland said. Joel was really starting to hate his whiny voice. "Maybe Mr. Fowler here is innocent. Maybe Scott Murphy was acting on his own. He's the one who's been going after Doctor Hopkins. He disguised himself as a Bald Knobber in case he was spotted. Sheriff Taney caught him, and he had to shoot him to get free. The sheriff was shot by a Bald Knobber and Scott comes in claiming to have shot the bad guy."

Joel's head spun. "Scott Murphy's and Doctor Hopkins's families aren't feuding. They're sharing a roof right now. Besides, Scott's the one who raised the alarm when Hopkins's house was burning."

"The first one to ring the fire bell could be the one who started the fire," Detective Cleveland said. "The only mistake we've made so far is letting you interview Scott Murphy alone. Let's bring him in."

"What are you bringing him in for? I have his statement right here."

Detective Cleveland ran a finger over his brow as he dismissed the account on the desk. "We need transportation. Where can we find mounts?"

"See Mayor Walters." Fowler buttoned up his shirt. "He has a nice horse he'll let you borrow if the money talks."

The pony? Perfect. Joel only hoped it was in a biting mood.

"I don't understand why we need to bring the boy in," Joel said. "He's not going to run. His family is here." But even as he said the words, a bubble in the pit of his stomach rumbled. What kind of a man left everything behind? Him.

Ignoring him, Detective Cleveland turned to Fowler. "Where's the man with the horses?"

"At the dry goods store just across the street. Tell him you want the lawman special, and he'll hook you up."

With a long last look at Joel, the two men left, leaning together to share their thoughts as they took out to the general store.

Fowler shook his massive head like it was a barrel of molasses. "We should've kept the Murphy boy with us instead of sending him home. Sounds like them fellows are intent on wrapping this up quick."

"The truth is the truth. Even they can't convict an innocent man."

"I wouldn't be so sure. They sure let a lot of guilty walk free."

"We have to trust in the process," Joel said.

"Looks like it's going to be a busy night," Fowler said.

Joel's blood quickened at the threat. "You are staying out of this."

"And let you handle it? Come on, Deputy. I don't think you really want that. You know Scott needs help—help you can't give because you're too bound by the law and all. But not us. We can accomplish more."

"Clive." Joel swallowed. "We've been through a lot here, and so far we've both treated each other fair, but listen when I tell you that you cannot get involved. Not unless you want a whole troop of soldiers breathing down your neck."

Fowler's face hardened. He was growing more and more

intense. "We have to intervene. Don't you see what they have planned? Sheriff Taney was shot. Scott says he shot someone. What conclusion do you think they're going to reach?"

Joel's mind had been dancing around that possibility ever since Scott told his story. Of course that was what they'd assume, but it was more complicated than that. Scott wouldn't burn down Hopkins's house. Scott wouldn't dress like a Bald Knobber.

Except he wanted to be one more than anything. Was there something more at work here? Was Scott telling the truth? What if the sheriff thought he was Fowler and tried to arrest him? What if Fowler wasn't telling the whole story?

He really, really didn't want to do what he was fixing to do, but he had no choice. Joel moved back a step. The chair bounced against him, and before it hit the floor, his pistol was in his hand.

"In the cell," he said.

Fowler raised his hands but eyed him coolly. "Don't be an idiot, Puckett. You want Scott safe as much as I do. We can get him out of here."

"I can't let you do that. Get in the cell."

"You aren't going to shoot me." Fowler lowered his hands with a nonchalance that was convincing. "I haven't done anything wrong."

"I will. I don't want to, but I will." He'd done it before, but not to someone he respected as much as Fowler. "I'll nick you, right in the kneecap or maybe the foot. Give you another scar to be proud of. Whatever it takes to save your life, because that Officer Harrison, he'd just as soon shoot you as eat his next meal. Get in the cell."

Fowler studied him, searching for weakness, but he found none. Joel believed what he said, and Pine Gap couldn't take another loss. Finally, fuming, Fowler went to the cell. Keeping his gun on him, Joel followed and locked the padlock.

"So you're going to offer them a sacrificial lamb, are you?" Fowler sneered. "Give them Scott and hope they go away?"

Joel didn't answer. Fowler wasn't voicing anything he wasn't afraid of already.

CHAPTER 38

What was going on? Her pa, Uncle Fred, and Scott had sailed past the house like they had a strong wind at their backs. They didn't even stop to explain to her and Sissy where they were going or when they'd return.

Bouncing a slobber-covered infant on her hip, Betsy rested her forehead against the windowpane. She was sick with worry. Sick with uncertainty. She wanted things to be right with Joel. She wanted to apologize over the Kansas City stories, but now she had an even bigger fear.

If only she could roll back the clock—before he knew about the articles, before she knew about the other woman—and enjoy his company. If only her thoughts of him could be unstained by guilt and untroubled by doubts. Were the accusations true? How well did she know Joel?

Sissy came in, drying her hands on a cheesecloth towel. "Dinnertime."

Betsy bit her lip. She really didn't want to give up her post. The town was smoldering. Any minute now a flame would flare up, and she wanted to be ready.

There. Down the hill, the two government men left the jail-house and turned for Mayor Walters's store. What were they up to now? And where was Fowler?

"Betsy?"

Betsy spun. There was Sissy. What was she doing? And how was it that Betsy happened to have a baby on her hip? "I'm sorry. What did you say?"

"I said, 'Let's eat.'"

"I'm not hungry." Betsy deposited the baby into her mother's arms. "Here, I've got to go."

"Betsy," Sissy warned, "you know how I feel . . ."

And living under her roof, Betsy was obliged to respect her wishes, but respect didn't mean she had to obey.

"I'm sorry, Sissy, but this is important. You have your kids and your family to take care of. This is my duty, just the same." While she didn't change any diapers, she felt as protective of her town as any mother. She'd do what she could to fix this mess.

Sissy hugged Eloise tight and fixed Betsy with that look that her own ma had used for years. Finally, with a sigh, she stepped out of the way. "You do what you think is right."

Betsy would. At least today. Although she had a hundred reasons for writing the Dashing Deputy stories, she'd never done it because it was the right thing to do. For profit, ambition, excitement—but when she put pen on paper, she was only thinking about pleasing the newspaper men. Now her actions had nothing to do with ambition. She didn't care who got the glory, she just wanted justice for Sheriff Taney, and Fowler, and now . . . even Joel. No matter what had happened in Texas, Joel was their best chance for peace. If he needed help, she would do what she could.

She'd promised him that she wouldn't get involved, and that

was the only thing that kept her from skirting town and following the government men. Instead, she'd be up-front and ask Joel flat out if there was anything she could do to help. If he said no, then she reckoned she'd be back in the kitchen watching Sissy's babies for the rest of the night.

Not even taking time to grab the nearest coat, Betsy hurried out the door. But she wasn't going to the jailhouse, because Joel was on the road, walking toward her.

He was probably just passing by. Trying to start his work before she could interfere. The sun's rays came down from the south, shining beneath the brim of his hat. His mouth was set and his thoughts were miles away. Seeing him after she'd disappointed him made her shy. Obviously he wasn't looking for her. Maybe she'd ease back inside and save herself the embarrassment—

"Betsy."

She rocked in place. The wind pierced through her blouse and made her shiver. Had he been coming to her? Finally daring a look, she found him watching her, eyes wary and shoulders squared.

"I don't want to upset you," he said, "but there's something you need to know."

Betsy clasped her hands over her heart. Was she ready to hear his tale right here? In the middle of the street? "I've heard, but I'm waiting for your side of the story. I promise I won't be angry as long as you tell me the truth."

Joel looked up and down the road. His forehead wrinkled beneath his hat. He stepped closer and asked with a lowered voice, "Why would I lie to you? I just wanted you and Sissy to know before we come back with Scott in custody."

"What?" Another shot of cold air blasted through Betsy, making her lungs feel like chunks of ice. Had he lost his mind?

"What does Scott have to do with the woman in Texas and you losing your job?"

"Who told you that?"

Layer after layer of confusion. "Detective Cleveland had a lot of questions about you. Questions about you taking, you know . . . liberties?"

Joel's face disappeared for a moment while he studied the ground.

Betsy's unease grew. "What's this about Scott?"

He lifted his eyes, and the pain she saw scared her. "Fred and your pa brought Scott in this morning. Scott says he shot a man. It sounds like self-defense, but those detectives are bringing him in for more questioning."

Betsy shook her head. "Scott wouldn't shoot someone."

"It was the same night Taney was shot. Hopefully it was Taney's attacker that he got, but the officers have other ideas."

The officers? It was too much to take in. Betsy cast a nervous look at the cabin. "Sissy doesn't know."

"And maybe she shouldn't. Not yet. But I wanted you to know." There it was again—that wounded expression that meant he had cared so much about her but didn't anymore.

"What can I do?" Betsy asked. "You know I'll go crazy sitting at home and worrying about him."

"That's why I'm telling you," said Joel. "I don't expect you to sit at home. The government men have my hands tied, but I'd like another set of eyes out there. Someone I can trust to tell me the truth without prejudice."

The word *trust* stung like a wasp. "I'll do it right. You are the only one I'll report to."

He looked at her long and hard. "If they told you that I was fired for compromising a lady, why are you talking to me?"

She pushed a stray lock of hair behind her ear. "I've made

a mistake recently, and I'm learning how hard it is to make amends. If there's anything I'd like to see more of around here, it's mercy."

"Aren't you afraid it's true?"

She would be honest with him, no matter the consequences. "I'm terrified. If it is, then I've lost . . ." She searched for the words. "After writing those articles, I have no claim to your friendship, but I have the idea of you—brave, honorable, just. That's what I want to hold on to, even if I lose everything else."

They stood there with the cold winter wind driving between them. Both of them hurt, both looking to the other for comfort but knowing that they had miles to cover before any could be found.

"Those lawmen," Betsy said. "They found horses."

Or at least partial horses. True to his nature, good Mayor Walters had given them the least he could and probably took top dollar. Officer Harrison balanced on the ill-tempered pony, nearly jostling out of the saddle with each of its tiny steps. Detective Cleveland looked elegantly bored, or as bored as you could appear on a mule. Headed toward the jail, they didn't see Joel.

Joel's chest stretched with a sigh. "I have to go. Be careful."

Scott needed her. Everyone needed her. And she had Joel's blessing.

"You be careful, too," she said. Before he could leave, she stopped him. "Joel?"

"Yes."

"I'm sorry for hiding my stories from you. I knew better. And I don't know how you happened to be here, but I'm glad you are. God put you here for a reason."

He reached up to hold onto the badge pinned to his vest.

His fingers tapped against the metal. "Thank you. I guess it's time to see exactly what that reason is."

The coast was finally clear. Joel and the lawmen had headed out of town, and she was going to follow, but no sooner had her boot hit the hard-packed dirt of the road than a shrill whistle broke goosebumps out on her skin. Betsy spun toward the jail, where it was coming from. Long, wavering, and high—it was human, but just barely.

As if orchestrated by a choir director, doors opened up and down the street. Men with their napkins tucked into their collars, some holding a bowl, others pushing their wives and children back inside as they closed the door behind them and sent questioning gazes to their neighbors. Another whistle, and they began to move. Cautiously at first, but with more ease once they joined in the street, ignoring the dark looks of the men who opted to go back to their hearth with their family and wait out whatever mischief occurred.

What was calling them all to the jailhouse? Joel wasn't there. Betsy bit her lip even as she skirted around to the wooded path that led to the back of the jail. By the time she'd crept past the door of the jailhouse, the meeting was in full swing. Who'd have ever thought the Bald Knobbers would conduct their business right in the jailhouse?

"They can't take Scott in." She couldn't exactly place the voice, but it sounded like a middle-aged man. That narrowed it down to three or four townspeople who lived close enough to answer the call. "Even if he wasn't a Bald Knobber proper, we stick together. The boy didn't burn Hopkins's house."

"They're out for blood." That was Fowler, no doubt. "They want to blame one of us for shooting the sheriff, and they've got a confused young man on their hands. Now, Fred Murphy has never been one of us, but he's a fine fellow, no doubt." Agreement murmured around. "And Scott's heart is in the right place. Had we not turned him away that night, he wouldn't be in this mess, so I don't know about you'uns, but I feel honor bound to defend the boy."

Betsy wrapped her arms around her stomach as she balanced, crouching against the wall. Scott must be saved, but at what cost? How obligated were you to intervene when justice was running amok? When others were abusing their power, how far could you break the rules to stop them? She feared what chaos Fowler's orders would bring, but without his intervention, what could befall? She had no way of stopping the men, but she knew Joel would want her here. He wanted her to be his eyes and ears while he was otherwise occupied.

"We could get you out of there," someone said. "If we tied rope to the bars, we could pull it out of the floor."

Betsy covered her mouth. Was Fowler in jail? Pieces began to fall into place. Of course Clive would've tried to warn Scott. Of course he wouldn't let strangers ride out of town to arrest him. And what had Joel done? Same thing he'd done to her that night at the gang's meeting. Well, not exactly the same, but Deputy Puckett needed to get over this habit of tying up his friends. It really spoke poorly of his social aptitudes.

"You don't need me," Fowler said. "You'uns have every right to ride tonight, but seeing how I was put under arrest . . . well, let's not give them more cause. So get your hoods, get your horses, and ride to Huckabee's place. No bloodshed, but we can't let Scott fall into their hands. Help him disappear."

She remained with her back to the wall as they surged out. Voices thinned as they headed home to gear up and go, which was precisely what she would be doing as well. She already had

Scott's britches, but she needed to borrow Pritchard's hood once more. She knew where Joel kept his confiscated masquerade pieces, and locked up, Fowler couldn't stop her either. She would borrow Isaac's horse again, and she could ride with the posse . . . or in this case, the outlaws.

Sometimes it was hard to tell the two apart.

CHAPTER 39

"I'll take responsibility for his whereabouts. I'll even stay here at the house if that's what you want. Just don't lock him up. It's uncalled for." Fred pushed his glasses up on his forehead, which was slick with sweat.

Joel leaned against the doorframe of the log cabin, his arm propped above his head. With a gesture, he declined Mrs. Huckabee's offer of coffee. She moved on to the next man, undoubtedly thinking the same thing Joel was—that arresting Scott was over-reaching and calculated.

Detective Cleveland, usually so alert, hadn't seemed too interested in anything Scott said but had merely rushed him through his account, taking no notes at all. Now he seemed to be done with the whole exercise and didn't give Joel's suggestions about Bullard any credibility. They'd made up their minds that Scott was somehow involved in a larger conspiracy long before they heard his testimony. They'd been sent to investigate Joel, but if they could wrap up an arson and assault on a sheriff, then that'd be another star in their crown. And if they couldn't bag Fowler, Scott made an easy sack.

Officer Harrison fought against a yawn and lost. He took another drink of his coffee and with a casualness that had to break Fred's heart, gave his verdict. "The boy is a confessed criminal. Criminals belong in jail."

Fred's inky hands tensed, but the strangers didn't seem to notice. Mrs. Huckabee, whose bright eyes and sure gestures recalled her daughter, turned her back on Detective Cleveland, ignored his outstretched hand, and tossed the coffee into the basin.

Scott looked sickly, but he was true to his raisings. He stood. "Aunt Irma has my laundry done. Let me get a clean shirt." He squeezed his aunt's shoulder as he passed and left the kitchen to go to the loft in the low-ceilinged cabin.

For the first time in his life, Joel began to contemplate the consequences of doing something illegal. He didn't trust these men. But surely the detective would be content with a fair trial. Joel had to lecture himself with the same stern warning he'd give Fred as he watched his son be hustled off to jail—trust the process, truth will prevail, an innocent man has nothing to fear. But hadn't his own experience proven that wrong? Expediency coupled with a chance to further a career had convicted a host of innocent men.

"People are coming," Calbert said. He stood and frowned at the window.

People? More than one? All Joel saw was trees, but then from the shadows emerged the horrifying but familiar shape of horned men on horses. Proof that Clive Fowler had not been idle in his threats.

"What the devil?" Officer Harrison shuddered. The detective's throat jogged as he reached beneath his coat and loosened his gun.

Joel stretched a restraining arm across them. "Don't shoot. Likely they've come to talk."

"People don't need masks to have a conversation." A line of sweat ran down Detective Cleveland's neck.

"Stay inside." Joel pushed away from the window. "And don't you dare fire. I'm the law here, and I'll have your neck faster than the wire can tap out the message to Jeff City."

He didn't favor talking down the mob, but if bullets started flying, he wouldn't have a beetle's chance in a chicken coop of getting out unscathed.

Dear Lord, would he have the words to say? Would he have the wisdom to see everything through this encounter without more pain and more consequences? He knew he couldn't do it, but God could. If only Joel could hear Him over the roaring of his own worries and inadequacies.

The doorknob was ice in his hand. He turned it and slid one hand out, palm up, before stepping gingerly into the open. The door swung wider, exposing his whole body to the gang's drawn weapons. Slowly, he stepped forward and eased the door closed behind him. His throat jogged as the latch caught, leaving him cut off from any retreat. A slow scan showed that the whole gang had fallen out but with no giant at the lead. Fowler had remained in the cell.

"Who's in charge?" Joel scanned the crowd, their horses billowing steam in the frosty air. A few men he recognized, and then with a drop in his stomach, he caught sight of a familiar mask—the same one that'd been in his office for the last few weeks. Combined with the small size of the rider, he knew it had to be Betsy. He'd asked her to come along to observe, but it still shocked him to see her consorting with the vigilantes.

A slender man near the edge of the forest walked his horse forward. "We all want the same thing. We want Scott Murphy."

Joel's stomach dropped. A lynch mob? They didn't think Scott was guilty, did they? "What do you want the boy for?"

"To give him a chance," someone else hollered from the trees. "He didn't do anything wrong."

Joel prayed they were right, but he couldn't prove it. Not yet. "I understand why you'd think that," he said, "but I want to do what's best for the kid. The law says we've got to investigate what happened, and if the state decides to have a trial, then that's what we'll do."

Murmurs rose like an angry wind through dry leaves. Horses shifted nervously. Clouds of ill will were forming over the group. Again Joel held out his hand. "Let's say I let you take him. Then what?"

"Then he'd be free and wouldn't be accountable to those men who know nothing about what's happening here."

The city lawmen were getting a sharp education if they were still watching out the window. But this wasn't the lesson Joel wanted them to learn. He was surprised to find that he wanted them to respect these mountaineers. He wanted them to see that, although acting against the letter of the law, these men cared about their community and their neighbors. That was what they were doing this for. And if Joel could appeal to that care, then maybe he had a chance of convincing them to disperse without bloodshed.

"Yes, you could spirit Scott away—away from his home, his family—and then what? Would he really be free? Knowing that his name was besmirched and that somewhere on the trail behind him he was considered guilty, would that be free?"

"It's better than being locked up or hung." The slender man's hood moved over his mouth, muffling his words. "And we won't let that happen to him. He's innocent. We're the ones who went after Bullard, not Scott. If Sheriff insists on pointing a finger at Fowler, then let Fowler take the blame. And those are Fowler's words. We won't let this boy hang when we were the ones hunting for revenge."

Brave words from a masked man. Joel stepped out toward the

edge of the porch, leaving the protection of the shadows. "If you truly believe he's innocent, then why are you afraid of a trial?"

"Because we've seen how these courts run," hollered a man next to Betsy. She shied away as he continued. "Enough talking. Bring him out. We've lived here long enough to know there's no justice but what you find for yourself."

A handful of men began to dismount. Joel was running out of time. If they breached the door, Detective Cleveland and Officer Harrison would open fire. And then what about Fred and Mr. and Mrs. Huckabee inside? He had to convince the gang that no matter what they feared, hiding Scott away would not solve their problems.

"Stop right there." This time Joel forgot he was outnumbered. His words carried all the authority he'd ever earned, borrowed, or pretended to have during his six paltry years of law enforcement. "You can't take Scott. You can't hide him, because the day will come when he regrets leaving without clearing his name. Every day he'll regret it. I know, because that's what I live with."

He threw a nervous glance toward Betsy. He hadn't expected his shameful story to reach her, but it had, and she hadn't given up on him. She was there, head tilted, listening closely. He'd rather broach this subject with her alone, minus the burlap sack over her face, but right now the telling might make a difference to more than Betsy and him.

"Y'all have asked why in the world I'd leave Texas to come to Pine Gap. Well, it's not because I wanted to. It's because I had to. You see, I got accused by a young woman of being too familiar. It wasn't true, not a bit of it, but everyone figured that the easiest thing to do was for me to just marry her, and that'd be the end of it. No one wanted me to make a fuss. They just wanted the whole question to go away. So that was my choice—either marry her and by doing so forever be branded guilty, or leave so I could avoid the penalty of the accusations. I only wished someone would've counseled me that there was another choice. That I could fight the charges. I could stand tall and dispute her account and clear my name. But that was risky. I was promised safety and another chance at being a sheriff if I would go. So I fled."

Talking to a row of gunny sacks wasn't inspiring. Still, his story rolled out of his heart and echoed off the hills. Soon he'd feel relieved that it'd been released, but the shame hadn't lifted yet. "Every day I regret not defending myself. Every day I wish I had stood at the town square and let everyone know that I was not the man that woman accused me of being. Instead I left. I abandoned my home. It's lost to me. My friends know I'm innocent, but besides my parents, I couldn't even tell people where I had gone."

He searched the crowd. Their guns were lowered. Several scratched at their hoods. The tone had cooled.

"Don't do that to Scott," he said. "You aren't helping him by hiding him. He's a young man, a good boy. He doesn't want to spend the rest of his life avoiding the very part of the world that means the most to him."

With no leader, the gang didn't know what to do. They circled up, leaning forward on their horses to hear the verdict. Only then did Joel realize how tight his fists were. He stretched his fingers as the group broke their knot and a designated chief spoke up.

"You promise he'll get a fair trial?"

"As much as it's in my power." And he meant it.

"That's not saying much."

Behind him the hinges squawked and Fred stepped outside. "Gentlemen, I appreciate this show for my son, but the deputy is right. I can't let you take him. We're going to see him through this, and when it's over, we'll know we done the right thing."

And that seemed to be the last word.

Sensing that their rescue had no purpose if even Fred refused to turn Scott loose, the masked men peeled away a few at a time and blended into the forest. All but one stubborn little figure, who waited behind the brush pile.

Calbert Huckabee came out to the porch. "Seems like that Bald Knobber looks very familiar at this homestead—lot like a little girl I had borned and raised here."

And she was still there, even after hearing his story. Joel dug his toe into the porch. "Reckon I should go see what she wants?"

"Reckon so." Calbert patted him on the shoulder and returned inside.

Chapter 40

At first, Betsy had been rooting for the Bald Knobbers to free Scott. The threat of a trial terrified her, but Joel was right. If Scott ran, the charges would never be lifted. His name would always bear the smudge of suspicion. She wouldn't wish that on her enemy, yet that was what Joel lived under. And he wasn't her enemy—not at all—but the man she loved.

To be banished from home. To leave behind a bad reputation and unanswered questions. Betsy's heart ached for Joel. When she first met him that night at Mrs. Sanders's house, he'd acted bitter, cold, and now she knew the reason. How else had that ordeal injured him?

Joel stood beneath the cover of her parents' porch as the other riders vanished back into the woods. How hurt he must have been. How outraged that his precious character had been shredded with no hearing, no evidence, none of the process of justice that he cared so much for. And because of Betsy and her stories about a flirtatious deputy, his character had been attacked again. Now all of Pine Gap knew. An innocent man was living in the shadows of guilt, and it was because of her.

Tears streamed down her face. Suddenly the heavy fabric of her mask was suffocating. She tugged the front away from her face, bringing it tight against the back of her neck. Everyone else was headed the other way, back through the woods, but she couldn't get to Joel fast enough. He had to know how sorry she was, how she wanted to make it up to him. She slid off her horse and stumbled forward, losing sight of him. The harsh twine around the base of the mask was rough against her fingers. In her hurry she must've tied it into double-triple knots, and now it seemed impossible to undo. She bumped into a tree, ricocheting deeper into the forest where she'd spent her youth.

Grunting in frustration, she stopped at a new sound—boots rustling through dry leaves. Her arms were grasped, warm hands on both shoulders stopping her scrabbling at the mask. She cried out as the twine was snapped and the burlap trap was removed.

Cold air stung the tear tracks on her cheeks. Betsy lifted her hand to sweep the hair out of her face, but Joel was there first, his fingers sure as they pushed back the locks that had escaped from her braid. The sorrow on his face, the uncertainty, wrung her heart—as if his life depended on her reaction. She grasped his leather vest, sliding her fingers into the front pocket to hold on and share his warmth.

"I'm sorry," she said.

His eyes darted over her face, beseeching. "She'd plotted the whole thing. Thought I'd marry her, but I couldn't. I couldn't have a wife who would lie to me. I couldn't marry someone I didn't trust."

Betsy's grip on his vest tightened at his words. What did that mean for her? Was all hope gone for them?

But this wasn't about her. Joel was hurting. "I know the man you are. I shouldn't have given it a second thought. But to think what she did to you, and here she is, trying to ruin your life even further. . . ." Her head dropped. "I'm sorry for what you went through, and that I stirred it all up again. There has to be a way to fix this."

Joel drew in a deep breath and covered her hand with his own. "I thought she'd ruined my life, but if that hadn't happened, I would've never met you. I'm where I need to be."

She looked up at him. Could he forgive her? Could they truly start over? She tightened her grip on his pocket, and he kept her hand covered, protecting it from the chilling air. The scent of leather enveloped her in this warm cocoon that even the bitter wind couldn't pierce. If she didn't know better, she'd say that he wanted to reconcile as much as she did.

When he'd first arrived, he was the most handsome man she'd ever seen, but his looks were nothing compared to the earnest character he possessed—a character that would never be satisfied until the ghosts of the past had been laid to rest. But Betsy could only solve one significant problem at a time.

"There's something you can do for me," Joel said. "Something that will make this all better."

She wanted to hear it more than anything in the world, but hearing it would change everything. "What?"

His throat bounced as he swallowed. He tested his grip on her waist and shifted his weight. A little clearing of his throat, and then he was finally ready to make his request.

"Keep an eye on Fred and Sissy. They've got a tough row to hoe."

Betsy blinked. She pulled her hand free from his and shoved him to get away. "Take care of Fred and Sissy? That's all I can do to make you happy? That's all you can think of?"

Honestly, would the man ever come up with a hero-worthy statement?

His mouth curled into a smile and his eyes crinkled with amusement. "If you're willing to do more . . ."

"I'm not willing. I'm not." She stalked deeper into the woods, Joel hot on her heels. "Of course I'll take care of them. What do you think I was doing today?" She spun around to wave a dramatic arm in his face. "Scott is my cousin. I raised him, for crying aloud. But when you started talking about that woman in Texas and how . . . well, don't you worry about the Murphys. I'll take care of the Murphys."

Joel caught her by the wrist, which was swinging at a fair height. He pulled her into his arms, and with the kindest eyes that'd ever pierced her heart, asked, "But who's going to take care of me?"

Words were rolling around in her head too fast for her to make sense of Joel's question. She still had a bushelful of insults to rain down on him for leading her along, and here he was trying to make love to her again. "If you're fixing to tie me to this tree, then just do it," she said. "You're big enough to push me around. You don't need my cooperation."

"You said you'd do anything, and it seems you're insulted that I didn't ask enough. Well, I won't make that mistake twice." Still holding her wrist, he dropped to one knee. His smile disappeared and he looked as if he were watching for signs of a quick draw. "Betsy Huckabee, there'll be some who question my integrity, 'specially after I just spilled my guts to every man in town, but if you're willing to weather the scandal at my side, then I'd be honored if you'd be my wife."

She could feel her face growing warmer by the heartbeat. "Are you insane? You have a house full of detectives behind you. You best get up."

"No." He brought her hand to his mouth and planted a long, lingering kiss on the back of it. Awareness raced up her arm and did funny things to her belly. "No. I have to go back in that house and deal with something I can't bear to do alone.

Only knowing that you'll be waiting to see me again, waiting to be mine, will carry me through this. I'm not getting up until I have your answer."

Married to him? Her? Married? To this dashing, handsome Texas deputy? They would live together. Eat together. Have . . . all the other stuff married people had. For being a mature woman, she hadn't spent much time percolating over all that would entail. All she knew was that she couldn't give him up.

"I'll do it," she said at last. "For Scott. And partially to save your life, if you really think you'd be unable to survive without me."

One eyebrow raised. "You are a true civil servant, my lady." He rose to his feet. "As long as we're both in agreement that your affections are not involved in the least."

Again he was standing toe-to-toe with her. Again he was making her pulse race just below his warm touch. "What do affections have to do with it?" she squeaked.

"Maybe nothing for you, but I'm afraid I'm besotted. So whatever excuse you need to tell yourself doesn't matter to me, because you will love me. Just give me a little time, and you won't be able to help yourself."

Like she couldn't help the way the gravity of his nearness was tugging her closer? As if reading her mind, he wrapped her in his arms and pulled her against him. "My wife." His mouth hovered just above hers. "I never heard anything sound so sweet."

And sweet was plentiful at that moment.

He kissed her once, a solid, hearty kiss that strengthened her for what lay ahead. Her fears were real, but so was the hope that together they'd find Taney's attacker and clear Scott's name.

CHAPTER 41

The hinges on the cell squawked. Fowler marched out, dwarfing the men in their fancy clothes as he passed. Officer Harrison could've let Scott walk into the other cell on his own, but maybe dragging him by the arm made him feel big. Whatever the reason, Joel's teeth ground as the cell clanged shut.

Keeping the lawmen in the corner of his gaze, Fowler spoke. "What exactly is the boy accused of? Shooting a Bald Knobber?"

Detective Cleveland sat in Joel's chair and rummaged through his desk until he produced a sheet of writing paper. "The boy burned down Newton Hopkins's house. When Sheriff Taney caught him doing further mischief, Murphy shot him rather than confess his involvement with the arson."

Unfortunately, Scott had been out hunting the night Hopkins's house burned. Calbert Huckabee had dearly regretted not being able to provide an alibi for the boy.

The jailhouse door swung open, and the gray-headed postmaster stepped inside. "Telegram for the deputy."

Joel had seen more life in the eyes of a stone-dead lizard. "Is this about Bullard?"

"I hope you're satisfied with the answer." Finley threw the telegram on the desk and slammed the door behind him as he left.

"That's right," Fowler said. "You'uns are blaming the boy and neglecting the fact that we have a killer prowling about."

"Not anymore." Joel lowered the paper. "It's from Hot Springs. Bullard was shot there two weeks ago in a robbery attempt. His Arkansas kin identified him."

"Two weeks? Then he didn't set fire to the doctor's house, either?" Fowler wiped his mouth as he cut a nervous look at Scott.

Joel blinked twice, then focused on the message again, making sure there was no mistake. But the words were clear.

Could it be that Scott had shot the sheriff? But why would Taney put a knife to Scott's throat? Or was that a lie, too?

Sissy's tears had finally come, and they'd lasted all night. Hearing that her stepson had been arrested and accused of masquerading as a Bald Knobber only justified every fear she'd ever harbored against the gang. No matter how Uncle Fred pleaded with her, he could not convince her that Scott hadn't been involved with Fowler's men. She cried, she mourned, but she was convinced that the poor boy had been led astray by the troublemakers, and now he would pay for all their iniquities.

"Keep her away from the detective," Betsy warned Uncle Fred over the latest innocuous edition of the *Hart County Herald*. "Tell everyone she has scarlet fever or something, because you can't let her talk to people in this condition."

"She's just upset." He cranked down the bar, pressing the platen against the inked type blocks. "She loves Scott, and that's why she's taking it so hard. She's afraid for him. If only the district attorney would let us know whether he'll stand trial or not. Then we could breathe again."

Well, Betsy was even more afraid of what would happen if

her aunt didn't stop blaming Fowler for dragging the boy into delinquency. Sissy had let the fears fester for so long, they were blown-up out of all reasonability now. Didn't she understand that accusations against Fowler only made Scott look guiltier?

Betsy had just bent over the third page of type she was setting for that week's edition when Joel blew in. The combination of the frigid air and his general presence made her shiver. He doffed his cowboy hat, displaying a knit skullcap that made him look less like a hardened lawman and more like a mischievous schoolboy. Betsy bit her lip. He allowed a trace of amusement to cross his face.

"It's from Mrs. Sanders. She noticed my clothes weren't stout enough for winter here. Got me some fleece-lined gloves, too." He held up his hand and wiggled his fingers.

"I should've thought of that," Betsy said. "There's been so much going on."

"I wanted you to know that Scott's doing fine this morning," Joel said. Then with a weighty look toward Fred, he asked, "How's the family?"

"We're holding on," Fred said, never breaking his rhythm at the press. Getting the paper out was his livelihood, even if nothing printed in its pages mattered a jot to him. "My mind keeps going over the same questions, trying to figure out how I can help him. It would've been much simpler if we could've proven that Bullard did this."

"We're missing something," Joel said. "In fact, I came to see if Betsy would ride with me. I want to examine that ravine again, and where we found Taney."

"You want me to come?" Betsy asked.

Joel nodded, then looked to Uncle Fred.

"If it could help Scott," he said.

Betsy held up a finger, requesting a moment, and then dug

through the hooks on the wall to find a complementary set of outerwear rather than just grabbing something. She covered her mouth and nose with a scarf she'd knitted herself one summer before she'd left home, the last bit of clothing she'd ever made with her mother, although frequent packages came from home to keep her in clothes.

How happy her ma had been at Joel's proposal. It was a crying shame they couldn't celebrate proper, but once Scott was free, they'd do it up right.

But there was still something unresolved, something that would shadow their happiness, and while Betsy knew it didn't possess the power to dislodge her affections, it was better to air it all out. In true journalistic fashion, Betsy would rather know all the facts than be left to speculate.

Joel mounted his horse and motioned to the borrowed one he had saddled for her. He didn't have to wait for her to lead, she noticed. How easily he'd become accustomed to the winding paths and trails.

Once they'd left town behind, they were free to speak.

"So Bullard is dead?" Betsy asked. "Then he can't be a suspect for the Hart County crimes."

"We have Scott and we have Taney, but we have to find the third man," Joel said. "Otherwise, Detective Cleveland has decided that if it's between Scott and Sheriff Taney, he figures Sheriff Taney is the victim and Scott's to blame. Even Scott's injury and the knife your pa found haven't convinced him that Scott was attacked. I'm afraid nothing's going to prove it to him."

"But if only Taney and Scott were there that night, why would Sheriff Taney hurt Scott?" she said. "Did Taney think that Scott was Bullard?"

"I've wondered that. And then instead of admitting his mistake, he swears that Fowler attacked him? Both Scott and Taney swear they were attacked by a Bald Knobber, so who was the man in the mask?"

Betsy had been over the conundrum dozens of times and still had no answers. But someone did have answers to another issue she'd been curious about. Unable to hold it in any longer, she blurted, "Tell me about Miss Blount."

His horse stumbled. "What do you want to know?" he asked.

"Everything."

She'd decided to believe him, decided that this woman had lied about him, but at the same time, she knew that she'd always wonder, always fear that some undisclosed, unsavory news would emerge. Even now her innards clutched, not sure she was going to like what she heard.

"I reckon that's your right," Joel said. They continued around the mountain toward the ravine as Joel started his story. "Back home, I didn't much care for the girls in town. I wanted to be a lawman. That's all I ever wanted, and that's all I had time for, much to my ma's consternation. I did a fair job at scaring all the girls away, but one day Mary up and appointed herself as my handler. She pretended to shield me from the girls trying to get my attention. I didn't need her to do that, so I mostly just ignored her."

"Was she vulgar? Unladylike?"

"No, just persistent. And counterfeit. I'd sit on the porch of the hotel for half an hour and not say a word. If I cleared my throat, she'd hoot and carry on like I'd said something hilarious. Didn't take long to grow tired of that." His voice slowed. "I was at the jail with Sheriff Green when we got word that a buggy had been overturned out by the river. It was nearly dark, but I set out to check on them. When I got there, sure enough, it was Mary's buggy, and she was left stranded."

Betsy's head popped up. "Wait a minute. Who told you it was overturned? Why didn't they bring her back?"

"Good questions I should've asked at the onset. When I got there, I thought she was alone, but her brother stood up from behind the buggy. I got off my horse and walked around the wagon to see if there was anything to use as leverage and get it right-side up again. As I was scouring the banks of the river, I heard a horse. It was mine, and it was leaving." The last words were spoken through grinding teeth.

"Go on," she said.

"Mary laughed, like it was a joke, but it wasn't no joke to me. A deputy losing his horse is a serious matter, but what was I supposed to do? Shoot her brother? If I'd known what they had in mind, I don't think I would've regretted doing it." He ran a hand over his face. "That's how I came to be stuck all night with her. We could've walked to town and made it before morning, but she refused to even try. And then the next day . . . well, you can imagine how it went. She and her pa were at the sheriff's office, insisting that his deputy had compromised a young lady."

"Didn't they believe you?"

"It didn't matter. All I had to do was marry her, which is what she was after all along, and the problem would go away—protect my honor and her reputation. Sheriff Green was running for re-election and didn't want a stink. Everyone thought that was the simplest solution."

"Everyone?"

"Even my mother. She was furious with Mary and her brother, but she thought me tying the knot was long overdue. It's no surprise she saw this as her best chance."

Betsy's eyes narrowed. "It's hard to believe she'd do that out of the blue. Did you talk all sweet to her, or . . . ?"

"Like I did to you?" He rode closer. His leg brushed against hers. "Think, Betsy. What did I say when we first met? I told you to leave me alone. I told you that I didn't want to talk to any women because I feared for my reputation. Remember that?"

"You weren't very friendly, I do recall."

"And this is why. Her accusations drew questions about my character and affected my job, but anything I said to defend myself was seen as unchivalrous toward a lady. I couldn't win for losing."

"I can't imagine how frustrating that was for you." She let her eyes linger as some of the angst melted off his face.

"You don't blame me?"

"Not at all. Especially since I'm the one who informed her of your whereabouts."

"Wait." Joel stopped on the road. A mischievous glint danced in his eyes. "The Dashing Deputy articles were distributed in Fort Worth, right?" His gaze settled somewhere on the horizon. He already knew she was to blame, so what was bothering him now? "I wonder how many people in Garber read about my brooding eyes and strong jaw. How many could tell I'd stolen the heart of the famous E. M. Buckahee?"

Betsy reined her horse into his, pretending to smash his legs, but it was only an excuse to bump against him.

Joel tsked. "Assaulting a deputy. Gonna have to write you up for that." But instead he caught her hand. Would he still want to hold it after she shared her opinion?

Betsy tightened her grip. "Joel?"

"Mm-hmm?"

"I can't help but think that you need to go back to Texas."

His face tightened. "I can't. If I want to be a deputy and someday a sheriff, there's no reason to go back."

"But you miss Texas and your family. And there's your name to clear. Like you said about Scott—"

"We're here," he interrupted.

His brow was troubled. Betsy didn't like it. She didn't like there being anything in the world that could disturb her man like that, but for the time being, she had to set it aside.

First they had a problem that was closer to home.

CHAPTER 42

The wind whistled above them like a lonesome banshee look-ing for a place to rest. Joel's boot splashed in a puddle at the bottom of the ravine. The jagged rocks and broken tree limbs made the place feel like a valley of the shadow of death, even if no one had died there. With all the debris and boulders, a body could've been lost down there, which was why he'd come back despite Calbert's claim to have checked it. Now he was here again, but this time he was looking for some-thing smaller. Something that both Scott and Sheriff Taney had mentioned—a Bald Knobber's mask that'd been worn by their assailant.

Betsy scrambled over the rocks and thrust a stick into dark crevices. "It hasn't rained enough to wash anything away," she said, "unless there was rain up on the mountain."

"We'll go downstream a bit, just in case."

He didn't know what finding the mask would prove, just that he had to do something for Scott. Scott was a good kid—in fact, he'd soon be family—and Joel couldn't let this mistake ruin his life.

"I've got something!" Betsy called.

Joel turned to see her with one arm swallowed up by a hole in the ground. Her head was turned and she squinted against the sharp branches that guarded the den.

"Get your hand out of there," he ordered. "You're going to get bit."

"It's almost free." Her eyes widened. "There!" Slowly she pulled her arm out of the hole to produce a battered piece of burlap.

With two horns.

"Some animal wanted it for its nest." Betsy shook it out straight. Clumps of mud sloughed off as she straightened one of the horns. "This mask is different from the others. Look."

Joel's mind spun as he took the mask from Betsy. It wasn't like Fowler's hood. Like Betsy'd said, it was different, and different from Pritchard's, too. This mask wasn't painted in the same way, and the horns were stuffed, not solid like the others. Someone hadn't gone to Bald Knobbers' Academy and learned how to fashion the hoods in the correct manner.

"The others have horns made of cork," Joel said.

"I remember back when I was a pup, everyone would sit on their porches of the evening and whittle on them," Betsy said.

Joel pushed his hand up the neck of the mask and jammed his fingers into the cone. He pulled out a handful of its stuffing.

"That's not the work of any seamstress." Betsy leaned over him for a better look. "Those horns are pathetic. What all is stuffed in there?"

"Feathers." Joel sent a dozen gray feathers floating in the air. "But it looks like they started with cloth scraps before they resorted to tearing up their tick."

Betsy tilted her head. "Let me see. Maybe I'll recognize a pattern from a shirt or dress." But the material didn't look like anything a woman would sew with. Burlap, canvas, and more feathers spilled out as the horn grew softer and emptier. "A bachelor," she said. "Nothing feminine . . . except for this." The worn red velvet was bunched into a tight ball. Betsy tried to straighten it, but it sprang back into its wrinkled form. She rubbed the material between her finger and thumb. "Who would have a dress made of this?"

"Mrs. Rinehart or Abigail Calhoun?" Joel suggested. "But you'd know better than I."

"Not Abigail. I've snooped through her wardrobe and trunks since I was little. And if she got something new, I'd know it. Mrs. Rinehart orders everything from the catalog, so it is possible, but I don't think she'd keep something this worn. She'd throw it out at the first sign of wear."

"So not a dress. Do men wear velvet here?"

"Maybe it's not clothing," Betsy said. "A pillow, or a lining?" She continued to rub the material between her fingers.

Joel had seen it before. He tried placing it in different settings. Was it in Walters's dry goods store? No. A cushion at Mrs. Sanders's? No. Some kind of lining. It was in a box . . .

"A banjo case," he blurted.

Betsy's brow furrowed. "A banjo?"

Suddenly the outlaw that attacked Scott had a definite identity. The pieces of the stories began to fall in place.

"There's only one person I know in town who has a banjo," she said. "Are you sure that's where it's from?"

"Unfortunately, yes." There wasn't a third man, after all. Just a scared boy and a crooked sheriff.

"Why would he do this?" Betsy began pacing, and despite her question, she seemed intent to answer it herself. "I bet it was just killing Sheriff Taney that they replaced him. He couldn't let you win. He needed outrage so people wouldn't trust you.

Everyone loves Doctor Hopkins, and burning his house was the worst thing he could do."

"He blamed Fowler for causing him to lose his job, so he framed the Bald Knobbers wherever he could to prove that I wasn't up to the task. Went around dressed like one of them, doing mischief."

"But Scott caught him," Betsy said. "Scott shot him, and Taney fell in the ravine."

Joel nodded. "That's why he looked so beat up, falling through the brush and rocks. But he managed to climb out before he got too weak. Which is why we found him up the trail."

"You don't think he would've really killed Scott, do you? I can't imagine."

"Desperate men know no bounds. No telling what could've happened. We have to find him. He has to know we'll figure it out soon enough."

"I don't guess there's any chance you'd let me go with you." Betsy huddled inside her coat, maybe for the first time looking like she wanted him to say no.

"I'll get Officer Harrison and Detective Cleveland from Mrs. Sanders's before I head out. By the time we get to Taney's, they'll be caught up, but don't say anything to your uncle. We have to make sure word doesn't get around. We don't know who might be helping him."

Solving the case, finally knowing who the bad guy was—and most importantly, knowing that both Scott and Fowler weren't to blame—made Joel want to sing. And dance. With Betsy. But he swallowed down that thought. He had a job to do first.

"I'll be waiting for you to get back," she said. "But for now I'm dying to get a pen and paper and write about what we found out."

"Betsy . . ." he growled.

"I won't write about the case," she said. "Maybe I just need to fill a few pages with praise for my Dashing Deputy and how proud I am of him. That'd be okay, wouldn't it?"

"As long as it's for my eyes only. We're allowed to keep some of our story private, you know."

Was that a blush? It was hard to tell in the frosty air. But with a wink, she spun on her heel and started the climb out of the ravine.

Betsy paced the cabin, not sure what to do with herself. Uncle Fred and Sissy had gone to visit Scott at the jail again. The news that he'd soon be free nearly carved its way out of her throat and made its own announcement, but Betsy had persevered. And now there was nothing to do but keep Amelia and Eloise entertained until she heard from Joel.

Being a lawman's wife must taste like this—the metallic worry always in the back of her throat. How many hours would she spend pacing in front of a window, watching children play while dreading news that could change their lives and throw their future into jeopardy?

Betsy pounded the windowsill with a clenched fist. She'd do it every day if need be. Was life measured by the trouble you avoided, or by the obstacles you overcame? God had made her for trouble, equipped her for hardship. She'd do her share and then some. Most of all, she'd buttress the man who faced the dangers for all of them. He wouldn't do it alone. Not while she had blood pumping in her veins.

Uncle Fred and Sissy came up the hill, their breath turning white in the chilly evening air. Betsy gave the stew another stir, making sure nothing had stuck to the bottom of the kettle while she daydreamed. They were back earlier than she'd thought. She'd have to bite her tongue or she might let the news slip.

Sissy was crying again. Betsy bent to pick up Amelia, who'd thrown herself against Sissy's leg and bawled as if she hadn't seen her ma in months. Uncle Fred sat at the table and settled in as if content to stay there for years.

"You're back early." Betsy dished out a bowl of stew. The bowl clattered on the table in front of Uncle Fred.

"They're taking Scott to another jail." He pushed the bowl away. "They said he can't get a fair trial here, so he's going to Springfield."

Betsy lowered the spoon. Her eyes darted from Uncle Fred to Sissy. "Who took Scott?"

"Sheriff Taney. We tried talking him out of taking Scott on the trip himself. He looks awful."

Betsy dropped the spoon. She rushed to her uncle and clutched his sleeve. "Sheriff Taney came to the jail and took Scott? Is that what you're saying?"

Fred's face tightened. "I thought it odd that Joel wasn't there, or the Jeff City men, but Taney said it was urgent. He had the key to the cell and everything."

"No, no, no." Betsy pushed past her uncle, ran to the coat rack, and began fighting her way into her coat. This couldn't happen. She had to get help.

"Betsy, what's the matter?" Uncle Fred had her arm and wasn't about to let her slip away. No time for secrecy now.

"Taney is the one who attacked Scott. He staged the whole thing. He wanted Joel to fail, so he made like the Bald Knobbers were out of control, burning Hopkins's place and raising trouble. It was Taney wearing the mask."

Uncle Fred shook his head, but slowly understanding settled. He jumped up and ran out the door. Sissy collapsed on the bench with Amelia patting her, but Betsy couldn't stick around to comfort her. They had no time.

They had to catch Taney. Had to save Scott from Taney's devious plans. Where was Joel?

"I'm going to the sale barn for a horse," she hollered. They had to hurry.

But Uncle Fred knew which direction to run.

To Fowler.

Before Betsy could return with a horse, a clump of men seethed beneath the hanging oak. Most, if not all, had a hood in hand. Those with horses had familiar horns peeping out of the saddlebags. Fowler stood in their midst, stoking their outrage.

"He pretended to be us and burned down Hopkins's house?" one man exclaimed.

"We knew you didn't shoot him, boss. We knew he was lying."

"If he lays a finger on Scott Murphy——"

"He already hurt the boy. Did you see his neck?"

The sound of beating hooves raced toward them. Joel tore over the hill on his black horse, throwing clumps of soil behind him, and in his wake, the two city gentlemen tried to keep pace on their inferior mounts.

The crowd parted with barely enough time to give Joel safe passage to the front. The horse pawed the ground, unable to tether its spirit, while Joel kept the reins close to his chest.

"Sheriff Taney is missing," he said. "We suspect him——"

"We know already," Pritchard cried. "He took Scott."

Joel found her in the crowd. Betsy nodded. "He told Uncle Fred and Sissy that he had to take him to Springfield. They left fifteen minutes ago."

Even Officer Harrison understood that was no good.

"Here's what we're going to do," Fowler said. "We're going to divide up—"

"Wait!" Joel kept the men in sight, even as his horse paced and swayed, bellowing its eagerness to run again. "We don't need a group of masked vigilantes. We've had that. You've hidden your identity and robbed everyone in this town of knowing who to blame." The murmurs weren't friendly, but Joel raised his hand. "You've also robbed the town of knowing who to thank when they were helped. Hide your face and you miss out on the responsibility, but also on the blessing. Don't you think it's time the people here know their heroes?"

Detective Cleveland and Officer Harrison tried to squeeze into the group, but the men tightened around Joel as he continued.

"And look where the disguises have gotten you. They've shielded the guilty one and let him make accusations against honorable men. Isn't it time to take away the mask and let us see people for who they are?"

Pritchard was the first. He tossed his new hood against the base of the hanging oak. Then Mr. Rinehart. One by one, they threw the symbol of their heroism against the tree. Finally, Fowler tossed his crooked-horned sack.

"It won't be the same," he said.

"It'll be better," Joel promised. "Because what we need isn't a group of disguised men acting without accountability. We need a posse. We need people who say who they are, what they're going to do, and why. Those are the men we need to find Sheriff Taney."

"We got to catch him," Fowler roared.

"Find Scott," Uncle Fred hollered.

"Just like the Dashing Deputy!" Pritchard yelled, much to Betsy's chagrin. When had he gotten hold of a paper?

"When you find them, fire two shots to let us know." Joel's eyes flashed. "We'll come running to help."

And with that, they split into as many different directions as there were men. Without a doubt, many of them would enlist more men along the way. Every hollow would have a watcher, and soon they'd find their man.

If it wasn't too late.

CHAPTER 43

"The train comes at six," Betsy yelled over the sound of crashing branches. They broke out of the trees and thundered into a shallow river, breaking the icy crust along the bank and crashing through the freezing water. "If they are sure enough going to Springfield, we don't have long."

"But that was a lie." Joel leaned forward to duck beneath the limbs once they'd gained the opposite bank. "The trial isn't in Springfield. Taney is out of options."

He didn't want to scare her, but he didn't give Scott much of a chance once Taney got him well enough away from town that no one could hear a pistol shot. Scott was the one witness who might be able to convince a jury that the man in the mask he'd tussled with was none other than the sheriff. For Taney's purposes, Scott had to disappear.

They cut across trails, bounded through thickets, and took shortcuts that felt impossibly treacherous, but their mountain-bred mounts never faltered—something that even this Texan was beginning to appreciate about the Ozark horses. The train whistle sounded. Betsy spurred her horse again as they flew down the last section of road before reaching the depot.

There it was. The same sorry log depot with the stubby rock chimney he'd encountered when he arrived. But if he could see it, they could see him.

"Whoa!" He pulled up short before cresting the hill. Betsy skidded to a stop, then her agile pony reversed back down the road.

"What are you stopping for?" she asked.

"Taney might be watching. We don't want to scare him away."

"You *want* me to hide? That's a change."

They directed their horses off the road and waited for the churning, smoking engine to pull into the station.

Only a porter got off the train. He stood on the empty deck. The door to the depot opened, and a woodsman in moccasins chewing a piece of straw came over. They talked until the porter checked his pocket watch. Joel's legs tightened in the saddle. If Taney wasn't here, then his intentions were much darker.

But then a figure emerged from the trees. Two figures. Scott's head hung, his shoulders slumped. Taney's hand rested on his shoulder in a fatherly manner. At Joel's side, Betsy made a strangled noise. He laid a hand on her arm to calm her. So far Scott hadn't been harmed.

The porter waved the sheriff over. Taney handed the depot man some cash, and he hurried away to return with a slip of paper for the porter. The porter nodded, then motioned Scott toward the train. Scott halted at the doorway and turned to face the mountains.

Joel felt that moment with his whole heart—the moment a man said good-bye forever to his homeland. A moment he'd always regret.

The horses leapt forward and tore up the road like they were fleeing a pack of wolves. Scott looked up and rubbed his eyes, then, realizing they weren't a mirage, his face crumpled in wonder. Taney, too, stood in shock, but when he tried to move, it was too late. With his recent injuries, escape was impossible.

Betsy flung herself off the horse and, ignoring Joel's caution, ran to her cousin. She didn't care that Taney wasn't secured. She knew Joel was right behind her, and the sheriff would dearly regret any move he made against her person.

"On account of your age and injury, I won't throw you on the ground just yet." Joel held Taney's arms behind him. "But give me an excuse, and you'll see how fast you eat dirt."

Scott shook his head. "It's not his fault. He's trying to help me. Don't blame him."

Betsy threw her arm around her cousin's shoulders—a feat, considering his height. "How is he trying to help you?"

"He thought they'd find me guilty, so he told me to run. Even gave me some money to get a new start."

Betsy closed her eyes and thanked God for the bit of conscience Taney had retained.

"Is that what he told you?" Joel asked.

Taney studied the ground. "I never was going to kill him. Even that night, I wanted to scare him with the knife so he'd come back to town and insist that the Bald Knobbers had roughed him up. Then you'd need my help and I could prove myself. I didn't know he had a gun."

"That was you?" Scott's upper lip rose as he stared at the sheriff. "Why would you do that to me?" He turned his face away, hiding his anguish.

Betsy rubbed his back. "We've got it all figured out, Scott.

You're not in any trouble. No more hiding. You can come home."

Joel's eyes flickered to hers, but she didn't see the joy she expected. His head dropped as he led Taney away, and only then did she realize that going home to his family was the one thing Joel couldn't do.

CHAPTER 44

One Week Later

"Three cheers for Sheriff Puckett!" Uncle Fred punched his fist into the air and led the townspeople gathered at the jailhouse. "Hip, hip, hooray! Hip, hip, hooray! Hip, hip, hooray!"

Betsy's laughter turned to cheering when Joel removed his Stetson and waved it grandly from the step.

"I knew he'd make a fine sheriff," Pritchard boasted.

"Once he survived that pony, I figured he was a decent fellow," Mayor Walters added.

Josiah elbowed her. "He'll make a good sheriff, but I ain't too sure about a brother-in-law."

Betsy kicked him in the knee. He groaned and bent to rub it while she continued clapping.

Joel would be their sheriff. He'd have a secure job, a full salary, and a house of his own. A house of their own. But there was something that needed fixing first, if he was willing to admit it.

The ladies of town had prepared a potluck and everyone had turned out. Even Abigail and Jeremiah rode into town in a wagon with her folks. Doctor Hopkins and Laurel came, too, although their eldest daughter hadn't been as friendly since word of Betsy's engagement spread. Clive Fowler carried on like the party was for him, and in a way it was. Finally he'd found someone he trusted with the role of protector of Pine Gap. He could retire. The only ones missing were Detective Cleveland and Officer Harrison, called back to Jeff City now that Joel's character had been verified and the true story of Sheriff Taney's attack had been told.

Betsy's heart swelled as she surveyed the folks scattered across the lawn on the square. Everyone within sight was happy. And for today, everything in view was perfect. But there was damage not visible that had to be reckoned with. One burr that still rubbed her sore.

By the time the desserts had been consumed and the wind grew fiercer with the lowering of the sun, Joel had made the rounds once, twice, and in some cases three times. When he finally joined her next to the hanging tree, she knew her patience had paid off.

"May I escort you home?" He offered his arm.

"Of course, Sheriff Puckett."

They made their way to Uncle Fred's house. According to the original plan, that hellfire and brimstone preacher Silas Ruger would marry them, and they'd be man and wife before the week was over. But Betsy had been pushing for something different.

They reached the house, but instead of going to the office door, they took off down the path to the woods behind. Slowly they covered the soggy ground that cradled patches of snow on the north side of the trees and valleys until they reached a lookout spot. Betsy gained the platform, then turned to face Joel. His close-cut beard couldn't hide the dimple in his cheek. The shadow of his hat didn't cover the wistfulness of his eyes.

"Did you ask permission?" she asked.

The smile faded. His chest filled. "Mayor Walters said Fowler could handle things if I had to go, but I don't have to. You're worried about nothing."

Betsy pressed both arms over her stomach. How she wished she could ignore the obvious—wished she could revel in the joy that had found them—but it wasn't time yet.

"I saw you at the train station, Joel. I saw how you looked when Scott decided to come home. You aren't free. You have unfinished business in Garber."

He slipped his hands into his pockets. "I *will* go someday, but what's the hurry? Let's get married first—"

"No." The most painful word she'd ever had to utter. She cleared her throat and continued. "Living in Pine Gap—living with me—can't be your second choice. Go home to your beloved Texas. Clear your name. If you love me, if you love this town, you'll come back. If not"—she pressed her lips tightly together before finding the courage—"well, it's better to know now than to wait."

He walked past her and stood at the edge of the ravine. The sun was dipping into the mountain, melting its honeyed syrup on the crest and making the edge of his hat glow.

"I wanted everything to be perfect before I went back—job as a sheriff, a lovely wife, maybe even a child or two to prove that I'm a decent family man. But it's like . . . like every day I'm gone is a banishment." He clasped his hands behind his back and watched the colors melt behind the bare limbs on the mountain. "I'd do it in a heartbeat if it weren't for you." He turned to her, his eyes full of worry. "I love you, Betsy. I don't want to risk our future. Whatever I have to gain in Texas isn't worth losing you."

"Who said you would?" Her fingers dug into her ribcage. "I've waited twenty-four years for my man. Don't you imagine I can wait a few more months?"

322

But maybe his concern wasn't that she'd change her mind. Maybe he was afraid he would.

Her side ached. She eased her fingers. "You gave me a stern lecture not too long ago about how I had to trust you where your profession was concerned. I learned to do that. I respected your role as a leader and as the deputy. This . . . this is where you have to trust me. This is where you can honor my wishes and acknowledge that my insight, even though inconvenient, has value."

He took her hand, pulled her to the edge to stand next to him and watch the shadows grow. Their fingers threaded together as Betsy prayed for his decision, even though she dreaded it. Finally, as the sun dropped out of sight, he answered.

"I'm going to miss you." His jaw clenched. "Betsy, you don't know how I'll miss you, but I'll hurry back, and everything will be just the same as when I left. You wait and see." His words were commands, daring her to suggest any alternative. "And in the meantime, you keep writing. Naturally you won't have me to inspire you, but I'm sure Fowler will make enough drama for a few stories."

She laid her hand on his arm. "And you keep track of your daring deeds so I'll have abundant material when you return."

"It's a deal." He squeezed her hand. "I can't wait to see what the future has in store for your hero—the real one, that is."

She searched his profile, wishing she knew, too. Joel would do what was right, that was certain, and hopefully doing right would lead him back to her.

By the time he left that night, Betsy was content with what they'd decided. Joel would publicly declare his innocence and challenge the lies about him, even if it meant facing more scandal. He was brave, honorable, and determined—all qualities that were taking him from her for a little while but would hopefully lead him back as soon as his duty was done.

And no matter when or if he returned, knowing Joel had changed her life. Just like the men of her town had set aside their disguises, she no longer hid her intelligence behind a juvenile mask. She'd yoke up with a woman's mind and a woman's heart and answer for herself. Responsible. Trustworthy. Accountable. If she had to make it on her own, she could. But that didn't mean she wanted to.

It'd be many days before she stopped watching for his black horse. Many nights before she stopped setting the table for one extra. But before spring came, she'd start listening for the train whistle. When the crocus returned, she'd begin watching at the road for her Dashing Deputy to return and claim her.

Because a hero always came back for his lady.

EPILOGUE

Joel shoved a plate of food through the door of the cell and locked it.

"This isn't hot." Leland Moore's words slurred. "It's not even warm."

"You showed up at my wedding nimptopsical, and you expect me to cook you up something fresh? You're lucky you've got anything at all."

Leland held his head with both hands. "Thought you'd be in a better mood, having just got married. No use yelling at me."

Joel wasn't yelling, just anxious to get home, to his new home and to Betsy. He'd sent word ahead on his way from Texas for her to be ready to wed, and she'd succeeded spectacularly. Her ma and Sissy had helped her set up the cabin he'd leased so that it was right homey. Abigail Calhoun and Laurel Hopkins had sewn her a new dress for the wedding, and Joel had never seen anything so fetching. Two days after he stepped foot off the train—two whirlwind days of meeting with her family, hauling furniture and whatnot, consulting with Fowler, and stealing away to be alone with his intended—and he was married.

And even though he'd had his hands full of work to catch up on, his heart was light. Joel was cleared in Texas. Commissioner

Anderson and the rest of the Blackstone County Commissioners had held a hearing. Sheriff Green spoke on his behalf, recounting the details of that night and apologizing for not speaking up sooner. Mary and her folks carried on about her ruined reputation, but Joel was able to produce the crumpled letter she'd written him just that winter. Knowing Betsy's proclivity to snoop, he'd gone back to pull it out of the trash bin, and once he started thinking about it, burning it felt akin to destroying evidence. So he'd tucked it inside the band of his Stetson and hoped he could forget about it.

Once the commissioners read Mary's description of how hard she'd worked to ensure his capture and how bitter she was that her plans hadn't succeeded, they cleared him on the spot. A letter was drafted to the State of Missouri to clear up any misinformation they might have gathered, and Joel was once again free to wear a badge in Texas.

But he doubted he ever would.

He hung the keys to the cell on the peg and grabbed his hat. Fowler would have to come by in the morning to release Leland, because Joel didn't plan to make an appearance before breakfast.

Betsy tidied the cans in her kitchen pantry for the hundredth time. Helping Mayor Walters arrange the tall displays he couldn't reach had let her stock her new house with plenty of necessaries.

Her new house. She looked about the one-room cabin, the table for two against the wall, the stove that could keep the whole house toasty on the coldest of days, the bed laid out smooth with quilts from her grandmother's trunk. It was small, but it was hers. And there was nothing else she could do besides sit down and, for the first time, wait for her husband to come home.

Betsy had never been good at waiting.

She'd changed into her nightgown early since she wasn't sure how to go about getting dressed with a man in the room. But after padding around the room in her bare feet for an hour, she was wishing she could go to town and look for him. That morning a few friends had joined her family for the ceremony, but now she was by herself and not taking to the solitude with good grace.

She heard hooves on the rocky road outside. She wadded her white nightgown in her hands and scurried to the window. The thin clouds in the sky only diffused the moonlight, making it easy to see him coming up the path.

Oh, what a pity she couldn't have included illustrations for her articles. Astride a horse that did him justice, Betsy knew that if Joel's likeness were included on the page, numerous young ladies would find the time to make a clipping of the Dashing Deputy and probably save the image along with pressed flowers in their thick volume of *Shakespeare's Complete Works*. But she wanted no pictures now. He was her Stalwart Sheriff, and she wouldn't share him with anyone, although he promised to give her plenty of material for her Dashing Deputy stories. Because they would be stories, not news. And she wasn't hiding them from anyone.

The time it took him to stable his horse was enough time to make her jittery. Not knowing what to do with herself, she sat in the rocker and pulled her feet up beneath her gown. She'd debated on whether she should unbraid her hair and had decided not to, just in case something should happen and she needed to get dressed and run to town again. What could make a woman leave her house on her wedding night, Betsy had no idea, but it paid to be prepared.

The door swung open. His silhouette, from his boots all the

way up to his hat, filled the doorway. He scanned the room, his eyes seeming to rest on everything she'd shuffled around or moved since she'd been confined there to wait, then came to rest on her. He smiled gently and pulled the door closed behind him.

"Do you want some supper?" she asked.

"They fed us enough at the wedding." He hooked the latch on the door and set about removing his boots. "How about you? Are you hungry?"

Betsy squirmed. "I can't think about food right now."

He smiled as he removed his hat, his vest, and hung his gun belt by the door. He had a routine, and while it was new to Betsy, she was comforted by the mundane activity. This was her new life. It would be normal soon.

"Is there anything I can get you?" Betsy asked. "If you need—"

"Just you," Joel said.

She put her feet down, but even by the light of one lamp, she felt exposed in her nightgown. She reached for a quilt to drape over her shoulders, but he caught her hand.

"Are you cold?" He kept his eyes on her face, even though her blush must have been noticeable all the way down the scooped neck of her gown.

"I . . . I don't know." Chilled, hot, flushed. "I guess I'm just . . ."

"Excited?"

There was so much love in his gaze. She was going to say *embarrassed*, but maybe excited was better. She squeezed his hand as her answer.

"I've been thinking of you the whole way—"

An explosion of noise sounded outside. Chaos erupted in the form of drums, bugles, and kettles banging together. Joel shoved her down on the bed, then threw himself over her, covering her with his body. Nervous or not, Betsy couldn't suppress the laughter that rolled out of her and shook the bed.

Before Joel could spring for his gun, she grabbed him around the neck. "It's a shivaree." She nearly had to yell for him to hear her above the din. "They're just being ornery."

Raised voices sang off-key to the accompaniment of every noisemaker invented, but Betsy was more distracted by the proximity of her husband. He reached forward enough to peer out the window. He was talking to her, but she couldn't hear him. He swung the shutters closed. Only by watching his lips could she make out something about *everybody* and *even your brother*. Then more clearly she heard, "I'll tell them to stop."

"No." She was starting to relax. Starting to enjoy the weight of him, the closeness. Starting to realize that whatever she feared, him leaving was worse. She pulled his head down so he could hear her. "You can't go out there until after."

His mouth repeated the word. "*After?*" His eyes traveled to her lips. The sternness melted from his face. "Are you sure?" he mouthed.

Somehow the noise made their space seem cozier. Made him feel closer. Regular music had broken out as dozens of voices belted out the lyrics to some nonsensical song. It drowned out the sound of her answer, but when Joel turned down the lamp, she knew he'd heard.

It wasn't until much later, as Betsy dozed in his arms, that she realized the night was quiet. There were no revelers, no riders, no whoops and hollers coming from the mountains. All was quiet. All was peaceful.

And he'd never left her side.

Regina Jennings is a graduate of Oklahoma Baptist University with a degree in English and a minor in history. She has worked at the *Mustang News* and at First Baptist Church of Mustang, along with time at the Oklahoma National Stockyards and various livestock shows. She lives outside of Oklahoma City with her husband and four children.

Sign up for Regina's newsletter!

Keep up to date with Regina's news on upcoming book releases and events by signing up for her email list at www.reginajennings.com

More From Regina Jennings

When Miranda Wimplegate mistakenly sells a prized portrait, her grandfather buys an entire auction house to get it back. But they soon learn their new business deals in livestock—not antiques! While Miranda searches for the portrait, the handsome manager tries to salvage the failing business. Will either succeed?

At Love's Bidding

You May Also Enjoy . . .

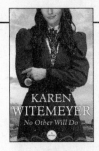

When the women's colony of Harper's Station is threatened, founder Emma Chandler is forced to admit she needs help. The only man she trusts enough to ask is Malachi Shaw, whose life she once saved. As Mal returns the favor, danger mounts—and so does the attraction between them.

No Other Will Do by Karen Witemeyer
karenwitemeyer.com

Lady Ella Myerston is determined to put an end to the danger that haunts her brother. While visiting her friend Brook, the owner of the Fire Eyes jewels, Ella gets entangled in an attempt to blackmail the newly reformed Lord Cayton. Will she become the next casualty of the "curse"?

A Lady Unrivaled by Roseanna M. White
LADIES OF THE MANOR
roseannamwhite.com

At Irish Meadows horse farm, two sisters struggle to reconcile their dreams with their father's demanding marriage expectations. Brianna longs to attend college, while Colleen is happy to marry, as long as the man meets *her* standards. Will they find the courage to follow their hearts?

Irish Meadows by Susan Anne Mason
COURAGE TO DREAM #1
susanannemason.com

BETHANYHOUSE